barely

NEAR MISS BOOK #3: AN INDIGO KING ROCK STAR ROMANCE

NEAR MISS
BOOK 3

AMY BOOKER

Barely

Near Miss, Book #3

by
AMY BOOKER

ISBN: 979-8-9859875-4-6

Published by Renaissan Publishing Limited, Cuyahoga Falls, Ohio

www.amybookerauthor.com

If you've read any of my books, you'll know that the chapter names are all song titles. Music has been an integral part of my life, and it always sets the mood. Whether it's the overall energy of a song, the lyrics, or even just the title, that tone carries through into my written words on the page. The playlist and a link can be found at the back of each book, or you can find them on my website: www.amybookerauthor.com.

dedication

May your face be ever shiny.
(you'll get it later)

When I open the door to my friend Ren's store, Vital Records, off the Sunset Strip, I am greeted with the most blood-curdling scream I have ever heard. And that's saying a lot since, being in a rock band, there are plenty of screams to compare it to. *Holy Hell.* I glance around, and I appear to be the only person in the store. *What the fuck?*

"Ren?" I wait for an answer and don't hear anything but the music coming from the sound system. I'm now slightly concerned my friend was just murdered or accidentally killed by one of the many chandeliers falling on top of her. "Rena?"

A small giggle comes from somewhere behind the counter, and I make my way slowly towards it to investigate. Leaning over, I see a giant baby in a playpen of some sort sitting up and grinning toothlessly at me, a stuffed donkey in one hand. The mop of curly red hair is a dead giveaway; this is Ren's daughter, Charlotte. So, this must be what Ren looked like as a baby. *Ha. Cute.*

"Jude?" Ren's voice calls from behind me. I turn to find a blur of red hair rushing toward me in time to catch her as she hurls herself at me. She wraps her arms and legs around me, and my senses are attacked by the fragrance of her peach shampoo mixed with baby powder as we spin around. "You didn't tell me you were back in town! When did you get in?"

I was not expecting that enthusiastic of a reunion with Ren. We've been friends since I moved to LA from New York almost eleven years ago, and this is the first time she's ever jumped on me in greeting. I'm not sure what to make of it. I let her slide off me and take a step back to try to compose myself.

"A couple days ago." Now I'm nervous and awkward and can't figure out how to stand still or where to look. My muscles tense up, and my stomach goes all fluttery. That surprise attack threw me way off. "Was that you screaming when I came in? It sounded like someone getting utterly murderized."

She laughs and runs her fingers through her long red curly mane of hair, trying to tame the wild strands to no avail.

"No, that was Charlotte. She's discovered her voice, which is *so* awesome for her...and everyone who hears it." Her expression tells me this is, in fact, not so awesome. She leans down and lifts the baby out of her playpen, resting her on a hip, and the two of them are unmistakably mother and daughter.

Charlotte puts her hand in her mouth, slobbering all over, her bright grey eyes scrutinizing me. I examine her right back, narrowing my eyes at her. She's fucking cute in a little Vital Records t-shirt, but I know absolutely zip, zero, zilch about kids. Or babies, for that matter. Especially baby girls. And seeing Ren with one that is now a permanent part of her life is surreal. The adjustment is going to be tricky.

"How old is she now? Ten?" She's a lot bigger than the last time I saw her when we played LA in the summer. "Got her learner's permit yet?" This makes Ren laugh again, and this time Charlotte joins her while gumming her fingers to death.

"She's six months old exactly tomorrow."

"Oh no," I groan.

"What?"

"Are you going to be one of those annoying moms refusing to use the month-to-year conversion chart? Is she going to someday be 43.2 months old?" Parents are usually annoying about their kids anyway, but stuff like that makes it even worse. Don't make me fucking do math to figure out your kid's age. "That converts to three and a half years, by the way."

"Well, not around you now, obviously. Spoilsport." Her sarcastic grin lights her face. There she is. The Ren I knew before the baby came is still in there. *Good.* I was worried motherhood would soften her rough edges too much. Those edges are what I like the most about her and why we get along so well. We can snark at each other and not be offended.

"How are things going?" I glance around at the empty store and wonder about the lack of foot traffic coming through. "Slow day in the record biz?"

A shadow crosses her face before she paints another smile over it.

"Um...I just re-opened after closing for a couple of weeks, so things are a little slow."

This is the first I'm hearing of the store having to close. That is pretty major for her. This store has been her focus for a few years now. Well, until Charlotte came along. Ren isn't one to keep stuff like that from me. We don't talk as often as before I started touring, but still.

"Why did you have to close?"

She turns as if looking for something, but I catch her expression; she's about to cry. Before I can say anything, though, she's back around with a wide grin and eyes glistening. A fake smile if ever there was one.

"Oh, you know. Decent daycares around here can be a bitch to find, so I stayed home with Charlotte while she went through a bout of croup. Not a huge deal." Something in her eyes is extremely sad. She's lying through her big fat teeth.

"Nice one. Try again. This time with feeling."

The smile slides into a brief frown, then into a full-blown glare.

"Damn you, Jude." She's shaking her head, knowing she can't pull that shit with me. *Sorry, not sorry*.

"Many have tried. Talk to me." I can wait her out all day if I need to. I've got nothing better to do. "What's going on? Where's 'Brad the Dad' in all this? I thought he was back for good and supposed to be helping out."

Brad is Ren's on-and-off-again boyfriend and Charlotte's father. I hate every single one of his guts. And the rest of him too. I may be a player, but I'm careful. Brad is literally a reckless dick. Who knows how many illegitimate kids he has around the country. He's a lousy singer who gets kicked out of every band stupid enough to let him join. I can't believe people still hire him. Thinking about him makes my blood boil.

Ren is swaying with Charlotte, making faces at her, and avoiding my questions. I lean back against the counter and cross my arms, indicating I'm ready to wait her out.

"I need to go to the bathroom. Hold her a sec." There's another blur of motion, and suddenly, I'm catching another female redhead. This one's a little more fragile than the last one.

"What the hell...heck?" I call after Ren, but she's not looking back. What is she thinking? I don't have the first clue what the fuck to do with a baby.

I position her on my hip like Ren did and sway a little, and Charlotte starts giggling again, her full chubby fist shoved in her drooling mouth. *Fuck yeah. This is easy. I'm the God-damned Baby Whisperer.* I add a bounce to the sway, which results in throaty laughs I can't help but join. The game becomes trying to make her laugh harder with each bounce. This is a fucking challenge I'm determined to conquer because that little laugh is addictive.

I get a whiff of peaches and powder again, this time coming from Charlotte, and it's like I'm holding a little piece of home. I don't know how to describe the emotion, but it scares the God-damned shit out of me as soon as I feel it. My chest tightens just considering it. This is not cool. I had wondered how I would react to Charlotte but didn't expect this. Whatever *this* even fucking is. The reaction is so foreign I still can't give it a name.

I stop swaying and put a hand up for a high-five, curious if she's learned this yet. She looks at my hand, then at me, then back and forth for about an hour.

"C'mon, Charlie, high-five!" I smile encouragingly. She finally catches on to what I'm asking, takes her slobber-coated fist, and hits my outstretched hand. "Yeah!" I cheer, and she screams with that voice she's recently found. I think my ears break. Or maybe my skull. I feel about ten feet tall. *Holy shit*. She high-fived me. That was the best thing ever. *What just happened here? And where the fuck is Brad?*

two

MY BEST FRIEND

REN

Well, there's something I never thought I would witness; Jude holding and playing with my daughter. And doing both masterfully. I thought for sure he'd set her back in her playpen like a typical guy, but for him to keep her and entertain her says a lot about his character. I always knew Jude was one of the good guys, but this reinforces it for me.

I feel bad handing her off like that, but the questions about her father, Brad, brought up pain I don't want to deal with. I don't need to be throwing all my troubles into Jude's lap. He's been a great friend to me and has seen me through many difficult times, but he's got an enormous career happening now and doesn't need stupid distractions from me and my wreck of a personal life.

I lean against the wall and watch them playing

and high-fiving each other. Charlotte is having a blast with this new stranger. I need to be careful. She has enough male figures earning her trust and then bailing on her. With Jude's almost constant touring, I'm afraid he'll bail on her too. Not on purpose, of course, but kids don't know that, unlike her asshole father, who purposely chose to run away from his responsibilities.

"She likes you." I reach for Charlotte to come to me, but she turns and buries her head into Jude's chest, refusing to move. "Um...Wow. Okay."

"Sorry, Ren, but you've been replaced. Charlie is my new best friend now." He grins, now relaxed with a baby on his hip, and his smile is so sincere something in my heart melts a little. "We had a meeting while you were gone, and it's been decided."

"A meeting, huh? Well, I'm heartbroken. I just got you back." I study my daughter, facing me again, but still leaning against Jude, drooling all over his shirt. "Was there any discussion about the maximum quantity of drool allowed on your clothing?"

He glances down, sees what I'm referring to, and frowns.

"Is this normal? To be leaking at the mouth so much? Maybe she's broke. You should have her checked."

"Did you call my child broken?" I pry her out of Jude's arms despite her complaints.

"No. I said maybe. I would never say it outright. To your face." His crooked smile is infectious, and he shoves his hands into his pockets, looking a little lost now that Charlotte is no longer in his arms. It's kind of cute.

"She's due for a nap, and I think the excitement of her new BFF tired her out." I rock her from side to side, watching her eyes grow heavier with each movement. Yup, she'll be out in no time. "Also, did you call her Charlie?"

"Yeah...why?"

"I wanted to keep away from giving her nick-names, but everyone is hellbent on calling her anything but her actual name." I sigh and can't keep a yawn from escaping. The fatigue in my muscles from carrying Charlotte so much is taking its toll on me. My lack of sleep isn't helping, either.

"But she likes 'Charlie.'" Jude's earnest face is too much for me to take.

"Fine." I carry Charlotte over to her playpen behind the register and lay her down. Luckily, she doesn't put up a fuss. She can be an easy baby when she wants. "Not like you'll be around to call her that anyway." I see Jude flinch, hurt flashing in his eyes, and I bite my lip. I didn't mean to hurt him. "Shoot. I said that out loud, didn't I?"

"You did." He gazes out the window, a grimace taking over his face. He's pretending to survey the traffic, but I know better. He's avoiding looking at me. "I heard it and everything." The humor is gone, which is a rare thing for Jude. He's almost always amused by something. *Shit.* I didn't mean to take my frustration with Brad out on Jude. He doesn't deserve it.

"Sorry about that." I lean on the counter behind him, putting my head down on my arms; the glass counter is cool against my skin. "I'm so tired anymore, I barely know if I'm awake or dreaming, let alone saying words aloud or in my head."

"Don't you get any breaks?"

"Pops comes and takes her in the afternoons. And I still have Sawyer here part-time and weekends."

The next thing I know, Jude is smoothing my hair out of my face, and I swear he's going to put me to sleep if he keeps it up. The gentle touch is mesmerizing.

"So, where is Brad?" His voice is concerned, and he doesn't stop touching my hair. I close my eyes, enjoying an elusive moment of peace. But it's fleeting now that I need to talk about my ex.

"Gone." I may need to, but I really don't want to talk about him. I just want to have my hair played with until I fall asleep for about fourteen hours. That shouldn't be too much to ask.

"C'mon, Ren. You're going to tell me eventually, so you may as well get it over with."

"There's not much to tell. It's always the same with him. You know how he is. He doesn't want to be tied down, so he goes out and screws whatever's available and then plays the martyr when I kick him to the curb. Meanwhile, we're left to take care of ourselves." Tears I didn't think I had left run down the tip of my nose and drop onto the glass of the counter display case. I think the tears are mostly because I'm so tired, but I hate that I still get upset about it. It's been a few months now, and we're figuring it out without him. It just takes a while.

Jude's hand stops stroking my hair, and I can sense him tensing up even with my eyes closed. I turn my head to the side and peek up at him. His sharp jawline is clenched, and his eyes are closed as if he's trying to calm himself down.

"Where did he go?" He opens his eyes and gazes down at me, his gray, trying to read my gray. The furrow in his brow is deep, and I can't tell if it's contained anger or what it is. If I thought for a second it was directed at me, I'd be scared.

"I don't know, and I don't care." The first part is absolutely true; I have no idea where Brad went when I kicked him out. As for not caring, that one is still up in the air. A part of me still dreams of us being a family, but I don't know why I'm holding on to that. It's stupid, and I'm not a stupid person. Each day that passes without him is chipping away at that hope, though. Maybe someday soon, I'll come to my senses. As of right now, I care enough to hate him, but I can feel even that waning.

"Good girl." His grimace softens as he pats my head and pushes off the counter, heading toward the exit. I don't want him to leave yet. He just got here.

"Where are you going? I haven't seen you in forever."

"I'm making the 'back in LA' rounds and have a few more stops." He gives me a quick but unconvincing smile as he pushes on the door. "I'll text you later."

I don't even have a chance to say goodbye before his back is to me, and he's heading down the sidewalk. The troubled look on his face when he left worries me. I wonder what is bothering him so badly. He asked about Brad, but I didn't get a chance to ask him about anything in his life. It was nice to see him, though. I've missed him.

three

HATE TO SAY I TOLD YOU SO

JUDE

I still smell like baby. I'm not sure how I feel about it. It was great to officially meet Charlie since she was way too small to be any fun last time. Man, who knew making a baby laugh could be so rewarding? Craziness. Seeing Ren was cool too, but I do not like seeing her so upset, especially due to Brad's bullshit. I can't believe him. No, I can because he's the biggest fuckhead to walk the planet. Guys like him need to grow up. You make it, you take care of it, or at the very least pay for it. It's not complicated.

I saw Brad last when we were in town for the Hollywood Bowl shows in the summer, and at the time, he was 'helping' with Charlie while Ren took care of her store. What it looked like was Ren taking care of everything while Brad hung out at the store, hitting on other chicks. I didn't say anything at the time because it's not my business, and secondly, it's not my fucking business. Third, Ren would have my head if I interfered in her love life, especially now with Charlie in the picture.

We are and always have been zero judgment friends, but man, sometimes it is so hard not to ask her what the fuck she's thinking when it comes to Brad. The dude is a fucking loser. And he only brings her heartache, and now he's going to do the same thing to Charlie, and I do not like that. I'm not sure I can sit on the sidelines anymore while he walks all over them. I don't think Ren is weak; far from it. She's one of the strongest people in the world. But I think she wanted a family, and the guy she picked to do that with is a dick. When assholes like that promise someone the world, all they can do is believe it's deliverable. It's not.

And then, these jerkoffs end up hurting all of these fantastic women, who then can't trust good guys because of the bullshit they get put through. And, when did I become a fucking relationship expert? Maybe I should stay in my lane and let Ren handle this herself. I know that's what she would want. She'd kill me if she knew I got involved. But fuck me if I can stay out of it.

I send a text to Vanessa, our band manager. Out of everyone I know, she's the most likely to know what's going on with Brad.

ME: Hey, Van. Any idea where Brad Chambers

landed band wise? Or where he's staying? Kind of important. Thanks.

I walk for a while as I wait for a response, stopping at the Rainbow to grab a quick lunch on the patio. It's a typical LA day, with plenty of sunshine and a warm breeze pushing the smog around. As I take a seat at the outdoor bar and order a drink, Vanessa texts me back.

> VANESSA: Just found out he's with Chaos Fuel in Pasadena. For now. What's up?

> ME: Any word on where he's staying?

> VANESSA: You didn't answer my question. But no.

> ME: Thanks.

> VANESSA: Jude?

I ignore the question, not wanting to get into details with her. She'll forgive me. Chaos Fuel? They must be new; I've never heard of them. Interesting name, though, and it is so Brad. He definitely fuels his own kind of chaos. I try to think of who I know in Pasadena who might be part of that crew, but I blank.

How deep do I want to go with this? Something inside is nagging at me that this is not the right road to go down, but the rest of me is like, *fuck yeah*, it is. The dude needs his head screwed back on straight. *Shit.* Am I volunteering for that? Not sure my original intentions were violence. That doesn't make it out of the question, though.

It is more than obvious Ren is having a hard time being a single parent. She looked like she could fall asleep on her feet. *Damn.* Maybe I should've stayed and offered to help out, but I know fuck all about taking care of babies or record stores. If anything, I could make things worse for Ren if I tried to help and just got in the way. But I can't do nothing.

I do a search for Chaos Fuel to see if they have any shows coming up. Maybe if they're playing out somewhere, I can coincidentally 'run into' him and have a little chat. Man to man. Amazingly enough, they are playing tonight at a dive bar that, if I remember correctly, barely fits people, let alone a band. Interesting.

Before I text the rest of my band to see if they'll go with me tonight, I reconsider my options. That's usually a good thing to do, right? *Right.* Okay, I can do nothing and sit by and watch my best friend struggle being a single mom. I can offer to help her and get shot right down for offering, or, I can go talk to her shithead ex and try to get him to see the error of his ways. That last one is really looking like a winner to me. I text my bandmates in Indigo King, Ryan, and Matt, to see if they're up for an adventure.

> ME: Hey group text we all hate, I need you to come with me tonight to a hole in the wall to kick someone's ass.

MATT: I told you to take me off of this stupid group text.

MATT: Who's ass?

> ME: Ren's ex, Brad. Now in Chaos Fuel

MATT: Is this the same Ren that is just a friend?

RYAN: Who the fuck started this group text again? Jesus.

I wait before I respond again as they each get their shit together. They'll come around eventually, one way or another. I know it's last minute, but we'll go stir crazy if we don't ease back into home life after being on the road for so long. I know I'm already antsy to keep moving. It only takes a few minutes to hear back.

MATT: I'm in. Which hole?

> ME: Old Town

RYAN: Fine.

MATT: Seriously. Delete me from this group.

We make arrangements to meet up later tonight. And...I instantly regret doing this, and I haven't even done anything yet. My appetite is long gone, so I pay for my liquid lunch and start walking the strip again. It's still only afternoon, but I need to figure out a game plan for how to approach this tonight. I am not one for confrontation, so I have no clue what the fuck I'm thinking doing this. Matt's the fighter, and Ryan is the diplomat of our group. What does that leave me? Ladies' man, of course. While the coolest of the three, that is no help for tonight.

Memories of Charlie high-fiving me with her drool-soaked hand and then laughing her head off crash into me. That's why I need to do this. Charlie needs her fucking father in her life. Even if he is the lowest of the dregs of humanity. Is that right? Is any of this right? Aren't they better off without him? Even if it's going to be hard? Ren can take care of herself. *Fuck me running*. I'm spinning myself in circles with this and getting nowhere fast. This is going to be a clusterfuck. Chaos Fuel, huh? How fitting.

four

STUPID THING

REN

Charlotte wakes up from her nap just as I reach one of my distributors on the phone that I've been trying to get ahold of for days to discuss their bill. Of course. And two customers just walked in. *Shit.*

"I'll call you back," I say into the phone before hanging up while waving at the new customers. The pitch of Charlotte's screams increases along with its volume, even as I pick her up to calm her. "Shhhh. Shhhh." She's got napping-baby sweat plastering her hair to her forehead, and her face is flushed. She's so damned cute; it's hard to be mad at her for screaming bloody-fucking-murder upon waking. I'd do the same thing if it were an acceptable behavior for adults.

I pace one of the isles with her on my hip, trying to cool her down, and ease her crying. It's times like these that my decision not to use a daycare yet becomes a real problem. I check the time on my phone, noting that my grandfather should be here soon to pick up Charlotte. He's been helping me with her in the afternoons since Brad and I broke up, and he really is a Godsend. Charlotte loves spending time with him, and she lights up whenever she sees him.

The couple leaves without buying anything, *damn it*, but it gives me a chance to get Charlotte changed and ready to go. A few minutes later, and punctual as always, my grandfather walks in with his baseball cap pulled down low on his face, hiding from Charlotte. She's not fooled and lets out a happy screech as she leans toward him so he can pick her up. He obliges and gives her a few twirls around.

"You spoil her." I grin at them, so thankful that Charlotte spends time with her great-grandfather like this. He was the leading man in my life growing up, too, since my father left my mother and me when I was twelve. He doesn't have to help out like this, but he offered as soon as he found out about Brad leaving. He learned of my predicament only when he tried to come to the store and discovered it was closed. I hadn't wanted to bother him or anyone with my childcare issues, but he insisted he take her late afternoons until the store closes. So, Charlotte gets to have dinner with her great-grandfather most nights, and I get a few hours of actual work done.

"Little girls should be spoiled. Look what happens later on." He waves in my direction, but he's got a smile a mile wide, crinkling the corners of his eyes. He starts dancing with Charlotte, bouncing her with the beat of the music playing in the store, and she's suddenly not grumpy anymore. *Hallelujah*.

"Very funny, Pops." I pretend to glare at him. This is how it's always been with him, light and easy, fun and games. It's never the end of the world when he's around, and every problem has an easy solution. I try to adopt his attitude, but sometimes it's so damned hard. I'm too high-strung and over-think everything to be so carefree. It doesn't stop me from wishing I could change to be more like him.

"You sure you don't want me to take her overnight?" The concern on his face deepens his wrinkles. "I don't mind, and you look like you could use the sleep." Bless him for offering, but I can't.

"Thanks, Pops, but no." I take Charlotte for another hug before handing her back. "I'd miss my girl too much. You know how I get without her." I get major separation anxiety when we're apart, but it's more that. I don't want to be a further burden to this saint of a man who has already done too much for me. More than anyone else in this world ever has. I hand over her diaper bag and favorite donkey toy that's about to lose an eye. *I'll need to fix that*. "I'll be by later to pick her up."

Once they leave, I examine the boxes of records

delivered earlier today and take them over to the lounge area of the store, where there are soft couches for customers to sit and listen to their purchases. After a few loud yawns in a row, I start taking inventory.

"I could watch you sleep all morning," Jude whispers in my ear.

The sound of his voice stirs something in me, and I roll over to wrap my arms around him. His strong muscles under my hands send shivers rushing across my skin. I pull him into a kiss, letting our tongues slide and dance, running my fingers through his dark, auburn hair. We break the kiss, and my mouth goes to his neck, my teeth nipping lightly.

"Jude..." I can't get enough of him. I've missed him so much. He's been gone for far too long.

"Ren..."

I love the way he says my name. It's almost like a growl; it's so low and husky. Such a turn-on.

"Rena." Now he sounds irritated.

I lean back and open my eyes to see what's bothering him. I'm not in bed. I'm not even at home. I'm still at the store, on the couch where I was taking inventory just a minute ago. Obviously, some time has passed, and much more than a minute. However, this is not my worst realization. No, that honor goes to the fact that Judę is next to me, wrapped in my arms, with my fingers threaded in his hair. *What the...?*

Releasing Jude and his hair from my grasp, I fly back and roll ungracefully onto the floor, my tailbone none too happy with the impact.

"What are you doing here? What time is it? What are you doing here?" I repeat, the magnitude and awkwardness of the situation dawning on me, not like a slow sunrise but like a tsunami breaking onto the shore. *Holy shit*. That dream about Jude was intense. I can still taste his skin on my lips. I'm afraid to look at him. I *need* to look at him.

When I glance up, Jude is staring at me with a confused look on his face, as if he doesn't understand what just happened between us. He's not the only one. I need to find a nearby rock to crawl under right away. *Jesus*. I look away quickly, scramble to my feet, and rush to the front of the store to find my phone to check the time, getting as far away from him as I can.

There's still daylight coming through the store windows, so maybe I wasn't out of it for too long. I find my phone and discover I was out for about an hour. I have a lot of time before I need to pick up Charlotte. *Whew*. That's not as bad as I thought it was. I was sleeping so deeply that it was highly disorienting to wake up with the subject of my erotic dream right there in my face. Up close and personal. Where he's never been before.

This brings my mind to Jude here in the store. I'm afraid to look toward the back for fear that he's still sitting there with that dazed look on his face. I don't blame him, though. I'm just as confused about it. What the hell am I doing, dreaming about Jude? I've got him on my brain since he came in today, and I hadn't seen him in a long time. Nothing more. Absolutely nothing more than that.

"You could have been robbed...or worse." Jude's voice is right behind me and full of anger. Not what I was expecting, to be honest. Part of me is almost relieved that he's approaching the situation this way instead of directly addressing what happened.

I still can't look him in the eye, though, and I can feel a blush that probably matches my hair rising in my cheeks. Hopefully, it conveys the mortification I'm feeling, and we can cut the lecture short. I clear my throat and look down at my very interesting shoes.

"I am aware of the position I just put myself in." Wow, what a poor choice of words. The flush deepens as I add embarrassment on top of everything else. And now I think I'm breaking out in a sweat. *Lovely*. How can this situation get any worse?

"And why were you just kissing my neck?"

Shit. So, that's how it gets worse. How do I

answer that? *Duh, I was having an erotic dream about us waking up together about to have hot sex. That's what I do when that happens.* I can't think of a single response that will get me out of this. Maybe mistaken identity...

"I was dreaming about Harry Styles, I think. Sorry about that." I try to laugh it off, but inside I'm cringing hard. *Drop it, Jude.*

"Rena. You said my name..." He's not dropping this. *Crap.* And I still can't meet his eyes.

"Yeah, right. In your dreams. I said, 'dude.' You know I call everyone that." I turn away, letting my hair cover my face some, trying to find something to look busy with. Now my ears are hot.

"You call guys 'dude' while you're having sex?"

I can't take it anymore. He needs to drop this so we can get on with our lives as though this never happened, like normal adults who find themselves in this situation all the time. This has to be a common occurrence, right?

I turn to face him, a hand on my hip in exasperation, pushing through my embarrassment. "As a matter of fact, yes. I do. I call guys 'dude' during sex, and they usually like it. What are you doing here again, anyway?"

He's unfazed for a minute, but he points back to the lounge area after eyeing me warily for way too long. "I brought you dinner."

I now see the bags of take-out on the coffee

table. I guess I was too flustered to notice them when I woke up.

"Oh. Wow." I don't think Jude has ever brought me food before without me asking him to. How strange. "Are you feeling okay?"

"What? Can't I do something nice for my friend?"

The word 'friend' hits me wrong when he says it now, and I don't know why. But at least we're off the topic of my kissing his neck. Hopefully, it was just his neck. *Good lord.* I'm never going to live this down. It's too good of fodder for Jude not to use against me in inopportune times like he does all of my embarrassing moments. I hate when I give him ammunition like this.

"Did you bring enough for both of us?" I ask, gravitating toward the food, suddenly very hungry and happy to have something else to focus on besides kissing him.

"I brought enough for the whole class."

five

DIE ALONE

JUDE

I'm trying to put the sensation of Ren's lips on my neck out of my mind, but God damn, it's hard. On the one hand, it's fucking hilarious she did that to me, but on the other, my initial welcoming reaction, which is still echoing through me, is driving me nuts. Even when we've both been sloppy drunk and hanging all over each other, we've never crossed that line. There's an unwritten rule between us we won't. We value our friendship too much to risk it for anything.

At least, that's what I *think* we've agreed on. We've never talked about it because it's weird, and we haven't needed to. Do we need to talk about it now? It will be more bizarre if we talk about it, so no. Not doing that. I need to let this go and forget about it. She was sleeping, so she didn't know what she was doing. And she's obviously embarrassed, so she didn't mean anything. So, I need to stop thinking about it already. *Jesus.*

"How's your pad Thai?" Ren interrupts my thoughts and expertly uses her chopsticks to grab at the noodles in my container.

I yank the box out of her reach.

"Mine. Eat your own food, wench."

"Damn. We used to share food all the time. Life on the road's hardened you, son."

I came here intending to feel her out about telling her my plans to talk to Brad tonight. Now I'm at a loss for what to do. Do I tell her and risk bringing up pain she's now starting to move past? Or do I act behind the scenes and hope things work out without her knowing I interfered? I sense I could be risking our friendship by doing anything, but I know within myself doing nothing is not an option. I need to at least try if I'm going to be able to look at myself in the mirror or into Charlie's bright eyes.

"Earth to Jude. Come in, Jude." She's snapping her chopsticks at me.

"Sorry, I'm still working out the jet lag since getting back from Europe." Which isn't a complete lie. I have been having trouble getting my sleep schedule on track.

"So, how was Europe? Is it true both Ryan and Matt got engaged while you were over there?"

"Yup." It still hasn't completely hit that they're engaged. But then, nothing's changed in our relationships yet. I'm wondering if it will. Who am I kidding? It totally will.

"Geez. What's in the water over there? Love Potion #9?" She gives me a sideways glance I can't read, but then her features turn sad or melancholy, but it vanishes as quickly.

I'm not sure what's going on with her, but something is indeed up. I know we haven't spent much time together lately, but usually, we fall right back into our familiar orbits when I come back from a tour. I think the addition of Charlie into our universe might be throwing our equilibrium out of whack.

"Well, for Ryan and Sarah, that's been coming for about a year now. Ryan was just waiting for the 'perfect time,' whatever that meant. And Matt and Samantha, that one came out of nowhere. But, she's good for him." I shrug, not sure what else to say.

"So, now it's your turn?" She grins wickedly at me, and her voice switches to something like an old-time radio announcer. "Will the Romeo of Rock 'n Roll, the Casanova of Concert Halls, the Don Juan of...crap, what goes with that? Um... the Don Juan of Dive Bars finally become shackled to a ball and chain any time soon? Stay tuned to find out..."

I can't help but smile, but that's as far as it goes. I'm not laughing like Ren, and I couldn't say why not. She often jokes about my sex life, hell, I even join in picking fun at myself in that regard, but I'm in a funk tonight. Everything is just feeling *off*.

"Yeah. Yeah. Very funny. You know that's not happening." I scoff at the suggestion of me getting married. My cards have been dealt, and Marriage isn't one of them. And I'm not mad about it. "I'll get married on a day of the week not ending in a 'Y.'" I am not the marrying kind of guy. Hell, I'm not a relationship kind of guy. I'm not any kind of guy. I'm just a guy. *I need to stop thinking the word 'guy' for fuck's sake.*

"Are you still hell-bent on never getting married?" She frowns as if the thought troubles her. "Who will take care of you when you're old?"

"My adoring fans, of course. Who do you think?" Honestly, I don't think that far ahead. I'm not a planner like Ren is. I don't have my entire life mapped out. Life is something that happens *to* me, not *because* of me. "I'm not in a band because I like playing music. I'm in Indigo King because I'm seeking home health aides for my retirement."

"Ugh, Jude. You and your groupies." She physically shudders, and I'm almost offended.

"Everyone serves a purpose in life. Some purposes are more fun than others." I wink at her and laugh when she turns beet red. "What are you getting embarrassed about? Did you revert to being a virgin after having Charlie? Is that a thing?"

"What? No." Her flush is only deepening, and I'm reminded why picking on her like this is so much fun. "And no, that's not a thing."

"So, you're not thinking about dating now that asshole's out of the picture?" I am purposely not bringing up the kisses on my neck she woke up to. I don't figure in this equation. Well, I shouldn't.

"I've thought about it, sure. But when do I have time to date? I barely have time to eat most days."

"You're eating today."

"Yeah, because you brought me food. I probably wouldn't otherwise."

"You need to take care of yourself, Ren. You're useless to Charlie if you're a zombie."

She sighs and yawns, rubbing her eyes, obviously tired.

"I know. I know."

I examine her more closely, and she is beyond exhausted. No wonder she fell asleep on the job when she got a minute of quiet. This makes me want to talk to 'Brad the Dad' even more and kick his ass into gear to help out. And most definitely to do so without telling Ren.

We finish our dinners, slowly returning to ourselves like we used to be before I left and before Ren had Charlie. I wonder if it will take longer to settle back to this comfort level with each other next time we spend any time away from each other. I can see that being the case, but I hope it isn't.

Everyone around me is either getting married or having babies, but none of that makes me want to follow suit. If anything, it makes me want to stay away from it all the more. I don't do feelings, and I absolutely don't do relationships. They've never been in my DNA, and I know for a fact your DNA doesn't change. It can't change. So, neither will I, and I'm okay with that.

J ude takes off on some secret adventure as I close up the store, and I eventually make my way toward my grandfather's condo in Santa Monica to pick up Charlotte. Jude's probably got a hot date with one of those home health aide applicants he was talking about. He's too funny. While we joke about him being a player, I never press him for details. I don't want to know details, to be honest. In all the years we've been friends, he's never had a real girlfriend. Or at least not one that lasted more than a few months. That can't be a healthy way to live; without real love in his life. While sure, I'm there for him as a friend, and his bandmates are too, he doesn't have a 'person.' Everyone should have a 'person.'

Then again, neither do I anymore. Well, that isn't entirely true. I have Charlotte. Even with the bullshit I have to put up with in Brad, I'd not give her up for the world. There are zero regrets when it comes to having her. Parenting can be a nightmare sometimes, like when I needed to close the store when she was sick, but she's worth everything I need to do for her to be happy and healthy.

My phone rings and I notice Sawyer, my part-time employee and friend, is calling. It's not unusual for him to call, but it's typically during the day if he does. I answer with the car's hands-free button.

"Hey, Sawyer, what's up?"

"Hey, Rena." He sounds nervous. "Did you know that Jude was back in town?"

"Yeah...I just saw him a little while ago. Why?"

"Okay. Well, I'm at this dive bar in Pasadena to check out this new band, Chaos Fuel, and he's here with the rest of Indigo King."

"Chaos Fuel? Cool band name. Are they decent?" I wonder if Jude's band is scoping out the competition or something. He didn't mention going to see a band tonight, though. Not like he's obligated to tell me his plans or anything.

"Um. Don't know yet; they haven't gone on. But..." he stalls, not telling me something.

"What is it, Sawyer?" The hair on my arms stands at attention, anticipating whatever is coming next because it will not be anything I want to hear.

"Brad is the singer for Chaos Fuel. And Jude is here looking a little amped up." Loud music starts up in the background. "Hang on. Let me head back outside."

"Well, I take back my 'cool band name' comment. Chaos Fuel is the dumbest band name I've ever heard. Has Jude seen you yet?" Both Jude and Brad know Sawyer, so it's not like he will go unnoticed in a small dive bar.

"Nope. Shit. Yup. He just did, and I think he knows I'm talking to you. Maybe. Shit. I don't know." He's becoming unglued. "Hey man, what's up? Yeah, he definitely spotted me."

"Dude. Chill. Everything's fine. Jude won't do anything stupid." *Yes, he totally would.* What is he doing there? Something in my spine catches fire as I think about Brad out partying around town while I'm on my way to pick up our daughter, too exhausted to think. A small part of me almost hopes that Jude does do something stupid to Brad. He deserves it. "Is that Brad's band playing in the background now?" The sound is too distorted to tell if the band is any good, but curiosity grabs me.

"No. They go on last." He pauses, "Hey man, how's it going? Shit. Now Brad's noticed me too. I feel like I'm in the middle of some weird living chessboard, and I don't know how to play chess."

That makes me laugh. Sawyer can be overly dramatic when he wants to be.

"So, what do you expect me to do from my car on

my way to pick up Charlotte about any of this? Or was this a 411 tip?"

He sighs loudly into the phone.

"Just information, I guess. You didn't mention that Jude was back, and they're both here together, which is odd."

"Well, people are allowed to be in the same public place together." I'm not convinced by my words, but I have to say something. "Thanks for letting me know, Sawyer. Even though I already knew about Jude being back."

"Yeah, okay. Cool. Sorry to bring up the Brad stuff."

"No worries. I'm sure I'll hear his name again at some point in my life. May as well get used to it now." That's the truth enough, though I still flinch inwardly when his name is said.

"Uh oh."

"Uh oh? What 'uh oh?'" I don't like the sound of that.

"Jude broke away from the guys in his band and is heading over in Brad's direction."

"What?" What the hell is Jude doing? "What's happening?"

"I'll call you back."

The call disconnects, and I'm left to wonder what the hell is going on at some nameless dive bar somewhere in Pasadena between my best friend and my ex-boyfriend.

seven

BOUND FOR THE FLOOR
JUDE

I make my way to the Old Town Bar to meet up with Ryan and Matt. I didn't tell Ren what I planned to do, and while the thought of her wrath still makes me nervous, I think the move is worth the risk for Charlie to have her father in her life. If Ren finds out I interfered and won't talk to me, but Charlie has her dad, I'm cool. This whole thing affects me way more than it should, but I can't stop myself from doing this, either.

By the time I arrive at the bar, the bands are ready to start, and Ryan and Matt are huddled in the corner leaning against a defunct pinball machine. The place is beginning to fill up, which isn't hard to do, considering how fucking small this place is, but there are more people than I expected for a Thursday night. It hasn't changed much since the last time I was here, like five years ago, if at all. More neon tubes have died in the signs on the walls, but otherwise, status quo.

"We haven't seen Brad yet," Matt yells because it's so fucking loud in here.

"Did you check the courtyard?" The enclosed outdoor area usually gets more crowded than the inside. They both shake their heads and follow me outside to see if I can find Brad out there.

The patio is crowded, but I spot him right away, surrounded by his latest admirers. Victims, more like it. My fists are clenching of their own volition, and I need to get myself in check before I do something stupid. I wasn't expecting to react this way to seeing him, but after seeing Charlie... How the fuck can he screw over his own daughter like this?

"Dude." Ryan maneuvers himself between Brad and me. "What's going on here? You mentioned kicking his ass, but why? Other than his obvious douchebaggery."

"You know my friend Ren, who had a baby about six months ago?"

"Actually, no. We've never had the pleasure of meeting your so-called BFF." Matt appears mad at this. "Now she has a baby? Is it yours?"

"Yeah, why haven't we met this chick yet? If she's your 'BFF,' I can't believe she hasn't met your fucking band. What's up with that?" Now Ryan is mad too. "And why don't you talk about her?" What the fuck are they doing? Interrogating me now?

"Seriously, guys? This isn't the time." I try to step around Ryan, but Matt now blocks my way.

"You're not going anywhere or kicking anyone's ass until we know what the fuck is going on." Matt glances around, surveying the crowd, always looking for enemies. "We could do without another round of bad press because of violence, okay?"

He would know. His name got dragged through the mud this past summer after a violent altercation with his brother, who popped up out of his past to blackmail him. It was not fun. But we survived it relatively unscathed.

"Fine," I sigh, resolved to explain everything. I guess they have a right to know why they're here to back me up. Though I never talk about Ren for a reason. She's the one and only normal thing in my life, and I want to keep it that way. I want to keep her separate from the craziness of this lifestyle. I don't know why; I've always shielded our friend-ship like that. "My friend Ren, who I've known almost eleven years now. *Damn*. Anyway, she had a baby six months ago tomorrow, and asshat Brad over there is the father. He is supposed to be helping her out with Charlie, but he can't keep it in his pants, and now he's left them to fend for themselves. As you would say, Matt, it can't stand."

They stare at me with strange expressions I can't quite decipher. Ryan even cocks his head as he stares at me. I wipe my face, thinking I must have food or something still stuck to it.

"Huh," Ryan says as if something makes sense to him all of a sudden. He glances over at Matt, who nods at him in agreement with something I don't understand.

"What the fuck is wrong with you guys? Do I have Sharpie on my face or something? What the hell are you looking at me like that for?" These two are starting to piss me off. I didn't ask them here to judge me. I asked for their support.

Matt shakes his head with a chuckle and a quick sideways look at Ryan. So fucking cryptic.

"Never mind us. What's your plan here?"

I run a hand through my hair and grab my neck, trying to work out the tension building there.

"Yeah...I didn't make a plan. I was going to wing it."

"Dude. No." Ryan grabs my arm and pulls me to the opposite corner from Brad like we're in a boxing ring, and Matt follows. "First of all, does Ren know you're here?"

I glare at him. They're going to try to talk me out of this.

"Of course not. I'm impulsive, not suicidal." I see Sawyer, a friend of Ren's who also works at her store, out of the corner of my eye. I give him a quick chin tip and a wave. He's acting like he's spooked about something, but he can sometimes be dramatic. Maybe he's guessing something's going down between Brad and me. *Great*. He better not tell Ren I'm here.

"Well, if she wouldn't want anyone interfering, why are we interfering?" Ryan is still trying to be the diplomat, like always. Don't they understand when you have a kid, your kid should be your world? They're not that daft.

"Alright, Ryan. If you had a baby daughter, would you leave Sarah to do everything herself if things didn't work out between you two?"

He seems insulted.

"Of course not. That's ridiculous."

"And you, Matt? If you and Samantha had a child and you broke up for whatever reason, would you make her fend for herself and your baby?"

He, too, scoffs like this is the most ludicrous thought in the universe.

"No fucking way."

"Well, there you go. That's why I'm interfering. Because dick waffle over there is doing just that to his baby daughter."

"But Jude..." Matt starts, but I ignore him and push past him. I don't understand why they aren't getting it. This shouldn't need a second thought.

I spot Brad still in his corner with his victims; I'm just going to call them that from now on. As I'm about halfway to him, a group of women surrounds mc, and Matt and Ryan, apparently right behind me.

"Oh my God, look who it is," One of them growls. She has so much makeup on that it cracks in her wrinkles, and she's not even that old. *Shit*. I think I know her. Vaguely. "Jude the very rude boy."

I rack my brain, trying to remember her name. Celeste? Cherise? Something with a "C."

"Hey there. Good to see you. Sorry I can't chat at the moment." I eye Brad to make sure he's not sneaking off if he saw me heading his way.

"On another hit and run mission, are you?" She sneers at me, a wicked smile on her over-filled lips, and it dawns on me that I've slept with this woman. A long time ago, but it definitely happened. Good lord, I must have been drunk, or at least I hope I was. "You'll never change, huh, Jude?"

"What? What does that mean?" Who the fuck is this chick to judge me right now? Has she seen herself? I can't believe I slept with this woman. Did I sleep with this woman? Shit. How the fuck don't I remember if I slept with her? What is so different with me now that I can't imagine doing that again? I can't be that changed. I guess if I squint my eyes in the dark while drunk, she'd be attractive. Jesus. I'm such an asshole.

"Oh, honey. I'm not saying it's all a bad thing..." She smiles at me from under her fake lashes, and something inside me curdles at the look.

"Hey ladies," Ryan distracts them and stops me from responding disrespectfully to a woman in public and gives me a nod to go ahead. He probably saw my mood go dark. Matt stays vigilant, half in the conversation with the surrounding group and half in the crowd.

I'm probably going to need to revisit what she said at a later date because I know there's some issues in there that I need to address and deal with. Just not fucking tonight. I am not in the mood for soul searching tonight.

I press forward, making it to Brad without another interruption. I know he saw me heading this way, but he's acting like he didn't. *What a dickhead*. He's leaning against the gate, a girl on each side of him. Such a pretty boy with his open shirt and chains. I still don't comprehend what Ren sees in him. This dude is about as deep as a puddle.

"Yo. Baby Daddy. We need to talk." My tone is brooking no argument, and I see him stiffen.

He glares at me but pushes off the wrought iron and mutters something to the women. I shove my hands in my pockets, so I at least have some barrier between my fists and his fucking face.

"What's up, Lockwood? Didn't know you were a fan." He smirks to himself like he said something clever. *What a dipshit.*

"Really not a fan, and most definitely *not* why I'm here."

"Oh? Why are you here then? Crawling for leftovers?" He winks at one of the women against the gate, waiting for him. The only thing crawling is my skin, thinking of this guy with Ren. I visibly shudder at the thought.

I decide to cut the bullshit and drive straight to the point.

"You do realize you have a daughter? A baby? Right?"

"So? What's that got to do with anything?" As if Charlie is an afterthought. The fists in my pockets clench tighter, my nails digging painfully into my palms.

"So? So, you need to support her, you fuckhead."

"Last time I checked, which was, oh," he looks down at his bare wrist, "just now, that's none of your fucking business." He steps forward and gets an inch away from my nose. The reek of whiskey is pungent on his breath, and his dark eyes are concentrated on mine, daring me to do something dumb in public.

I don't need to turn around to know Ryan and Matt just stepped up behind me because Brad takes a small step back, trying to be subtle about it, but he's obviously backing down. *Chicken shit*.

"Anything to do with Ren is my business," I growl. "And that now includes Charlie."

"Her name is Charlotte."

"No. If you were at the meeting today like a real dad, you'd know there have been some changes in the nickname department."

"Meeting? What the fuck, man?" He's baffled, and I love it. Messing with him is too easy.

I step up to him, pulling myself up to my full height to look down on him, even if it is just a little.

"Be a man for once and take care of your shit like a real adult." I put a finger on his chest, pressing only slightly. "Faithless is he who says farewell when the road darkens, bitch."

I turn away before he can reply or haul off and punch me like I think he was about to. A small group is starting to congregate around us, and Matt and Ryan drag me out to the alley next to the bar, then to the nearby parking garage.

"Feel better now?" Ryan's at least not being facetious.

"I'll feel better if it makes a difference." I don't get the sense there's any getting through to Brad about responsibility and consequences for actions.

"Good luck with that." Matt grips my shoulder and gives it a squeeze.

They were the perfect wingmen tonight. They tried to talk me out of the crazy shit but then supported me when I went ahead with it anyway. Can't ask for more than that.

"Thanks, guys." As much as we can dance on each other's nerves, we are a chosen family. We stick together when it's important.

"What was all that about dark roads you were

saying? It sounded familiar?" I'm instantly disappointed in Matt.

"Duh, that was Lord of the Rings. Obviously."
Ryan looks proud of himself, and he should be. The
movie sessions on the bus, making them sit through
extended versions, are starting to pay off. If they're
not going to read good books like I do, they may as
well watch good movies. My work with him might
be done.

I smile to myself, remembering Brad's bewildered face. I hope I got through to him, for Charlie's
sake.

eight

SAVE ME

REN

When I arrive at my grandfather's condo, I try calling Sawyer back before going in. I have been on pins and needles waiting to hear back from him to tell me what happened, if anything, between Jude and Brad. He answers right before it switches to his voicemail.

"Hey, so crisis averted, I think." The relief in his voice is evident.

"Oh? What the hell happened?"

"I don't know exactly, but Jude went over to Brad and got in his face all serious-like. And then he poked a finger at his chest and said something, and the rest of his band pulled him away and out of here. Things were kind of intense."

What the heck is Jude playing at? Getting in Brad's face? That is so unlike him.

"So, Jude left? What did Brad do after that?" I hate asking, but curiosity is murdering this cat.

"Um...well..."

"Spit it out, Sawyer. I can take it. I know what he's doing." I say that but steel myself against what comes next.

"Okay. He laughed it off and went back to the chicks he was talking to before Jude got in his face."

Surprisingly or not, I'm not as affected as I thought I would be hearing confirmation of my suspicions. I think I might be too tired to care about what Brad does and who he does it with. I've got more important things to worry about than who my ex is sleeping with. I only care if he provides for his daughter, which he's not currently doing.

"Well, thanks for the heads up on tonight's excitement. You're working tomorrow night and this weekend, right?" I cross my fingers that he hasn't come upon some music festival that he absolutely must go to this weekend at the last minute. It wouldn't be the first time.

"Yup. I'll be there."

I let out a relieved breath after we hang up. I need a break from the store this weekend. My laundry pile alone will take up most of Saturday. I'll never cease to be amazed at how many clothes a little person can go through in a week.

The following day when I show up at the store, Charlotte perched on a hip, I find Jude waiting out front, leaning against the door and scrolling on his phone. Something inside my chest does a little dance.

"You're late." He doesn't glance up.

"Top of the morning to you too," I smirk, pushing him off the door with the hip not holding Charlotte. She giggles furiously and reaches out for Jude, but I distract her as I unlock the door. I need to figure out what he's doing here before we turn all friendly. "To what do we owe this great honor?" I start to make my way to the back to turn the lights on.

"Today is Friday."

"Yeah, I know. That doesn't explain why you're here." Charlotte gets antsy as we walk further away from Jude. She really wants to go to him. *Oh boy.*

"Fridays are release day." He's now yelling from the front of the store to me in the back. "I figured you could use some help with Charlie."

I stop in the middle of flipping switches for all the chandeliers and glance at Charlotte. I give her my most confused face and mouth the word, *'What?'* to her, and she starts belly laughing. Jude never helps me with the store. If he's here and a customer accidentally asks him anything, he always replies, *'Does it look like I work here?'* The customer typically says, *'Yes.'*

Heading back up to the front of the store, I eye Jude warily. I don't understand where this is all coming from. It's not like him to be so helpful. I mean, he's a nice guy, but he's not one to go out of his way to be one. I think about what Sawyer told me that happened between Jude and Brad last night. I don't know if I should bring anything up or not. I don't want him to think I'm spying on him or Brad. Nothing happened between them but an intense conversation, apparently. Nothing to be upset about. Even though the whole situation was all I thought about last night as I tried to fall asleep. Well, that and the crazy dream I had about Jude. Between both of those bizarre items, I didn't sleep much. *Again*. Maybe Jude being here today to help is a good thing.

"So, you're helping with Charlotte? Or the new releases?" I want to make sure I understand the boundaries of his charity.

"Just Charlie." He puts his phone away and takes Charlotte from me. She goes more than willingly and was leaning toward him the whole time. I only had to let her go as she basically jumped into his arms.

"I think she's smitten with you. Better watch out." Seeing the two of them together tugs at my heartstrings. Jude clearly has no idea what to do with her, but Charlotte's total trust in him despite that is so sweet.

"Yeah, well, I'm smittenable. Obviously." He glances around, unsure what to do now. The hapless expression on his face is priceless. Jude is usually confident, but he's out of his element with a baby girl in the mix.

"Why don't you guys hang out in the sitting area with her toys while I work?" I offer.

"Sure, we'll do that." He moves to grab her diaper bag with her toys.

"Jude?" He stops and finally looks at me for the first time today, and when our eyes meet, something is different. Our friendship hit another level, a grown-up level that we'd never been a part of before. We see each other as adults and not crazy twenty-somethings still figuring out life. My stomach does a flip, or cartwheel, or some acrobatic move. "Thanks."

His cheeks grow red, which I don't think I have ever seen before in all the years we've been friends, and I have to bite my lip to not laugh aloud. He's freaking cute when he blushes.

He takes Charlotte to the back area, and I put the latest Indigo King record on the store's sound system. Charlotte starts screaming in joy. She loves music, especially Indigo King.

Jude is back at the counter when I turn around,

slightly panicked. "She screamed. But she's laughing."

Now I can't help but laugh at him. He is completely lost.

"She did, and she is. She likes your band."

"Oh. Okay." He glares at me, presumably for laughing at him, and retreats toward the back again.

"Everything she does is probably normal. You'll know when something isn't."

The doubt crossing his face is fleeting, but I can tell he thinks, *'No, I won't.'*

"Yes, you will."

"How do you know?" His voice is quiet and unsure, and so unlike him.

"Because I know you. And I trust you." I try to make my smile as encouraging as possible for him. I'm amazed he's trying this, and while I half expect this to go horribly, I'm hoping everything goes well. I want it to go well. And more for Jude than for Charlotte. He's putting himself out on a limb for me, and I want this to be worth it for him. I want there to be a payoff. I'm more than sure that Charlotte will deliver on her end. She's a good girl. *Usually*.

nine

BOOM SWAGGER BOOM

JUDE

My first impression of babies – they're fun. My second impression of babies – they're boring as hell. My third – What the fuck was I thinking? She wants attention, like, *all the time*. I was not prepared for this. I should have Googled this or something before volunteering. Not the most brilliant move on my part.

Charlie puts everything in her mouth. *Every fucking thing*. She's needed two diaper changes in the same number of hours, which I absolutely will not handle, but Ren took care of it. I need to buy stock in freaking diapers. *Jesus*. She's been chattering nonstop with silly sounds as though she's having a conversation with me, which, okay, that's pretty damned cute. And now we've started crawling around in a weird floor version of Tag, and I can't tell who's It. It's me. I'm It.

"What is going on here?" Ren hasn't had much of a break from customers this morning, so I am glad I can help out.

"We're playing Tag. I'm It." I smack her calf lightly. "Now you're It."

"Jude. She's crawling."

"Yeah. That's how we're moving around for the game. Though she's not very good, she mostly goes backward, but she's funny as hell."

"She's never crawled before." Her voice sounds amazed and almost a little sad. I don't understand why that would bum her out.

"Really? Because she seems to be a natural. Except for the going backward thing." Did I witness one of her milestones and not even know? *Wow*. I got to be present for one of her firsts. *Very fucking cool*. "Should we video it or something?" I pull my phone out of my pocket and start recording Charlie scooting backward around the blanket on the floor and laughing. Ren gets down on her hands and knees and chases her, and they are the most wholesome thing I've ever seen; a mom playing on the floor with her kid.

My heart grows three sizes larger like the Grinch on Christmas. I get it now. I get why people do this. And I don't get how Brad could leave all this behind for some random piece of ass. His loss.

Little things like crawling, albeit incorrectly, are

actually gigantic things. Things that need to be celebrated. It *should* be celebrated.

"So, what else should I keep an eye out for her doing that she hasn't done yet?" I'm excited that this shit is happening on my watch. Like I have anything to do with it.

Ren sits back on her heels, considering my question.

"Hard to say, she's ahead in some stuff, but every baby is different."

Charlie backs herself into my leg, and I pick her up, turning her to look at me.

"So, what's your next trick, huh? You gonna start running around here in a minute?" She giggles and drools. I reach up to wipe her chin with my thumb, and she bites me.

"Ow! She fucking bit me. I mean, she bit me." I examine my thumb for signs of broken skin or blood, but only a dent in the skin shows. "That hurt, little lady."

"She can't gum you to death." Ren stands and glances around the store, which is currently empty of customers.

"That wasn't gums." I lift Charlie's upper lip, and sure enough, a bit of a white tooth peeks through her upper gum. "There's the culprit."

"What? What is?" Ren comes over and leans down to inspect Charlie's mouth, her red hair falling in my face and blocking my view. "Oh my gosh, a tooth! She's got a tooth!" She turns her head and is only a few inches from my face, and I have to lean back to see her clearly without my glasses. Her smile couldn't be any bigger, and the light spray of freckles on her nose and cheeks are brighter. I almost want to reach out and run a finger along her cheekbone to see how they feel right now.

I snap out of my daze and back to the present.

"Yeah, and the thing is friggin' sharp too. You didn't tell me you spawned a vampire."

"I'm surprised the tooth isn't bothering her." And as if on cue, Charlie starts howling, with tears streaking down her face, mixing with the drool and now snot. She's a fucking mess. My heart gets ripped out of my chest by this little girl's tears. There is nothing I want more in this world than for her to stop crying. I can't stand her being so upset.

I start bouncing her on my knee.

"How do I make it stop?" I need to make this stop. I need to make her okay. I start making funny faces at her, but she's crying too hard to look at me.

Ren runs over to her bag to grab her favorite toys, but Charlie wants nothing to do with them. Now her cries have amped up to eleven, and her face is turning red as she goes so long between breaths. *Jesus, that can't be normal.*

"Should we call her doctor or something?" I am freaking the fuck out.

Ren laughs at this, and I glare at her.

"She's just teething." She rummages through her bag some more, searching for something and not finding it. "Shoot."

I sit up, aware that I may have an errand to run, which will allow me to run away from the screaming that my heart can't take another minute of.

"What? What do you need?"

"Baby pain reliever. And I thought I had some numbing gel and a teething ring in here, but I guess not. I didn't think we needed it yet."

I hurl Charlie at her; carefully.

"I'm on it." And I'm out the door before Ren can let a single protest out.

I rush to the drug store down the road in record time and enlist the pharmacist on duty to help me procure everything a baby would need while they're teething. They are, of course, out of the baby-safe numbing gel, which would solve it instantly. Once I pay for about half of the baby aisle, I make my way back to Vital Records. I go to the back room where Ren has a mini-refrigerator and start putting the teething rings and other baby-related accessories in to cool down. Then I take a clean washcloth from the bathroom and run it under ice-cold water.

When I arrive back at the seating area, I take screaming Charlie from Ren, who looks like she's about to lose her cool, and give the cloth to Charlie to chew on. She instantly stops crying and starts gnawing on the cool material, her breath easing in small hitches. *Yup. Fucking Baby Whisperer.*

ten

Wow. Jude saved the day today. I don't know how I would have gotten through this morning without him with Charlotte's teething suddenly. And now he's snoring softly on the couch in the sitting area of the store with Charlotte sleeping on his chest, wrapped in his arms snugly. I had to take both a picture and record a video of them. They are so darned cute.

Jude has always been a dichotomy; the book nerd with glasses in a rocker's body. Even his tattoos are all literary in theme. It's why we've always gotten along so well, sharing so many of the same interests. Witnessing him being so involved in Charlotte's care today and so concerned for her well-being is a side of Jude I did not expect to encounter. We barely saw him when he was in town in the summer, and he had little to do with Charlotte. He wouldn't hold her back then. It wasn't anything personal; she was too small and didn't have a personality like she does now. And now she's sleeping on his chest? It's kind of wild.

When we met over a decade ago when I was a host on a vTV live music show, *Tour de Force*, I never thought we'd end up such good friends, or friends at all for that matter. I got him fired on his first day as an intern. Not on purpose, but the mistake on air was obvious, and it couldn't have been anyone else's fault but his. I would have felt bad if he had cared about the job and not just pursued it to make music business and band connections since he was new to LA. Honestly, I did feel bad and insisted he let me buy him dinner that day. That's where I found out why he was really there. I admired his creativity, and we've been best friends ever since. Even though I'm a few years older than him (which he never lets me live down), we've always been at the same level of maturity.

I supported him through all the dead-end bands he played in before landing in Indigo King, and he supported me through all the dead-end communications jobs I had before opening my store. *Tour de Force* was short-lived, and I'm only rarely recognized, thank goodness. I've been quite happy running Vital Records for the last five years, and the store does pretty well. I'm not going to grow rich running this place, but it's enough to get by for the most part.

Jude stirs, and I realize I've been sitting and staring at the two of them for an extraordinary amount of time. I can't seem to take my eyes off them, and my mouth goes dry as I take in the picture. My best friend and my baby daughter are so comfortable together. I'd never imagined this was possible. I assumed that Jude would always be somewhere on the edges of Charlotte's life, not an integral part. I'm not sure what to think about it.

Jude is always on the go; even when he's home in LA, he's out and about somewhere. He is not one to be pinned down. It's why our friendship has worked. I don't expect or demand constancy from him. But I do know that if I need him, he will be there for me, no matter what, and I'd do the same for him. We can and do go for months without talking or texting while he's on the road, and when he's home, it's like he never left. We fall right back into our friendship without missing a beat.

For some reason, that feels different now, though. Things have been a little awkward between us since he came back this time, and I'm not sure what the cause is. Maybe the magnitude of Charlotte's presence in my life makes things different between us. Then there's Jude going and having some intense conversation with Brad that I still don't know what to think about. Add on top of that the crazy dream I had about Jude and waking up to him in my arms, and things are just plain weird now.

Watching them nap together is doing something to my heart too. It's constricting and making me wish for things I shouldn't ever wish for. Not with Jude, anyway. I value our friendship way too much to think about trying to be more with him. I also know it would be a fool's errand to try. Jude will never settle down. This means he, in all probability, won't ever have a family. That makes me sad for him. He would make a perfect dad.

Charlotte starts to wake up, which wakes up Jude, surprised to find her on his chest for a second, but then he shifts and wraps her tighter in his arms. I freeze, not wanting to draw attention to the fact that I've been staring at them this whole time. Luckily, they both nod off again without noticing me, and I stand up as quietly as possible and return to the front of the store.

Pops shows up a little while later to pick up Charlotte for the evening, and I didn't realize it was that late in the day; time went by so fast. A few minutes after Pops arrives, Sawyer shows up for his shift, and the store seems very crowded very quickly. They see Jude with Charlotte on the couch and stare in amazement. I purposely brush off the surprise and questions I know are coming.

"Gimme a minute to wake them," I say, not

wanting Jude or Charlotte to be jolted awake with a crowd around them.

I try to pry Charlotte out of Jude's arms gently and am making some progress, but he senses her movement and instinctively grabs onto her tighter. It's one of the cutest things I've ever seen, and my heart skips a couple of beats. Charlotte's now awake, though, and starts fussing, kicking her legs, lifting her head, and whimpering slightly. This gets Jude's attention, and his eyes fly open.

"Hey, sleepyhead," I whisper with a smile, finally getting him to release Charlotte to me. "Pops is here for her now." I nod in the direction of the front of the store where Pops and Sawyer are waiting and still watching in awe.

Jude glances over and then runs a hand down his face before sitting up.

"Hey guys," he says to them as cool as can be, as if he wasn't just sleeping with a baby in his arms like a teddy bear.

I get Charlotte ready to go with my grandfather and see them off for their evening together. Pops again asks if I want him to keep her overnight, lifting an inquisitive eyebrow in Jude's direction, but I again decline and promise to pick her up at the usual time.

Sawyer shifts gears and decides to pretend that nothing is odd about Jude being here and helping with Charlotte. As though it happens every day. It's almost weirder for him to act like everything is normal than to address it somehow, but I don't want to think about it anymore or make any more of it than I already have. So, I let it go.

"What are you doing now?" Jude stretches his arms over his head, lifting his shirt and exposing his stomach. I glimpse a six-pack I don't remember him having, and my pulse quickens against my will. I have to look away and try to think of something unsexy to clear my thoughts. *Shit.*

"Well, I only have a few hours, so I was going to grab some dinner and bring it back here to work on the books till I need to pick up Charlotte." I realize how boring that sounds, but it is what it is. "Another exciting Friday night for Rena Scott."

"C'mon. Let's hit the Pier."

We haven't hung out together at the Santa Monica Pier in years. It used to be our go-to place when he wasn't playing out somewhere on weekends.

"Aren't you going to get sick of me? You've been with me all day."

"Nope." He puts an arm around my shoulder and pulls me along towards the door. It's just like old times, but it's also different. I wish I could figure out what was going on between us. It's most likely nothing. It's probably just me.

eleven

ALRIGHT
JUDE

I need a major palate cleanse. Between Ren's crazily enticing neck kisses and the attachment that seems to be forming between Charlie and me, I am craving some semblance of normalcy. I'm itching for things to be the way they were between Ren and me before she went and had a baby, and I went and got a little famous. Shit is getting way too heavy.

We take Ren's car to the pier since she'll need to pick up Charlie later. It's only a half-hour drive, but we're already awkward halfway there. *What the hell?*

"Freaking Queen Bee." The statement from Ren comes out of nowhere.

"What are you talking about?"

She glances at me sideways, a disapproving scowl on her face.

"Seriously, dude?"

"Seriously. What or who is a Fucking Queen Bee? Are you going senile already in your old age?"

"I can't believe you right now, Jude." The disapproval deepens and now appears to have some hurt attached. *What the fuck?*

"Ren. All who wander may not be lost, but you just jumped off the damned map. Explain yourself and now why you can't believe me."

She sighs heavily and waves an exasperated hand toward the car in front of us.

"Freaking Queen Bee...?"

I glance at the car, and the realization hits me like a pie in the face; the license plate starts with FQB. Freaking Queen Bee. I smack my forehead in disbelief at my forgetfulness. We used to play this game to pass the time in LA traffic whenever we drove together, coming up with names for the people in the cars by their license plate letters. Considering at least half of the people in LA use vanity plates, because it is the most pretentious city on the planet, it's been our own way of creating them for the rest of us. We haven't been in the same car in I don't know how long, so the game slipped my mind.

"Wow, Ren. Nice one. She does look like a Queen Bee." The name works even better since the car is a yellow VW Bug. "I'm sorry I was so slow on the uptake there. We haven't played in forever."

"Are you okay? You've been awfully quiet since we left the store." Her tone shifts from exasperated to concerned.

"Am I okay? What an existential question. How does one define okay? And how does that apply to a human's existence? Does okay denote a positive or negative? Or somewhere in the gray area in between?" Maybe I've convoluted my answer enough for her to drop the subject, so I don't need to consider my answer.

"Alright, never mind. Forget I asked. Geez." Her giggle is like music to my ears.

Mission accomplished, but at least she's laughing. I still need to work out whether or not I'm okay when I get some time to myself, which is rarely. Of course, I do that on purpose to avoid those specific types of questions, so there's that.

An asshole in a classic Porsche cuts us off, and Ren slams on the brakes. His license plate is surprisingly not a vanity one and starts with KAW.

"King Ass Wipe," I say, pointing at the car.

"I was thinking the exact same thing."

"Great minds..." I don't finish the saying. We know it. We say it all the time since we practically share a brain. The energy in the car shifts, but I couldn't say how, exactly.

We get to the Santa Monica Pier without getting into an accident or either of us having an existential crisis and find the boardwalk fairly empty. In mid-

November, the evenings are getting a little cooler, so the night crowds should be lighter now. As we approach, I stop at a hat stand to find some celebrity camouflage. Everybody knows that famous people can't be recognized if they wear a hat. It's common knowledge in LA, which is likely why this hat stand is right at the entrance. Serving famous rock stars such as myself who are forgetful yet want to have a fun evening uninterrupted by perceptive fans.

While I peruse the various piles of different headwear, Ren is having fun trying on furry animal costume hats. She's wavering between a pink bunny with long ears and a raccoon. Either animal face perched on top of her head is absolutely ridiculous but fucking adorable at the same time.

"Bunny. Definitely bunny," I say, deciding for her. "Plus, Charlie will love it."

She looks at me funny but agrees with a grin.

"She will. But for now, it's mine." She studies me and my current LA Dodgers cap and wrinkles her nose at me. "You don't even like sports ball."

"That's what makes it a perfect disguise."

"Here, try one of these straw cowboy hats." She jumps up to grab one off the top of the cart and places it on my head. Something in her eyes glimmers as she assesses me. Now her face becomes unreadable, and I can't tell if it looks okay or not.

"What? Is it dumb? Don't make me look dumb."

I pull out my phone to examine myself since there isn't a mirror in sight. It looks okay.

"Yes. Dumb. It's perfectly dumb. Nobody will know it's you." Her voice is a little hoarse as she speaks.

"Something wrong with your voice?" I hope she's not getting sick.

"I'm fine." She clears her throat again and turns away quickly. She's acting so weird. "I'm fine. C'mon, let's pay and go."

We grab a couple of burgers and sit at a table to people-watch.

Ren points to a well-dressed middle-aged couple walking hand in hand on the boardwalk.

"He... is an oil tycoon from some unpronounceable country on holiday with his lifelong mistress who he has a second family with."

I raise an eyebrow at her, incredulous.

"Now we're playing Life Story? You're pulling out all the oldies but goodies today. What's next? Truth Or Dare?"

"So? It's fun." The brightness in her eyes does something weird to my insides, and I have to shift my gaze away from her. I turn back to inspect the couple in question.

"Okay. She's a mistress, but he's not an oil tycoon. She only *thinks* he is. He's actually a high school teacher who saves up every year to take her on an extravagant vacation."

"Aww. So romantic." She clutches at her heart as if the story pulls on her heartstrings.

"Really? What about his other family? They wouldn't think so."

"But they see him every day. The mistress only gets this short time together with him." She's getting kind of angry, defending their love story. "Plus, they think Santa Monica is an extravagant vacation. That's daft, but you have to admit it is sweet."

"Ren. You know we made this up, right? They're probably just bank tellers from Burbank or some shit."

"Fine. I'll keep their love affair as my secret." She huffs dramatically, turning away from me, then giggling again. I love seeing her in such a playful mood after watching her be so tired and stressed. This was a fantastic call on my part.

"What about those guys?" I point at three teenage guys leaning against the railing, checking out the passing girls and being blatantly obvious.

"Hmm. Let me think." She drums her fingers on the table, studying them closely. "They were forced to be in a boy band together after failing solo attempts on a singing competition show."

"Okay. Good start..." She's in her element now. I love it.

"But they've been fired by their label for alien-ating their teenage girl target audience by being complete chauvinistic asshats." She nods. Satisfied with her assessment of the situation.

"Ding, ding, ding. We have a winner!" I cheer and give her a round of applause, to which she takes a sitting half-bow and grins.

The purples of the sunset behind her are now pulling out the highlights of Ren's red hair that peeks out from under her bunny hat, magnifying the impression of a halo of fire surrounding her. When she smiles like this, she's luminous, lighting up the entire pier. I can't seem to pull my gaze away.

She stops laughing and meets my eyes, suddenly growing serious, but neither of us says anything. After a few moments of us staring at each other, she shivers and rubs her arms as if she's cold. I finally break my gaze, take off my denim jacket, and wrap it around her shoulders without thinking. I rub her upper arms for good measure, making sure she warms up. I don't want her to get sick with her hoarse voice earlier.

"Do you want to go?" Something in my chest tightens at the thought of ending our outing. It's too early to go home.

"No. I'm okay now. Thanks for the jacket." Her smile is hesitant, and I'm right there with her. Every thought I'm now having is making me hesitate. This is supposed to be a palate cleanser, not making my confusion worse.

"Cool. Let me go kick your ass in some air hockey." I wrap an arm around her shoulders as I always have, and we move on to the arcade, but it feels different now. Everything is different. *God damn it. Everything is fucking different.*

J ude does kick my ass in air hockey, as he always does. But I give it the old college try. He always picks that game because he's remarkably good at it. Then we move to the games against the wall, where I shine. I can always beat him at one of the many pinball machines or the proper video games of Centipede and Galaga. I'm on a good run, but I can sense Jude getting antsy next to me.

"What's up?" I ask, clearing another stage of alien invaders. "Are you getting bored with watching me winning at this?"

"Har." He glances around a little nervously. "No, there's a group of girls over there, I think recognize me, and I'm not in the mood for rock star shit tonight."

"It's the hot cowboy thing you got goin' on, I

bet." I give him a cheeky smile as I let my video game ship get destroyed. He blushes for the second time in as many days, and *damn*, he needs to stop doing that, or I'm going to have weirder dreams than I already have. "Come on, let's go."

I grab his hand and lead him out of the arcade, staring down and daring the group of girls to stop us or get in my way. Once we're outside, I can't help but start laughing uncontrollably.

"What's so funny?" His bewildered look makes me laugh even harder.

"I can remember when you first got to LA, you couldn't land a date to save your life."

"And?"

"And now, you're practically fighting them off with a stick. I can only imagine how bad the groupies are on the road. You want for nothing, I'm sure."

I think he's still blushing, but his head is down, so I can't see his face underneath the hat to know what he's thinking, but his shoulders do shrug in acknowledgment. He's probably proud of all his conquests. That's something Jude and Brad do have in common, unfortunately. I need to remind myself they're only different in responsibilities and how they deal with them. Which, I guess, can be a big deal. Okay, it is a huge deal. But it doesn't remove the fact that Jude is a player in the worst way. He's come a long way in eleven years but hasn't changed at the same time. To go so long without a real relationship can't be healthy.

Our hands are still intertwined, but it feels completely natural. Like we do this all the time. Which we don't. We can be affectionate with each other, but not like this. I glance down at our fingers laced together, then quickly up at him, but he's looking off in the distance, a pensive expression playing on his face. He's so damned handsome in that cowboy hat I need to shift my gaze away from him. I reluctantly pull my hand out of his and wrap my arms around myself.

I need to stop the strange thoughts popping in my head about Jude. I can't think of him that way. Firstly, because he's my best friend, a relationship would jeopardize everything, and I'm not willing to take that risk. Secondly, he's a total player and would never be able to settle down with one person in a million years. No matter how much it seems like he's changed with Charlotte in the picture, I don't know that he really has. It could wear off the next groupie he comes across. Third, he's sworn he's never going to have kids or get married, and well, I have a kid, and I do want to get married someday, so that precludes me from any equation with him. Lastly, he would never feel that way about me, even if I did for him. I'm sure any weird feelings between us are strictly on my side of the fence, so it would be dumb to consider.

"Penny for your thoughts." He's looking at me intensely now, and he pulls on one of the bunny ears on my fur hat.

"Oh no," I laugh, feeling my freckles warm my face considering what I've been thinking about. "These thoughts are way out of your price range."

He drapes an arm over my shoulder, pulling me back to him, and my knees get a little weak, and my heart flutters for a moment. *Can't he see I'm trying to separate myself from him?*

"Didn't you hear? I'm a famous rock star now. I can afford everyone's thoughts here." He snickers at his own words. "Jesus Christ. Shoot me and put me out of everyone else's misery."

"Ha! I've heard rumors you're kind of a big deal now."

"Yeah, I started those. But you're changing the subject. What were you thinking about a minute ago? You looked like you were trying to figure out how to find the square root of pi or something." He's not going to let this go. *Damnit.*

"Nope. My thoughts are not for sale, sir. Move along." I flash him a smile, letting him know I will be just as stubborn as he is, if not more.

"Fine. I'll let it go for now." He squeezes my shoulder lightly as we walk. "But when you least expect it, I'll pry it out of you."

"Oh, really? You think so?"

"Yup."

"We'll see about that." *God, no*. Don't ever let me tell him what I've been thinking about. I would be more mortified than waking up gnawing on his neck at the store, which was beyond embarrassing. I don't think our friendship or even I could survive that.

I pull myself from under his arm and take off his jacket to hand back to him. He grabs it but looks confused.

"Aren't you cold?" He hands the jacket out to me again. "You should keep it if your cold, Ren."

I catch something in the tone of his voice and his expression that makes my stomach do a full somersault. Am I imagining all of this? Now that I've got the thought of him that way in my head, am I going to be seeing into everything he says? *Ugh. I need to stop*.

"I'm fine," I lie. I am chilled, but I need to separate myself from him, including his jacket. It's too much right now. "The games and the walk have warmed me up. Thanks." I avoid looking into his eyes because he'll know I'm lying. We can read each other like open books most of the time. At least we used to. I don't see why that would change.

The rest of the walk to my car, picking up Charlotte from my grandfather's condo and driving back to his car, is as awkward as possible. And I know it's me. I'm making everything uncomfortable, but I can't help it. Now I've thought of Jude differently. I can't *unthink* it. So now I'm stuck in some limbo area of who Jude is, and what I want him to be to me. And it sucks. I want things to be how they used to be. I know they can't, especially now with Charlotte in my life, but I yearn for things to be normal between us again. This flustered wariness I now experience when I'm around him can't be sustained for much longer. Something's going to give.

thirteen

STOP THINKING ABOUT IT

JUDE

One week. That's the longest I can go without seeing Ren and Charlie again. I tried for longer, but the thought of Ren juggling family and business on the busiest day in her store doesn't sit right with me. I also wanted to give Brad a chance to step up and do the right thing since our little chat at Old Town. I'm curious if I got through to him. While I don't have high expectations for him to miraculously find and implement a moral compass, for Charlie's sake, I hope he has.

To hedge my bets, I'm outside of Vital Records again the following Friday morning, waiting for them to show up, so I can find out if Brad came through and, if not, to help with Charlie. As Ren approaches the store, I can tell from the dark shadows under her eyes Brad is still the biggest loser ever created. *Fucking asshole.* The muscles in my jaw clench and my teeth grind as I think about how the complete irresponsibility of one morally bankrupt individual can affect so many others. He's affecting *me*, which is highly uncool.

I force a smile I don't feel as they move closer and try to hide my annoyance. I pretty much counted on this being the result and is why I'm here in the first place. That's not entirely true, though. I missed spending time with them. And it's been messing with my head all freaking week.

I've been getting on Matt and his fiancée Samantha's nerves, dragging them out for meals, movies, and seeing bands, just to keep myself busy. They finally told me to get a life, and they aren't into threesomes. It was fucking hilarious. I was not amused.

The whole 'idle hands are the devil's playthings' is true when it comes to me. Reading, which has always been my favorite way to escape from my own thoughts, didn't work this week. So, I've been very idle, high-strung, and annoyed.

I almost miss the road, and the meaningless sex. I try to miss it, but for some reason, I don't. Instead of being hungry for something carnal and empty, I'm finding myself wanting something deeper and meaningful. It's disturbing how different my mindset is now that I've been home from Europe. It's like a switch was tripped inside of me that turned off all the immature rock star bullshit. I think

Charlie has a lot to do with that, if I'm being honest. Charlie seems to be changing a lot, and I'm not sure how I feel about that.

Despite Ren's apparent exhaustion, she grins when she sees me, as does Charlie, and my heart speeds up. The smile I forced a second ago transforms into a real one I couldn't hold back if I tried. The two of them in my presence, safe and well, unties a knot in my chest that tightened further each day I stayed away from them.

"You know you're not on the payroll, right?" Her smile grows as Charlie leans toward me, and I carefully take her into my arms.

"Shit. My dreams of becoming a Victorian governess are dashed. I guess I have to go back to being a famous rock star then." Charlies got a teething ring shoved in her mouth, so we're armed and ready to face the day without any trips to the drug store. *Fingers crossed.*

Ren unlocks the door and lets us in. "Oh no. I'd never trample your dreams. You can still be a Victorian governess. I just won't pay you for the privilege."

I head straight to the back to set up the blanket and toys that will be our designated play zone for the day, and as soon as I put Charlie down, she starts scooting backward in a circle and smiling at me. She knows what's up. I'm the Tag-playing dude.

"Jumping right into it, huh?" I say to her, getting

down to her level. "I didn't even warm up yet. You'll make me pull a hamstring. You're not playing fair."

"Are you really here to play with her again while I work?" Ren's tone is surprised.

I glance up to respond with a sarcastic comment, but the hopeful look in her eyes fractures my heart into a million smithereens. I bite the inside of my cheek to stop myself from saying something stupid. *That's a first.* I don't know when that filter got installed in my brain, but I'm grateful.

"Of course," is all I can manage to say. I think it comes off as nonchalant, like I tried for, but who knows. I've already looked away, so I miss her reaction. I can't look at her. That expression on her face just then, afraid to hope or even wish I could possibly be here to help her, slashed me deeply. It's making me rethink every life choice I've ever made for some reason.

"Well, cool." She hovers for a minute, not saying anything until she turns to the front of the store. "Thanks."

I watch her out of the corner of my eye as she moves around, stocking the new releases and interacting with her customers. Some regulars stop over to our blanket area to check on Charlie, and she's her delightful little self with everyone. She sure knows how to pour the charm on to grab attention when she wants it.

Around lunchtime, I leave to grab Ren and me

some food, and when I come back, Charlie is super annoyed and needs an obvious nap. Luckily, I left a book in my car for this very scenario. I run out and grab it, and when I sit on the couch with my arms out for Ren to hand me Charlie, she stares at me incredulously.

"Did you just grab that copy of *The Worst Witch* out of your car to read to her?"

"What?" I don't understand what the problem is. "It's got some pictures in it."

"It's a little above her comprehension level." She's still dubious.

"Nonsense. Everything is above her comprehension level. The sound of the words is what matters." I Googled this and everything baby-related during the week while unsuccessfully trying not to think about the two of them. I didn't like being utterly helpless last Friday and swore not to be that way again if I can help it. Though I still draw the line at diapers. "Besides, *The Worst Witch* is the OG Harry Potter. If we're going to start her fantasy literature programming, we may as well start with a magic school for girls."

"I don't remember approving any kind of programming, dude." Ren laughs and hands Charlie over to me. I put my glasses on and settle back into the couch for story time. I can feel Ren's eyes on me as I make Charlie comfortable and start reading aloud. After a few minutes, she's still watching and listening to me read.

"Want me to bring *50 Shades* or *Twilight* to read to you next week since you like hearing me read aloud so much?" I smirk at her and revel in the blush that spreads on her cheeks before she spins on her heel and walks away in an embarrassed huff. I knew that would rile her up. The thought of it, though, gets to me too. *Shit.*

I chase that thought away as quickly as possible and resume reading to Charlie. I do not want to go down that rabbit hole of irrationality. Lately, it seems like I'm playing a game of Whack-a-Mole with my feelings on hard mode. I don't know what the fuck my problem is. Charlie is the only thing different around us now, and I don't see how that would change my feelings for Ren. If anything, knowing me, that would push me away, not draw me to her.

I sneak glances at Ren as I read, saying random words if I stare too long, so I don't raise suspicion. I think Charlie's been asleep for a while, but this is an excellent cover to try to study Ren and figure out what is going on with me.

Other than being tired, she looks great, but she's always been beautiful in a wild, fiery way. *Fiery? Did I just describe her as fiery?* It's not inaccurate, just a bizarre descriptor. *So, Jude, how would you describe your friend Ren? Fiery. Totally fiery. Fuck me.* One different thing is the baby weight. Not that Ren was scrawny before she had Charlie, but she seems healthier or something since she had her. Like she has a little more to grab onto, if...you were... going to grab onto her. I think I like it. I don't know. *Fuck!*

This has not been helpful. I would like to go drink an adult beverage now. Please.

By giving in and coming here today, I thought I'd figure out what is so different between us now, making me act all crazy, but instead, all I did was confuse myself and trigger a headache.

Like the week prior, I'm woken up with Charlie on my chest and Ren gently lifting her from me. It can't be safe to sleep like that where she could fall. Next week I'll lay on the floor so if she does roll off, it's not a long drop. Next week? How long am I going to do this?

Ren's grandfather is sitting in a nearby chair, eyeing me with a slight smile on his lips.

"Hey Art, how's it going?" I sit up with my elbows on my knees, take my glasses off and rub the bridge of my nose, trying to shake off the sleep still clouding my mind.

"Better now that you're here."

I snap my head up to stare at him. What does he mean?

"Oh? Why's that?"

He taps his fingers on the arm of the chair slowly. Deliberately. But he meets my eyes with measured certainty.

"With you here, I don't need to worry about Rena as much."

"Why would you need to worry about Ren?" I glance around to check where she is and if she can hear any of this, but she must be in the back with Charlie. I'm not sure what he's getting at and what it has to do with me. Plus, *I just fucking woke up, man.*

"I always worry about Ren. Don't you?" He tips his head curiously. "Isn't that why we're both here right now?"

I study him, considering his question. Isn't that exactly why I'm here? Because I was worried about her? About Charlie?

"I come here for the awesome napping couch." My mouth is dry, and my chest is tight. The words sound empty, even to me. "It does wonders for my jet lag."

I've now joined some secret admiration society for Ren and Charlie, and to be honest, I don't neces- sarily feel mad about it. His smile broadens, and he nods his head, and I have to look away from him. Is Art detecting something more here? Or is all of this obvious to him?

"So, what are you two going to be up to this evening? Anything fun?" A twinkle in his eye is always kind of there, but it seems incredibly sparkly today.

"Oh, I don't know." I shrug. I haven't thought this far ahead in the day.

"I have some ideas," Ren says, coming up behind me with a wicked smile on her face. I can feel my brows draw together, wondering what those ideas could be. Could Ren be feeling something for me too? That's crazy. There's no way. Or is there? She has been acting weird since I got back. I suppose it's possible. The idea makes me a little lightheaded.

"Oh, really?" I'm trying for dismissive, but I don't think I'm pulling it off.

"Well, you kids have fun, whatever you end up doing." Art winks at me over Ren's shoulder as he gives her a hug and takes Charlie from her.

I wave goodbye to Charlie, feeling all kinds of awkward. Like we're one big happy family who just had a regular family unit visit with each other that happens all the fucking time. And now Art's gone; it's just Ren and me, left alone to be awkward with each other because today is apparently 'Let's All Be Fucking Awkward Day.' It's fucking weird.

"I should probably get going...." I start, not sure what the fuck I'm doing anymore. Art's words are bouncing off each other in my brain, and this small hope I feel there could be something more between

Ren and me isn't something I planned on. *Ever*. Not with my best friend. Not with Ren. Is it so far-fetched, though? If Art can see something, which I think he does, maybe there is something to it, and I should pursue it. But not right this minute. I need to get my bearings before I do or say something I regret.

"No! Don't go." Ren has that wicked smile back on her face, and I don't know what to make of it. It's making me have thoughts. *Those* kinds of thoughts. About Ren. *Fucking hell.* "I have an idea of something for us to do tonight...if you're not busy, that is."

I swallow hard, suddenly lacking any moisture in my mouth.

"I'm free." I still can't return her smile; I'm so dumbfounded. Surely, that smile, that statement, means something more?

"Good. Sawyer should be here any minute, and then I will help you fall in love."

What the hell does that mean?

fourteen

HUMAN
REN

After I tell him I'm going to help him fall in love, the confusion on Jude's face is priceless. I wish I had my phone to take a picture to capture it since he so rarely looks out of sorts like this.

Since our outing at the pier last Friday, I thought all week about him and decided to help him find his person. I think he puts up a decent front about not doing feelings or relationships, but I've seen a new side of Jude since he's been back. I think a side of him wants to fall in love and have a family. Maybe. I don't know. I could be projecting my feelings onto him.

I also spent the week thinking about how I woke up kissing him and the feelings that little incident brought to the surface. Maybe things got weird between us because we know each other so well.

We're comfortable enough to fall back into our usual patterns and routines, but we fell too far this time. I know I've been emotionally fragile since Brad and I broke up, so it would make sense for me to turn to a person of comfort, like Jude, for affection. That's all it is.

And while it's nice Jude showed up today, he didn't reach out to us all week. That makes it obvious anything I'm feeling for him isn't reciprocated. He probably spent the week hooking up with random chicks he met while out having fun. But he needs to meet someone who isn't after him just to hook up with a rock star. He should find someone who can see past all the bullshit he shows in public and love him for the hot and caring nerd he is. I think Jude is ready for some stability in his life.

"Once Sawyer gets here, let's grab some dinner at my place, okay?" When I ask Jude the question, I watch his face roll through at least sixty different emotions, and I don't recognize any of them. They seem new, even to him. This is getting way beyond weird now. "What's your deal, Jude?"

"What do you mean?" His voice is rough, and he's having difficulty meeting my eyes.

"I don't know. You've been acting strange since you woke up from your nap. Did you have a bad dream or something? You look kind of upset."

"Upset? Why would I be upset? I'm not upset."

He even looks like he's aware of the rambling but can't help himself. I don't know what to think.

"Okay, okay. You're not upset." I raise my hands in self-defense. "Saying it like that totally doesn't sound like you're upset."

"Can we stop saying the fucking word '*upset*?'" He's agitated. Tonight might not be the best night to initiate my plan. He might think I'm meddling or something.

"Done. That word is, from this moment, banned from being spoken within the walls of Vital Records." I laugh, trying to lighten the mood suddenly sparking with heavy energy between us, but Jude doesn't join in with me. "Man. Rough crowd."

"Sorry. Nap fog," he mutters, shoving his hands into his pockets and rocking from heel to toe.

Maybe he's not ready for this.

Jude meets me at my apartment and instantly makes himself comfortable on the couch, picking up the TV remote and switching channels. I order a pizza and then literally wrestle the remote away from him and turn off the TV.

"Dude. No TV. We've got important stuff to talk about." I drag his feet off the couch and sit next to him, pulling my laptop off the coffee table and booting it up.

"What is going on here? What is so important?" The anxiety on his face and in his voice is starting to worry me.

"Calm down. It's not a big deal. I thought it might be time for you to consider a more meaningful relationship."

"With...you?" I glance over at him and can swear I catch hope in his eyes, but that can't be right. Wishful thinking on my part.

"What? Ha, as if." I try to laugh it off, but something in me wants to pursue the line of thought some more. Could he be thinking about me that way? I catch his expression out of the corner of my eye and almost believe I see disappointment in him. His shoulders slump, and I think he winces at my words.

"Then who?" I want disappointment in his tone, and when I hear it, I don't know if I just imagine it or if it's really there.

"Well, that's what we need to find out." I start typing and pull up the dating website I came across that sounded perfect for him. "That's where 'Last-PersonOnEarth.com' comes in." I turn the laptop to show him the screen.

Jude takes one look at the website and laughs so hard he snorts and almost chokes.

"'Last Person On Earth?' As in, 'not if you were the last person on Earth?'"

"It's just a name; it doesn't mean anything. The site is kind of perfect for nerds like us. Here, look at all these women. One of them might be your person."

"I'm doubtful I'll find my person on the internet."

"You never know. And they might be pretty. That's important to you, right?"

"Actually, I do know. And pretty has nothing to do with my person. Can't my person be a hideous troll?"

"They can be whatever they and you want them to be. That's the point of this. Look. There are no pictures, and they use all sorts of algorithms that make their matches super-duper accurate. You're almost guaranteed to find your soulmate." I don't know if the last part is true, but it sounds good, and I want him to be excited about this.

"Super-duper, huh?" He eyes the laptop warily. "I don't know... I highly doubt my 'soulmate,' whatever that even means, out of everyone in the world, happens to be on this random, horribly named dating site. I don't think this is for me."

I give him the puppy dog eyes. I know he can't resist the puppy dog eyes.

"C'mon, Jude. All joking aside, I think you should try this." I need him to try this and find someone, so I can get him out of my mind. I might selfishly be doing this more for my own peace than to find his soulmate. I'm a horrible person.

"Okay, okay. But there's one tiny condition."

"Oh?" I don't like the sound of that.

"Yup. You need to sign up too." The crooked smile playing on his lips is so smug as if he won this battle, but he should know me better.

"Fine. I'll sign up too." I start opening a new profile to fill out for him.

"Wait, what? You will?" He sits forward and is stricken with fear. He didn't expect me to agree. *Silly man.*

"Of course. I'm not a monster. I wouldn't let you out into the wild unchaperoned."

The agitation pouring off of him is tangible. I rattled him. The unrattleable Jude. The ladies' man extraordinaire is nervous about a dating app. I bite my lip to keep from laughing out loud.

"I don't know about this, Ren..."

"Too late. I already agreed to your terms, and a verbal contract has been made between us."

"I don't think that'll hold up in court." He jumps up off the couch and starts pacing, fists in his pockets.

"Well, sue me, and let's find out." I smile up at him. "Come on. If nothing else, this could be freaking hilarious. Right?"

He stops his prowling and stares at me. "Why

are you doing this to me? Haven't I been a good friend to you? Why do you hate me so much?"

"You're whining. Come sit down and let's fill out your profile."

He sighs loudly and falls onto the couch next to me, making me bounce a little with the impact.

"Fine."

"Okay. Username? And don't say…"

"BigDick69."

"Damnit, Jude. No."

"Why not? I use that everywhere. The chicks love it."

"The chicks? Do you want to spend the rest of your life with someone who likes guys that use the name 'BigDick69?'"

"Rest of my life? Fuck no. But I don't see this panning out that far. I mean, really."

"Well, it won't work with that attitude." If he's not going to be serious about this, I don't know what I'm going to do.

"Fine. Jesus. Shadowfax95 then." He picks up one of Charlotte's blankets and pulls it to his nose, and inhales deeply, seeming to calm down after he does. It's the most benign yet impactful thing I've ever seen him do. My heart breaks and melts right in that instant. If only Jude could see me the way I just saw him, we wouldn't have to go through all of this.

I need to blink away tears threatening to show themselves and refocus myself on the task at hand.

"Okay, that one is available. Imagine that." I hand the laptop over to him. "Finish setting up your profile with a password and stuff. I'm going to grab a drink. You want anything?"

When I glance over at him after standing up, Jude has his glasses on, staring at the screen with a deep scowl, his brows drawn together.

"Nope. I'm good." He starts typing rapidly. "Oh, cool. There's an option to hide your username, and they'll assign you a random number. I'm doing that. Total fucking anonymity, like the rock star I am."

I hope he takes this seriously and finds someone soon. Since he's been home, the more time I spend with him, the harder it is to think of him as just my friend. I need a buffer. Someone between us to force me to get over these crazy thoughts. But what will I do when he does eventually find someone else?

L astPersonOnEarth.com, how fitting. I bet I wouldn't want to date anyone on the site if they were the last person on Earth for real. There's probably a reason they don't allow pictures, and that makes me a shallow fucking asshole. But, so what? I should be allowed to be shallow if it's my 'soulmate' I'm being shallow about.

I promised Ren I would take this seriously before leaving her apartment. I don't know why this is so important to her all of a sudden. And to be honest, I was hurt she even suggested it. I don't know why, but I was getting the sense she might be reciprocating my new weird feelings for her, but obviously, I was wrong. It was stupid of me to even consider she felt anything more than friendship for me. We've been friends for far too long, and something like that could ruin everything.

When I get home, I ignore Matt and Samantha making out on the couch and head to the balcony with my laptop to finish setting up my stupid profile. And surprisingly, I'm honest in my answers to all their questions. And there are a lot of questions. I guess that's how they get the algorithms to work.

> What are you passionate about in life?

> > ME: Music. Fantasy literature. My friends. Sarcasm.

> Would you consider your values more traditional or progressive?

> > ME: A mix of both. Equal rights, but I'm protective of my tribe.

> What scares you/what's your biggest fear in life?

Jeez. They get right to the heart of it, don't they? How honest do I want to be here?

> > ME: Losing someone close to me.

> What's your biggest dating pet peeve?

Do I have any pet peeves about dating? I don't go on dates.

ME: Not being punctual.

I don't fucking know. This is all pretty ridiculous. Where is the 'If you were a tree, what kind of tree would you be' question? This is dumb. I can't believe I let Ren talk me into this. At least she has to suffer through these questions too.

Do you enjoy traveling?

Do I enjoy it anymore? I used to love being on the road, but we don't see any of the cities we go to anymore since we've gotten popular. Europe was fun, but we won't be anonymous there again, either.

ME: I used to.

What's a typical day for you?

ME: I don't have typical days.

Sure, I'm being vague, but I'm being honest. I don't want to give away that I'm in a popular band in any way, so I need to be at least somewhat cryptic about what I do.

Do you want/have a family?

Damn. Again, with the existential questions. Do I want a family? Sure. Maybe. I don't know. Will I allow myself to try to have one? No. Not likely. The pain involved in outliving your loved ones is too much for me, regardless of their age. So, no family, no pain. I witnessed how my grandfather handled losing my uncle to cancer and then losing my grand-mother to it as well, and he became a shell of a human being afterward. That's no way to live. And he didn't. He died of a broken heart within a year of my grandmother. Some would say that's sweet or some bullshit, but it's not. He's fucking dead. And all because he let himself care about other people more than himself. That's what love does. *Fuck that.*

But then I think of Charlie and how fucking awesome she is. Remembering the feeling of being present at a couple of her firsts isn't something I'll forget anytime soon. To feel that way for a child that isn't mine makes me wonder how amazing it would be to have that for one of my own. It's probably mind-blowing. While it isn't something I think I'll want right away, just being able to say I'm open to the possibility is a massive step for me. And if I can feel this way about Ren's child, I suppose I could feel the same for another partner's child. So, to answer this question,

ME: Not currently, but open.

Matt peeks his head out onto the balcony. "Got a minute?"

I close the laptop in relief of having an excuse to get away from my dating profile. It was getting way too deep there.

"Yup. What's going on?"

He takes the seat across from me with a glazed look.

"And what is with the crazed look in your eyes? Are you feeling okay?"

"Ha, no. I just remember Samantha and my first date here." He laughs and shakes his head.

"Eww. You guys didn't screw in this chair, did you?" I pretend to almost jump out of my seat.

"And what if we did?" He raises an eyebrow, his grin spreading.

"It's cool. I just want to make sure my fantasies are accurate, that's all."

Matt's grin disappears. *That'll teach him.*

"Dude. What the fuck?"

I wave him off. We've said worse to each other.

"Whatever. What did you want to talk about?"

He settles himself in his chair, leaning forward, elbows on his thighs.

"A couple of things. The next album, the holidays, shit like that."

"Shouldn't we include Ryan in all of this?"

"We talked earlier. We tried calling you, but you apparently weren't answering your phone."

I think back to napping with Charlie this afternoon. *Shit.* My phone's been off since then. Not cool.

"Yeah. Sorry about that. What's up with the holidays? Are you going to Samantha's parents in Ohio or something?" Since they're engaged now, I assumed he'd be going to do the whole family thing with Samantha, seeing as how he doesn't have any family.

"We are, but we wanted to invite you along too." He hesitates slightly. "I know you don't really talk to your family, and I wasn't sure what your plans were. So, we wanted to make sure you weren't sitting here eating ramen or something."

Great. So now everyone else is getting married and shit, I'm the pitiful loser who needs charity invites? *Fuck me.*

"Thanks, but I have plans." I keep my face neutral, so he doesn't see the ire rising in my blood. It's irrational, but it's there. Of course, I don't have plans. I barely registered the holidays are coming up. They're never on my radar.

Matt looks surprised.

"Oh, with your mystery friend, Ren?"

"Haha. Maybe." The snide tone in my voice even annoys me. What the hell. Why am I being such a dick?

"Chill, man. I'm messing with you." He examines me more closely, though, and his eyes narrow. "But why haven't we met this secret friend of yours, anyway?"

I shrug. "No real reason. I just want that part of my life separate."

"Separate from what? Me and Ryan?" His tone is offended, and I never considered they would feel that way about how I handle my relationship with Ren.

"Yes. I mean, no. I don't know." I stare out at the dark street below us, trying to figure out a way to explain myself to Matt without alienating him at the same time. "She's the one thing in my life I really care about, and I don't want that mixed in with the insanity that is Indigo King. And you two are part of Indigo King, so you're lumped into the pile."

Matt nods but doesn't say anything. His expression goes from offended to unreadable. But I think he might understand where I'm coming from.

"Look at what happened on tour this summer with your crazy brother. Him trying to blackmail you, and the huge press fallout from that. I don't want Ren and Charlie to be involved in anything like that. Ever. So, I keep them separate."

He stares at me intensely for a minute. Matt is always so fucking intense.

"This summer was a bit nuts, so I get that. But Jude, I'd still like to meet your friend. We don't need to be best buddies like you are, but at least an introduction would be nice."

I consider that. Ren never expressed an interest in meeting the rest of the band. Shit like that doesn't impress her, and she's always been more than happy to stay away from it. She's said she met enough bands hosting her video television show to last her a lifetime. And she's sarcastically said she believes me when I tell her I'm in a rock band but doesn't need proof. Which is very funny, actually.

Is now the time to introduce everyone to each other? Would Ren want to? She's got enough going on with Charlie; I don't know if she'd be open to it.

"I'll think about it." That's the best I can give right now. I'll need to talk to Ren about it and see what her thoughts are.

"All right. Think about it. That's all I ask." He stands up and stretches. "As for new music and tour stuff, we'll deal with that after New Year's. Is that cool? Take a little break?"

"Yeah. That works for me. I've got some ideas for our new songs, but I could use the time off."

"Cool. I'm heading over to Samantha's for the night. I'll catch you later."

I wave and nod as he heads back into the house to leave.

So, I'll have the place to myself again tonight. Maybe I'll start a movie marathon of some sort to pass the time. *Another exciting night for International Ladies' Man, Jude Lockwood.* What the fuck am I doing? Nothing apparently.

sixteen

HAVE YOU SEEN MY LOVE?

REN

W hen I get home from picking up Charlotte and make sure she's asleep, I pull out my laptop again and start setting up my own dating profile on LastPersonOnEarth.com. I did promise to try this along with Jude, and honestly, I need the distraction from him. Who knows, maybe I will find somebody on here. It's worth a shot, at least.

I like the idea of only using a number like Jude is doing. Part of me is curious how accurate the algorithms might be and if somehow the username is included in that, using only a number will put it to the test. Here goes nothing.

What are you passionate about in life?

ME: My family. Music. Fantasy
novels.

Would you consider your values
more traditional or progressive?

ME: A mix of both. I believe in equal
rights, but I also like being made to
feel safe.

What scares you/what's your
biggest fear in life?

ME: Losing someone I love.

What's your biggest dating pet
peeve?

ME: Cheating is a pretty big pet
peeve.

Seriously? What are they expecting people to put there?

Do you enjoy traveling?

ME: I used to.

What's a typical day for you?

ME: Every day is a new adventure.

I have to answer at least a million more questions, and it takes me a long time to finish. When I hit the 'submit' button, I expect it to spit out matches right away, but I guess it doesn't work that way. Nothing happens, except I receive an email letting me know I've completed the questionnaire. *Yeah. I know that much. Ugh.* The email says it can take days to be matched with someone, and a match isn't always guaranteed. That's kind of lame. I wanted instant gratification. I need my Jude obsession fixed. *Now.* I can't wait days.

I sit and watch my profile, refreshing the page every other second on the off chance something will show up. Nothing. I wonder how Jude is fairing with his profile. I bet he's got a hundred matches already. *The jerk.* I turn the TV on to a random documentary to have something to half-watch as I repeatedly refresh the page.

About twenty minutes in, I get a notification of an incoming message. My heart jumps as I open it.

> Good news! You've been matched with user CD13978! Click their username to view their profile and if you like what you see, send them a message!

It goes on to list a bunch of sample introductions. This really is for nerds like me who aren't smooth in the dating arena.

I click on user CD13978 and review their bio and questionnaire answers. The first thing I look for is if they have or are open to children because I'm not going to bother if they're not okay with Charlotte. CD13978 has no children but is open to meeting someone with their own. Okay. Point one for him.

I note we have similar taste in books, music, and movies, so that's more added to this guy's point total. Their biggest pet peeve is if their date is late? *Wow*. There are so many more important things to worry about than that. This guy's had an easy time if that's his biggest hang-up. I can't blame people for their life experiences, though.

When I get to the question about why they're using the site, they say a friend made them do it. Could this be Jude? That would be crazy. Out of everyone on this site, there's no way we'd be matched with each other. Right? I review the answers more carefully, and most of the answers could be things Jude would say. The punctuality thing sticks out to me because I know that bugs him of people in general. He would totally put that as something a date would do to piss him off.

The statistical odds of this site matching me with Jude has to be astronomical. I can't believe that would happen. I'm not sure what to do here. I can't come right out and ask if he's Jude. How would I explain that their answers sound like my best friend, who I talked into using the site? That would be extremely hard to explain and not a great introduction to somebody.

My inbox dings again with another message. Lo

and behold, it's a message from CD13978 himself. I can't help but smile at possibly having someone interested in me. That sounds vain in my head, but it is coming more from a place of insecurity than anything, especially since having Charlotte. I'm not exactly feeling like the most attractive person in LA. It's not the city to live in to feel good about yourself.

I hesitate to open the message for a minute, relishing this feeling of possibility. Once I open this message or respond, this feeling could run away faster than a toddler about to put something in their mouth they shouldn't. I finally give in.

> CD13978: Hello there, fellow hostage! I see you, too, have been recruited to dive headfirst into the dating pool by someone who claims to be a friend. That claim, at least on my part, is now under suspicion.
>
> We are apparently soulmates! Imagine that. And this site knew that about us all along. Skynet should become aware in about two days now then. Hopefully, you got the Terminator reference. If not, maybe this website is wrong about everything, and there is hope for the human race after all.
>
> Feel free to respond to this madness at your earliest convenience if you're so inclined.

May the stars shine upon your face.

Wow. There is so much to unpack in one message. I'm still not entirely sure this isn't Jude. The Tolkien quote at the end makes me question it. But the Terminator reference is throwing me. Jude's not a huge Terminator fan, but then the bit about Skynet could be because the notion fits the scenario. And man, I am overthinking the crap out of this. Is that because I want this to be Jude? Or because I don't want it to be him? What will I do if it is? And what will I do if it isn't?

I push that all aside and concentrate on how to respond. I have to answer, right? I rub my hands on the thighs of my jeans since they're starting to sweat. *Okay*. I'm going to respond as if this is not Jude and just some new guy who happens to have a lot of the same interests.

> ME: Greetings, fellow captive. Indeed, I agreed to a quid pro quo to enlist a friend on their journey to happiness, at my own peril and detriment.

> Soulmates! That may still be too early to call, but I'm open to the possibility. Since you've been wrangled somehow, will you take this site seriously? Or are you merely window shopping? Albeit in the dark.

May your face be shiny as well.

I reread it about twenty times before hitting send. I suck at this so hard. That's one part about dating that is frustrating; the whole *'Once upon a time, Ren's life went like this...'* part gets old quickly. Retelling your life story to a stranger is not my idea of a good time. Plus, I don't like talking about myself, so I end up asking all the questions, and the other person learns absolutely zero about me.

After waiting for a few minutes to see if there is a response with no result, I shut down my laptop and get ready for bed. CD13978, who I think I'll dub 'Cool Dude' until he proves himself otherwise, may have gone to bed, or better yet, may have a life and went out to a club or something. It is a Friday night. Most of the cool kids are out and about around town, living it up. I used to be a cool kid. But cool kids do eventually need to grow up. Growing up sucks. Highly overrated. Zero stars. Would not recommend.

seventeen

I NEED TO KNOW

JUDE

Several messages are waiting for me when I wake up on Saturday morning. A few of them are responses to messages I sent last night, and a few are from new matches reaching out to me. I'm apparently very matchable, both an affirmation and a surprise. It confirms what I experience on the road, but that is a response to a persona I put on. To be matched with so many based on my honest answers to the questionnaire throws me a little. I didn't expect that. I thought I'd be too weird for the general public. Ren puts up with my weirdness because she's equally strange. Ryan and Matt do the same, but only because they don't have a choice if they want me in the band.

Out of all the messages I've gotten, a few pique my interest. One of them totally got my Lord of the Rings reference, and another made a cute joke in return. It makes me wonder if the site would ever match me to Ren. Surely the odds of that happening would be fucking astronomical. That would be hilarious though. Well, I'm sure Ren would laugh, I'd probably get my soul crushed as she doubled over in hilarity. Not something I'd appreciate.

I don't know what the next step is now. Do I keep playing the pen pal with these chicks? Or do I ask to meet them? I'm completely lost when it comes to this crap. Usually, it's just, *'your place or mine?'* Now I need to plan and arrange things and participate in honest conversations. I'm not used to this. I'll stick to the messages for now and see where it goes.

My phone dings, and I see a text from my oldest sister, Jessica.

> JESSICA: Are you going to mom and dad's for Thanksgiving?

> ME: No. You?

> JESSICA: No. Going to NC for Brian's family this year.

> ME: Cool. Have a good Thanksgiving.

> JESSICA: You too.

And that will be the extent of my family communication for this holiday. I may call my folks, but that will be a game-day decision and will depend on whether or not I remember the day is actually Thanksgiving. It's not that I don't like my family. We're just not close. Nothing happened. There was no fallout or anything. We've just never been the kind of family to keep in touch with each other. The goal was to grow up and get out, and I think that goal was our parents', too, not just us kids. I didn't have a shitty childhood like Matt. And I didn't have overly caring parents like Ryan. They were just there. I was closer to my grandparents than them, which is odd, but I know Ren is the same with her immediate family. Her mother is a yoga instructor or something in Malibu, which isn't that far away, but they almost never talk, either.

My family experiences can best be summarized as indifferent at best. It's not that there's love lost; there was never any love to start with. I think seeing Ren interact so lovingly with Charlie is striking a chord in me somewhere. As though I'm finally seeing how a family is supposed to be, and something in me wants to be a part of that now that I see how good it can be. How much caring and love can be involved if you let it. You must want it first, though.

As for the upcoming holiday, I don't celebrate anything. Even Christmas. Well, except for Hobbit Day on September 22nd, I observe that. And only because Ren and I were going through some websites with random holidays, like Microwave Oven Day and Be Kind to Lawyers Day, we found Hobbit Day. For some reason, that day always sticks in my head. Maybe because of how hard we laughed at all the different and stupid made-up holidays. Ren got a particular kick out of Something on a Stick Day and almost busted a gut laughing so hard naming different things to try eating on a stick. It was fucking hilarious. I wonder if any of the women I message with know about Hobbit Day or Something on a Stick Day. I highly doubt it.

My phone dings again, and this time it's Ren. Her ears must have been burning. *Does that work with thoughts or just talking about someone?*

> REN: You doing anything for Thanksgiving? I'm making dinner here for Pops.

> REN: It's this Thursday. In 5 days, FYI. 😊

> ME: Thanks for the heads up.

> REN: So...is that a yes, you'll come for dinner?

> ME: You didn't invite me. You asked if I was doing anything and then told me what you were doing.

I know this will drive her crazy, but it's too much

fun. And it takes a few minutes for her to respond, so I know she's typing and deleting snarky replies.

> REN: Jude. Would you honor us with your presence at a feast I will prepare in your honor this coming Thursday, which is also known as the American holiday of Thanksgiving?

> > ME: My honor? Wow. I don't want to commit to anything. I may have a date. You were right, I really do need to beat them off with a stick. There are so many interested on this site. 😏

> REN: Really? How many?

I also knew that would pique her interest. She's too easy to mess with sometimes.

> > ME: Six so far. You?

> REN: Six?? Wow. Not that many here.

> > ME: Yeah, right.

I can't believe a million guys aren't busting through her laptop for a chance to date her. She doesn't respond. *Is she serious?*

ME: How many is not that many?

REN: Just three.

What the fuck? How are only three guys inter-ested in her? *Wait. Shit.* Three guys are interested in her. I don't like that either. I should be happy there are only three. Why should I be happy about anybody interested in Ren?

ME: Well, you are a unicorn.

REN: Yeah. Imaginary.

Her response and the sad tone of her words tugs at me. While the possessive idiot in me doesn't want anyone to go after Ren, I also don't want her to be unhappy. I know she wanted this dating website to work for both of us. I'll feel like shit if I find some-one, and she doesn't. I can't believe that would be the case, but what if it is? What will I do?

ME: I'll be there for turkey. That is what's for dinner Thursday, right? What time?

REN: Way to change the subject back. Yes. Turkey. Dinner is at 4:00.

ME: Gotta run. Site messages are blowing up now.

REN: Fine. Jerk.

I don't know why I sent the last text. It was dumb. And rude. Especially since she seemed a little upset at only having three suitors. *Suitors*. I really would make a fantastic Victorian governess.

I narrow my online conversations on the dating site down to three women to keep an even playing field with Ren throughout the following week. I haven't brought up trying to meet any of them yet because I like how things are going now. I have a feeling meeting in person would ruin it somehow. I know that's a strange way to look at it, but there is something about getting to know someone without the expectations or distractions of physical appearance that is appealing. I don't want to burst the bubble of my anonymity yet, either. Once they find out who I am, it might get weird. It's been kind of cool just exchanging words. All of the women seem to be intelligent and funny. They at least use whole sentences and punctuation, which is always a plus in my book.

And speaking of books, one of them has read about every book I have, including some pretty obscure ones. She's the frontrunner for that reason alone. The only issue with her, and it's not an issue, more a hesitation, is that she is one of two who has a child. That's another reason I don't want to meet her yet. If things didn't work out for whatever reason, I don't want to be responsible for her kid's therapy when they grow up with a complex about me abandoning them. I need to be very careful how I deal with that.

Thinking about it makes me think of Ren, and I wonder if she's going to meet any of the guys she's talking to on the site. Shit, maybe she has already. Would she do that so soon? I don't think she would. She barely has time, working ten-hour days and then having to be a mom on top of that. When would she find time to go out on a date? That pisses me off. She deserves so much better than she's gotten. She works so hard to keep her store going, and she's a great mother to Charlie. Any guy would be lucky to have her in their life. I know I am. *Then what the fuck am I doing looking for somebody else?*

Thanksgiving is now my favorite holiday. Looking at the calendar of holidays, it appears to be the only major one that doesn't involve having to buy gifts for your child. Groceries, yes. And lots of them. But no gifts. Charlotte is too young to appreciate that fact yet, but I sure do. I know the years to come will be full of gifts we don't have the money or room for. Something to look forward to.

Today I am a cooking fool. The turkey is in the oven and smells delicious, and the pies I baked from scratch are cooling on the counter. Pops got here early to help with Charlotte while I made the pies and dressed the turkey. I can hear them giggling in the living room while playing on the floor, and the sound fills my heart. I'm so blessed to have him in our lives so much.

The doorbell rings, and I glance at the clock on the living room wall on my way to answer it. I can't imagine Jude being an hour early, but he is all about being punctual; maybe he figures early is better today. When I open the door, though, it's not Jude. It's Brad. My chest tightens, my breath catches in my throat, and I suddenly don't know what to do with my hands, so I cross my arms awkwardly.

"What are you doing here?" I hiss, glancing over my shoulder to make sure Pops is staying in the living room with Charlotte.

He has the nerve to look offended at my question.

"What do you mean? I'm here to see my daughter. It's Thanksgiving."

I stare at him, dumbfounded. Is he serious? I step outside my door and shut it behind me, so our voices don't carry into the house. I check the rest of the street and don't notice anyone outside, so hopefully, we won't attract an audience. Who knows how this is going to go. I never in a million years thought Brad would show up here like this, today of all days, and want to see his daughter. He's wanted nothing to do with us since I kicked him out four months ago after cheating on me for the last time. I've not heard one single word from him since then.

"Are you kidding me right now? You can't just show up here unannounced and uninvited after us not hearing from you for months. That's not how this is going to work." I step up to him, and he takes a step back. He must catch the fury that probably looks like crazy coming through in my eyes. *Good. Let him be afraid of me.*

"I thought you wanted me involved in Charlie's life?" He scoffs at me, and he shakes his head as if I'm the one being irrational. "I have a right to see my daughter whenever I want to." I can't believe he thinks that. I finally take a good look at him, and he looks like shit, like he just rolled out of bed and is still hungover. He still reeks like booze as well. There's no way I'm letting him near Charlotte in this state, regardless of the circumstances.

"Yeah, no. You don't." I take another step toward him, and he doesn't move this time. The spark in his eyes is almost like a dare for me to challenge him. He actually thinks he can do this. He's got a rude awakening coming. "Not whenever you want. When I say you can." My voice rises each time I speak as the anger inside me grows at his audacity. "When you call ahead. When you make arrangements that I agree to. That's when you have a right to see her. That's how this is going to work."

"That's bullshit, Ren. Why should my access only be when it's convenient for you?"

"Well, your way is when it's convenient for you. Do you not see the irony in your own question?"

"Is everything okay out here, Rena?" Pops shouts

from behind me. I turn my head and find him eyeing the situation with concern.

"It's fine, Pops. I'll be right in." I call over my shoulder and go back to glaring at Brad.

He has the gall to smile at my grandfather, and it's a con man's smile. A smile that now makes my skin crawl. A smile I fell for like an idiot more times than I care to count.

"Hey, Mr. Scott," he calls with a small wave. The door shuts behind me with no response from my grandfather. *That's right, asshole, you're not welcome here*. The smile slides off his face, and he shifts to glare back at me, picking right up where we left off.

"If you want to visit Charlotte, you need to arrange it with me first. I won't keep her from you if you do us both that courtesy." My muscles twitch at the thought of letting him take Charlotte, but I have to be fair. He is her father, as much as I regret that fact. "I don't intend to interfere with your relationship with your daughter." The words are sour in my mouth as I speak them. I would love nothing more than never to deal with him again, but I know I can't do that.

"It sure seems like you want to interfere." He takes a step closer, pulling himself up and trying to intimidate me. I don't back down. I'm not going to let him bully me. "It seems to me like you have to get your way, Ren. Just like always. You'll never change." He has the nerve to glare at me with hatred. As if I did something awful to him and not the other way around. He was the one who cheated on me, so where he gets the idea I'm the bad guy here is beyond my comprehension.

"If it isn't Brad the Dad. Is dickhead school closed for the holiday today?" Jude's voice is light, but the cutting edge to it could slice bone. I didn't notice him pull up or get out of his car. Of course, I've been preoccupied with my jerk of an ex showing up on my doorstep. I'm happy to know he's here. He'll have my back.

Neither Brad nor I look away from each other, our glares building intensity.

"Fuck you, Jude." Brad tries to sound tough, but it falls flat.

"Are you volunteering? Nah. That doesn't work for you. Never mind." Jude pushes between Brad and me, getting in his face and pulling himself taller than him. *How does he like it?* "How about you get lost, huh? You're obviously not welcome here."

"How about you mind your own fucking business, Lockwood? I told you that at Old Town." Brad sounds like a whiny child. The more I know him, the more I wonder what I ever saw in him. He's not even cute anymore.

"And I told you, pillock, that when it comes to Ren and Charlie, they *are* my business. So, you're going to want to back off and go home." Jude isn't kidding. I can see the rage emanating from him, and he's almost vibrating with it. Brad better listen to him, or I don't know what's going to happen here. I'm starting to really worry.

"You're the one that said I need to be involved in Charlotte's life. Well, here I am, and this is how I'm treated." He spreads his arms and scoffs as if in disbelief he's being treated so poorly. So that's what Jude said to him. *Good*.

They appear to be at a standoff for the moment, with neither one about to back down. I'm unsure what to do now, so I do nothing but back away from them both. I don't like the energy between these two. This is not how I thought this Thanksgiving would be going. I can't help but think about Pops with Charlotte inside right now. I don't know if he's watching all of this, but I hope not. I hope he's keeping her entertained and unaware of this shit show.

"Jude, let's go," I whisper and reach to put a hand on his back. I want this to be over already.

They stare for about another minute, then Brad backs up with a vicious grin, but his eyes never leave Jude.

"Fine. I'll go. But this isn't the end, Ren. Not even close."

Jude ignores this and wraps an arm around my shoulders, walking me back to the house. Not the end of this? What does that mean? What could he possibly think he could do?

"I always knew you two were fucking around," Brad yells, and I can feel Jude stiffen next to me. I grab his hand and squeeze it. *Ignore him, Jude.* "Shit. Now I wonder if Charlie's even mine."

"I am going to fuck him up..." Jude tries pulling away from me to go after Brad, but I hold on to his hand for dear life. I will not have these two fighting in the street.

"Jude, no. Don't take his bait. He's just being an asshole." I try to pull him back toward the house, but he's super strong, and it's hard to hold him back. "Don't stoop to his level."

"Ren, let me go," he growls, his jaw clenched. I've never seen Jude so irate.

"No. Don't let him get to you. Be the bigger man. Let's go inside."

"I don't want to be the bigger man." He's trying desperately to slide out of my grip, but I've been practicing these moves with a squirming baby for six months. Getting away from me now is going to be near impossible for him. "I'll give up a few inches if it means I get to kick his fucking ass."

Brad's laugh at us is chilling. I can tell he's not happy that Jude is restraining himself, or, more accurately, I'm restraining him. He'd like nothing more than to start something and make a scene so he could twist it later.

"Remember what happened with Matt and his brother this summer. Don't give him any fuel." I highly doubt that he wants to go through that again.

Sure enough, once my words needle their way through his consciousness, he relaxes and lets me pull him into the house. Neither of us gives Brad the satisfaction of a reply or a glance. *Jesus.* Wrestling with a twenty-eight-year-old human wasn't on the holiday menu today. Brad showing up out of the blue was surprising, but his last statements about Jude and me completely threw me. Where the hell did that come from?

Well, that was intense. I did not expect that to happen when I came over for Thanksgiving dinner. The last person I thought I'd find in Ren's front yard was Brad. After he didn't contact Ren to help her after my little chat with him, I figured that was the end of it. Showing up out of the blue and wanting to see Charlie is seriously insane. I wish Ren didn't hold me back. But then, violence would only make me feel better for a minute, if that. Knowing me, I'd hurt my fucking self in the process. I need to learn from Matt's incident this past summer. But his snide comment about Charlie's paternity and my possible involvement was way out of line. If I had gotten to him, he would have deserved everything he got and then some.

When Charlie's face lights up as she sees me, all

135

of that bullshit flies out the fucking window. I'm reduced to a puddle on the ground, but I don't let it show. At least, I hope I don't. I have a reputation to uphold.

"Look out, Pops," Ren jokes on her way into the kitchen. "Mr. Smittenable over here is vying for your position on Charlotte's dance card."

"Nah, we're just friends." I bow slightly to Charlie and smile at Ren's grandfather. "How's it going, Art?" I never could bring myself to call him Pops, plus he just looks like an Art.

He shakes my hand heartily, his eyes intense.

"Everything okay outside?"

I glance sideways in Ren's direction but nod at him.

"Yeah. It's all good for now." My eyes express that things may not stay good, and he nods his understanding. "Just had to bounce an uninvited guest. I have to do that all the time in my line of work, so it wasn't a big deal."

Ren laughs, coming back into the living room and handing me and Art beers.

"You're playing amphitheaters now. I highly doubt you get called on to bounce people anymore."

I puff my chest out a bit, ready to debunk that myth.

"Pfft. Shows what you know. I had to haul a guy out by his shirt at our show in Germany last month."

Art raises an eyebrow, impressed, but Ren is suspicious.

"Really? You had to bounce someone?" She sounds like she doesn't believe me. I'm almost offended.

"Really. This totally wasted dude jumped on stage in the middle of my solo in Hamburg. *My* solo. If it were Matt's or Ryan's, I wouldn't have cared, but mine crosses a line. I can't encourage that kind of behavior. So, out he went. Luckily the stage door exit was pretty close by. Now that I think about it, it was the loudest reaction I've had to my solo. I should arrange for that to happen every show."

Ren shakes her head at me.

"You're incorrigible."

"And smittenable. Don't forget that one." I set my beer aside and get down on the floor to play with Charlie. She starts doing her backward scoot, and I love she knows I'm the one she plays like that with. We play our modified tag game, and Art even joins us. Charlie is overjoyed at having more participants in our game, and my heart feels like it will burst in my chest.

Once we tire her out, Ren feeds her and puts her down for a nap so we can eat dinner.

"So, how long are you in LA for, Jude?" Art asks. We've finished dinner, and he's washing, and I'm drying the dishes. His idea, not mine, but it's cool. I guess it's fair.

"I don't know. We're going to be figuring that out after the New Year." I put the plate I just dried into the cupboard, sensing a bigger conversation coming. "So, I'm here at least another couple months or so."

He nods, and I don't know how to interpret the question and his response. Since I've been back in town, he's been acting weird, and I'm unsure what to make of his questions or statements.

I glance around to make sure Ren isn't in the kitchen with us, and it seems clear.

"Art, is something going on your not telling me?"

He scowls at me.

"What do you mean?"

I'm not buying the innocent act.

"You tell me. You've been acting kind of weird lately."

That makes him laugh as he hands me another clean plate to dry.

"Well, as you can tell from Rena, it's hereditary."

"C'mon, Art."

He considers me for a minute, pausing in his washing and turning to me head-on.

"How about you tell me what's going on between you and Rena? Or you and Lottie?"

The questions shock the shit out of me. *What the fuck? And he calls Charlie 'Lottie?'* That's odd. I guess Ren was right, and we really don't want to call Charlie by her full name. I had a feeling that Art was sensing something between us but didn't expect him to come right out and ask about it. His intense gaze makes me extremely nervous, and a slight sweat breaks out on my forehead. I hope he doesn't notice. How do I answer him? Truthfully? What is the truth about what's going on with us when I don't know myself?

"As far as I know, nothing. Things are status quo." I avoid his stare that seems to see right through me. *Damn.* "Why do you ask?" Maybe if I can find out what he thinks he sees between us, I'll better grasp what might be happening.

He keeps his stare locked on me, studying me, and I feel the weight of that examination. I'm being measured, but against what? I have no idea. I've never measured up against anything before, so I'm sure I don't again now in his estimation of me. He can probably tell I'm unworthy of Ren and Charlie, and I agree. He's been the most important man in their lives, and I could never dream of meeting him at his level. I'd never deserve them.

Art finally resumes the dishes, and the air leaves my chest in relief at the end of his scrutiny.

"While you may not see it, Jude, you've changed since the last time you were home."

What the hell is he talking about? I've changed?

"How have I changed?" I don't think I can keep the disbelief out of my voice. I can usually agree with Art on most things, but he's way off on this. I don't change. I'm the same sarcastic asshole I always have been.

He glances over his shoulder to check again if the coast is clear. I think it's hilarious we're trying so hard to keep our conversation from Ren, but then we both know the wrath we'll face if she hears us. We're not really talking about her, though.

"Jude. You're helping at the store every Friday and hanging out with Ren afterward? That's not the old Jude. The old Jude would be out prowling on Sunset for his next conquest, even though you didn't have to work that hard for it."

That makes me blush a little, I can even feel my ears heat up. Art sure knows how to get to the heart of the matter. He's not wrong there. I shrug. "Okay..."

"And, come on. I've seen you with Lottie. You can't tell me that little girl doesn't have you wrapped around her little finger very securely." He arches an eyebrow at me, and I can't help but agree with that much. *She does.*

"Well, yeah. But she does that with everyone she meets. She's a charmer. I'm not special."

"Did you not see her when you came in today,

and she saw you?" The eyebrow previously arched is now even higher. "That is special, son."

Remembering how Charlie's face lit up on my arrival makes me smile.

"Yeah, I saw that." I can't deny it. My heart completely melted when I saw it. "That was pretty cool. But I'm not seeing how that's changed me, Art. I'm still the same old me as far as I can tell."

"Well, maybe *you* haven't changed who you are as a person, but you can't tell me *things* haven't changed between you and Rena." He hands me another wet plate.

"Changed how?" I want details. I want him to tell me what is going on, so I can stop being so fucking confused when I'm around her. I need to know what he sees between us.

"First, there's you helping Rena at her store. You've never done that before."

"I'm helping with Charlie, not the store." Even I can hear the stupidity of that statement.

He ignores me and continues.

"Second, the way you two look at each other when the other is unaware is new."

"How are we looking at each other?" I haven't noticed Ren looking at me any differently. Whether I see Ren differently is another story and not one I want to admit to right now. Especially not to her grandfather. And I don't think I've been obvious about it either.

"Come on, Jude. Don't be coy."

"I'm not, Art. How is Ren looking at me?" I need to know if she's feeling anything like I am, but there is no way I'd ask her directly.

He glances over his shoulder again.

"Let's just say it's more than how a friend looks at another friend."

I almost drop the dish I'm drying but recover quickly. Can that be true? Is she considering me as more than a friend? I can't bring myself to believe it. Unless I see it myself, or she comes right out and tells me, I'm not going to put any stock into Art's claims. Especially after the whole LastPersonOn-Earth.com business.

"Well, if that were true, she wouldn't have coerced me to join a dating site."

"She did?" He sounds shocked. "And you agreed?"

I laugh, "I know. Yes. I agreed, but only on the condition she joined as well. I'm not going through this nightmare alone."

Art shakes his head in disbelief, with a tinge of sadness too. I don't know why any of this would make him sad. On the contrary, he should be happy Ren is moving on from Brad.

"I guess I'm an old fool who just sees what I want to see then."

"You'd want me and Ren to be together?" I can't believe that either. Art and I have always gotten along, but I never got the idea he saw Ren and me as more than friends. I can't believe we're talking about this.

"I want Rena to be happy." He drains the sink and dries his hands carefully. "And you too. That's all I want for you two; however that takes shape."

"Well, thanks, Art. That means a lot coming from you."

"Okay, I think that's enough of that and my queue to head home." He pats my shoulder and leads me out of the kitchen. "I'll go say my goodbyes."

Before I can take a seat on the couch, Art is back and whispers, "Both of them are sleeping, so I'll sneak out now." He shakes my hand and leaves with a nod.

I go down the hallway and peek in on Charlie, her little snores filling up the otherwise quiet of the space. I stand in her room, leaning on the edge of her crib, watching her sleep. Something inside me twists, wanting to protect this little girl from the big bad world. I want to build a huge impenetrable bubble around her, so she never hurts, and never knows any kind of pain.

I wonder if Ren does this, too, just staring at Charlie in complete awe of her existence in the world. If I were a parent, I'd do this all the time. If I were a parent...*cart, watch out for that horse behind you.*

I straighten and quietly pad to Ren's room to check on her too. I think the last time I was in here was when we moved her into the house a few years ago. Ren is snoring lightly like Charlie, the fading light of dusk casting its last orange hues across the room, her curls highlighted in the glow. *Fiery isn't wrong.* There is no way I'm waking her up. She needs this sleep and deserves it after cooking all day.

Glancing around, I spy a picture frame with a collage of photos of the two of us on her nightstand. The pictures are from the photo booth in the arcade at the Santa Monica Pier. Something inside me dances at the thought these pictures are the first thing she sees in the morning and the last thing at night. The photos are kind of great, though. I don't know why I let her take them all. At the time, I didn't realize their actual value, or Ren's, for that matter.

Does this mean Art is correct? Ren does have feelings for me? It could mean nothing at all. Maybe I'm like Art and only see what I want to see.

twenty

IT'S GOING TO TAKE SOME TIME

REN

I wake up to Charlotte crying and Jude trying his best to calm her down. I hurry to her room and find Jude holding her while pacing the floor, his face stricken with worry. My heart lurches a little at how sweet the two are together. He does hate when she cries.

I reach to take her from him.

"Let me take her. She probably needs a new diaper."

"No. I just changed her, so that's not it. I think it's her teething again bothering her. She should get some of that pain reliever stuff."

My mouth drops open in shock. *What did he just say?*

"You...what?" I can't believe what I just heard. He changed a diaper? Hell must have frozen over, pigs are flying somewhere, or something else fantastic. I never thought Jude would ever change a diaper in a million years of years. "You changed her diaper? Who are you, and what have you done with my friend, Jude? Oh, and welcome to the planet Earth."

"Should I not have changed her?" He looks confused and still so worried about Charlotte that my heart overflows. "I thought that was why she was crying in the first place, but she didn't stop after I changed her either."

"No, it's fine. You did the right thing. I'm just surprised by it, is all." Charlotte is starting to cry herself out as she leans her head against my chest.

"I know. I swore I'd never do it, but I couldn't stand hearing her cry like that. Plus, YouTube is there for a reason. Most people fail to see the resource it is for learning things."

"Really? You looked up how to change a diaper on YouTube?" I lead us out of the nursery and into the living room. I don't know why I'm surprised by this. I guess I'm shocked he changed a diaper after swearing it off so adamantly.

"Well, yeah. The point was to not wake you up." He's always so matter-of-fact with his words. As though these things should be common knowledge to everyone when there is no possible way on Earth everyone could know.

"Well, I appreciate the thought and the effort." I check out his handy work, and he did a decent job. I can't help but grin at him. "Good work. Hopefully, you smashed that 'Like' button and subscribed."

"So, where is the pain reliever stuff?" He searches around and finds her diaper bag and starts digging through it frantically, ignoring my attempt at a joke.

"It's in there. Keep searching." He's becoming distraught, and I'm worried what he's so upset about. Is it just Charlotte's crying? Or is it something more? I don't want to tell him to 'chill out' because that would be very unhelpful if he's genuinely freaking out. "And, Jude. Take a deep breath. It'll be okay."

He finally finds the medicine and gives it to me with shaky hands.

"What else do you need?"

"There should be a new box of cooling gel I picked up yesterday in the bag too." I sit with Charlotte on my lap and start to prepare a dropper full of medicine.

He finds the other box, opens it, and pulls out the tube. Unscrewing the cap, he discovers the tube needs to be cut open.

"What evil witchcraft is this? Why is there a cap if you have to cut it open too?" He hurries into the kitchen, opening and closing drawers quickly. "My kingdom for a pair of fucking scissors!"

I can't help but chuckle at his outburst but can compose myself before he returns with an open tube of cooling gel. Once everything is administered and Charlotte has calmed down on my chest, Jude releases a deep breath.

"You know, you've had it pretty easy with Charlotte," I say, eyeing Jude cautiously. He sits next to us on the couch carefully and starts smoothing Charlotte's hair. "She's been all 'good baby' with you, but you've seen her true self today here at home."

"Does she cry a lot like that?" And my heart is now mush. Everything is now mush. I have to look away from him. The compassionate sadness in his eyes is more than I can take. He is so affected by her emotional outbursts.

"Not a lot, no. But more than you've seen of her. Until today that is. This is all very normal."

"Geez. I could not handle that day in and day out. I don't know how you do it."

"Well, I don't have a choice in the matter. But look at this face." I pinch her cheek lightly, and she giggles a little. "I would honestly choose it anyway. How could I not?"

I glance up and catch Jude gazing at me with an admiration I've never gotten from him before. My first instinct is to turn away, but I force myself to hold still and return the expression. I am so pleasantly surprised at not only his changing a diaper, but the concern he showed for Charlotte when she was in distress was overwhelming. I don't know what to think about Jude anymore. When I think I know all there is to know about him, he shows me another, more amazing side I never knew existed.

He's making it so hard to not have feelings for him that go beyond friendship. How can I not when he is so invested in the well-being of my child? Or when he defends my honor with my ex-boyfriend? Things like that can't be typical friendship activities. And the way he's looking at me right now makes me think he might feel the same. *Geez. I'm going off the deep end*.

"So, how's your internet harem shaping up?" I tear my eyes away from him. If I'm going to talk to him about his love life, I don't need to look at him while I'm at it.

He shifts uncomfortably next to me, and I can see him frown out of the corner of my eye. I can tell my change of topic has unsettled him, and I'm not sure how I feel about that.

"I've whittled it down to three possible candidates." His tone is nonchalant, as if it's no big deal. I think it's significant.

"Wow. Why the culling of the herd?"

He reaches over and takes Charlotte from me, and she starts to beam like a spotlight on him.

"I wanted an even playing field in our game."

"What game?"

"Not a game. Contest or competition or whatever. You know what I mean." He shrugs it off. Again, as if it's not important.

"Jude. I thought you were taking this seriously." I can't keep the disappointment out of my voice. If he's treating this entire thing as a joke, I don't know what I'll do. He needs to find someone else so I can stop this downward spiral I'm in falling for him.

"I am taking it seriously, which is why it's down to three." He's back to being agitated, and I can't tell if it's me he's annoyed with or my talking about this. "Why string people along if you know it won't work out with them? I'm doing them a kindness."

I guess that makes sense. Since I'm only starting with three, removing any from the selection pool would be extreme. Considering Jude began with a lot more, cutting it down to a few seems like it would be more manageable.

"Are you thinking you might want to meet any of the three that are left?" I'm curious how far he's willing to go with it. There's a pang in my chest, thinking of his meeting and falling for one of these women. But isn't that why I started this in the first place?

He scowls slightly, his brows drawing down.

"Not yet." He's getting Charlotte to high-five him while he talks, and she's giggling away. "I want to see how things go for a while."

"Okay. I just wanted to check in with you on it." I can't hold back a yawn. Even with the nap, I'm exhausted. "Don't give yourself a wedgie."

"Shit. I mean, shoot." He sits up suddenly,

handing Charlotte off to me. "If today is Thanksgiving, tomorrow is Black Friday, isn't it?"

"It is indeed the biggest retail shopping day of the year tomorrow." I eye him curiously. I hope he's coming by tomorrow. Good or bad, I was kind of counting on it. I can get Pops to get Charlotte early if he doesn't, but I like hanging out with Jude. I can't bring myself to come right out and ask for his help with her for some reason. It still seems too huge to burden someone else with. But he's gone so often, I need to soak him in while I have him. "Why do you ask? Do you have shopping plans?"

"What? No. But you'll need help with Charlie at the store tomorrow, right?" I want to believe I see hope in his eyes, but I don't know if I really do.

"Sure, I could use the help, but Jude, you know I'd never ask you…"

He waves a dismissive hand at me.

"Bunk, bosh, hooey, and moonshine. You don't need to ask. I'm offering." He leans over and gives Charlotte a soft kiss on the top of her red curls, and I will need to be resuscitated in a minute. "So, I'm going to bail. I'll see you tomorrow." Our eyes meet, and it's as if he's contemplating something, but God help me if I can tell what it is. He can be so unreadable sometimes. Shaking off whatever he was just thinking, he stands and leaves, and I'm left wondering what he was thinking about.

I could jump to all kinds of crazy conclusions if I

let myself. That's just it, though. I can't let myself. I need to be realistic about all of this. It's why I suggested the dating site to begin with. I don't want to lose this friendship. I don't want to risk this because this is amazing as it is. What kills me is knowing how great things are between us now; I can only imagine how much better things could maybe be if we were together. We'd either be amazing or a complete catastrophe. I don't want to gamble on that future. Not when this now includes Charlotte in the picture. I need to be careful with her heart and my own.

twenty-one

RUBY
JUDE

When I get home from Ren's house, I bounce off the walls with energy. I got so riled up over Charlie's crying I think it's shorted the wires in my brain. I was tempted to see what was happening on the Strip since everything is open on Thanksgiving, but I wasn't feeling the vibe. I haven't cruised the Strip in over a year since our tour started, and I don't know what's wrong with me. I should be all over that. Matt's out of town for the weekend at Samantha's parent's in Ohio, and I have the whole place to myself. I should be living it up, having wild sex with random women on every available surface in the place while I can. But no. I can't do that because I'm too amped up from learning how to change a diaper and trying to calm a crying baby most of the evening.

I don't know what I'm doing anymore. Art's comment about Charlie having me wrapped around her finger sure nailed it. But the shit he said about Ren and me looking at each other differently doesn't seem right. I think he's got that part wrong. Ren has never and would never think of me as anything more than a friend. So, I'm not going to entertain that thought anymore. I just need to get over this somehow and focus on the stupid dating site. It will be a distraction if nothing else.

That's an idea. I pull out my laptop, grab a beer from the fridge, and take a seat on the balcony, putting my feet up on the chair across from me. The sun went down a while ago, but it's still warm enough to sit out here for a little bit yet. I need to cool off anyway.

When I open the website, I find messages from two of my...what do I call them? Conquests? Absolutely not. Art used that word to reference my previous proclivities. I need to open another tab and start searching for what to call them. Candidates? Fuck that, too. Paramours? Oh, wow, that refers to cheating married people. Never mind. Prospects? I guess that will do. I don't want to call them matches because I don't know that we are yet. Not in the true sense of the word, at least.

I open the one from the prospect I'm leaning toward, the similar reader with the kid, CF52951. I call her Catfish because she really is too good to be true. I'm sure there's a catch somewhere, or there will be hidden cameras to surprise me on the gag if we ever do meet. While she's the one I'm leaning toward, she's not a real person to me yet. Damn, she might actually be an AI.

> CATFISH: Hey there. I know it's a holiday, but I wanted to send a note to tell you I was thinking of you. I hope you had a good day with family, friends, or both.

Well, shit. That's fucking sweet. More proof for the AI argument. I don't know how to fucking respond. While I love reading lots of words, writing them? Not so much. I especially don't want to write about feelings or anything like that.

> ME: Thanks. You too.

Wow, Jude. That right there has got to be your finest work. You should print that out and frame it to hang on the wall. This is a fucking masterpiece. Jesus Christ. Why is this shit so hard? I open the second message. This one is from the woman I call Honey Bunny, HB64575, since she always jumps down random rabbit holes in her messages.

HONEY BUNNY: So I hope you had a great Turkey day. Have you ever wondered where names for certain body parts come from? I mean, I know it's Latin or Greek in origin, but what the hell? Like, gizzard. It's the weirdest word, don't you think? Or Coccyx. Why bother with the one vowel? Just go full-on consonants, I say. Hope your day was good.

ME: Thanks. You too. Don't forget the niddick – the nape of your neck. Or the minimus – aka, your little toe. Those are essential body parts with equally important names. The ancients were lucky to have first dibs on naming things. I definitely would have gone in a different direction on several names. Since we're on body parts, the funny bone is the first to go. Not a bone, and not funny. It's confusing the kids.

There. Now I can go to bed and not feel bad for not responding. This online dating thing is exhausting.

The next day at Vital Records is busy. Sawyer

even comes in early to help Ren with the shopping insanity. Surprisingly, she tells me at lunch, during a lull in the crowd, she was expecting it to be busier than it has been.

"I depend on this day for about fifteen percent of my annual sales. But I'm just not seeing the foot traffic I've had in years past." She shakes her head, worry crossing over her features. "I think being closed for those couple of weeks really hurt more than I thought it would."

Seeing Ren so worried tears me up inside. We don't usually talk financials when it comes to our businesses. It isn't like we discussed it and decided not to talk about it; we just never have, and I don't think now is the time to start. But I need to do something. I don't know where this urge to play the hero for Ren and Charlie is coming from. It ties in with my desire to protect them, which has taken me over. I never felt like this for anyone or anything before, not even my band or career. It's that deep.

This realization propels me to act, and an idea comes to me. I hand Charlie back to her mom and take my phone outside to send a text.

ME: Hey group text we all hate.

MATT: I see you still can't follow instructions. Delete this, and DON'T start it back up.

ME: I thought you wanted to meet Ren.

MATT: Go on…

ME: How about doing a pro bono in-store acoustic set and signing at her shop? Vital Records LA?

MATT: She owns Vital Records? No shit. When are we doing this?

RYAN: Who the fuck started up this group text again? What are we doing?

ME: A free acoustic set at Vital Records.

RYAN: Cool. When?

ME: I'll get back to you.

MATT: Individually?

ME: Fuck you.

MATT: Are you volunteering?

RYAN: Are you volunteering?

I should have seen that last bit coming. I'm just excited to have a possible plan to help Ren out. They didn't bat an eye at the part about the show being free. Not that I expected them to demand payment, but it's cool it's not even a topic of discussion.

As I'm entering the store again, I receive another text from Matt. This time it's a direct message and not part of the group.

> MATT: Is everything okay?

> > ME: Bad Black Friday, I guess. Just want to help.

> MATT: OK, cool. No problem. Let us know when.

> > ME: Will do. Thanks.

I can't contain my grin as I make my way back to Ren and Charlie inside the store.

"You look like the cat that nabbed the canary. What's up?"

"How do you feel about an Indigo King store takeover?" I'm internally crossing my fingers, toes, and eyeballs that she goes along with this. I *need* her to let me do this for her. I don't know why, but I don't care why, either. I need to do this.

She's skeptical but interested.

"What do you mean by 'takeover?'"

A few customers walk in, but Sawyer is on it and goes to help them.

"I mean, we'd like to do a signing here and a small acoustic set, maybe. If you agree... it's something...we could maybe do. If it's alright with you."

She runs a hand through her hair, her striking

gray eyes examining me closely, and I'm not sure what she's looking for or what she's seeing in me. I can't read this expression, though. It's not one I've seen before.

"What are you doing, Jude?" Her tone is angry, and I'm even more confused. I thought she'd be happy about this.

"What do you mean? I thought it would be good for the store." I glance around and wave a hand at the almost empty store, indicating the lack of customers. "I thought it would be good for you."

"What's with the white knight act from you? First, you're suddenly the damned Baby Whisperer, and now you want to try to somehow save my store? I didn't ask for any of this, Jude."

"Right. I'm offering these things." I shake my head in confusion at her. How is she not understanding this? "You do know how friendship works, right? We do stuff like this for each other, right? Oh, and thanks for the Baby Whisperer affirmation. I thought that one myself."

"Jude. You know we don't do stuff like this." She shifts her weight from side to side nervously, now very interested in her shoes. My heart is sinking. She can't be this proud. I know she's insanely independent, but she's got to see reason on this.

"That's bullshit, and you know it. Remember when I was with that band, Road Kill? And you came to our first show, and I wrangled you into doing the lights for us?"

A snort escapes her, and she covers her mouth quickly, trying to hold in her laugh.

"Oh my God, you guys were horribad. I forgot about that."

"Yeah, it wasn't my finest moment. But my point is you were there to help out when I needed you."

"Jude. I flipped the stage light switch on and off to make it look like a strobe light for twenty minutes. That's hardly the same thing, and you know it."

I've got to get her to let me help her somehow, and I think I might be winning her over. I know deep down I won't be okay until I know she and Charlie will be alright. It's just a fact of life now. They are now my worry.

"Well, I'm sorry you don't see your value as a lighting technician, but Ryan and Matt are on board and looking forward to it, so you're kind of stuck with us."

Her eyes widen, and her mouth drops open. Her entire demeanor shifts from laughing back to angry and then irate. The change is so fast and extreme it makes me dizzy.

"You already asked Matt and Ryan? Jude. This is my business you're messing with. *My* business. You can't go behind my back and arrange shit like this without my permission. You just can't do that." Her eyes are now steel, and her jaw is set. She's pissed. I can't believe she's fucking pissed about this. I don't think she's ever been this pissed at me before.

"Ren...I was trying to..."

"What? Swoop in and save the day? How about asking first?" She finally notices her voice has risen in volume, and the customers in the store are starting to give us strange looks. Her cheeks flush with anger and embarrassment, and she grabs my arm and drags me to the back room with Charlie in her other arm, a little unsure what's going on with her mom's mood. *I'm right with you, kid.*

"What is your problem, Ren? I'm trying to help you out here. I don't get why you're getting pissed at me about it."

"Since when did it become your full-time job to save me, Jude? You come back from your tour, and suddenly I'm your charity of choice for donating your time. What is with you lately?"

Her words land like punches on my soul. I don't understand what I did wrong. I thought this was what friends did for each other; help each other in times of need. *Times like this.*

twenty-two

BREAKING DOWN
REN

J ude has finally crossed a line with me. I can't
believe he just went and recruited the rest of
his band to do a signing and a set in my store.
My store. My business.

"Where exactly is your band going to set up?
Both to play and to sign? Do you see room out there
somewhere for either of those? Or is that your next
trick? You're going to magically create space in my
store for this too?" I'm so mad right now, and I'm
just getting started. I don't care if Jude now looks
like he wants to run into heavy traffic. "And what
about security? You guys need that kind of thing
now, right? Who's arranging and paying for that?
And stock? Where am I going to get enough inventory to support this? And how much time do I have?
You've apparently got this whole thing planned out
for me. Please, do tell me how this is going to work.

Oh, and are you going to arrange for daycare for Charlotte that day, too, while you're arranging our lives?"

Charlotte senses my mood and is starting to get agitated, making me even madder. Tears threaten themselves, and I need to look away from him. The defeated expression on Jude's face is now filling me with guilt for being mad at him. What the hell? We've never meddled in each other's businesses before. Why is he suddenly doing all this?

Jude is speechless for the first time in the eleven years I've known him. And this time, the flush in his face isn't cute; it's angry. I can't believe he's mad at me for reacting this way. What did he think I would do?

"Ren." He takes a deep breath and lets it out slowly. Obviously trying to calm himself down. "I am trying to help you."

"I didn't ask for your help, Jude. And you're not seeing how this is now a bigger problem for me."

"I'll admit I may not have thought this entirely all the way through. But we can work out the details. I'm sure we can." His anger is subsiding, and so is mine. Charlotte's fussing is making me calm myself down. She often feeds off my mood, so I need to keep myself in check.

I let out a deep sigh, physically deflating as well as mentally. I don't know why this hit such a nerve with me. I know Jude would never do anything purposely to make my life difficult. On the contrary, he does what he can to make my life easier. Like being here today in the first place. And I have to go and be a bitch and bite his head off for trying to do something nice for me.

Charlotte's got one of her fists wrapped around a section of my hair, and she gives it a pull, literally yanking me back to the present. I can't think of anything to say, though. I'm still angry, but I don't want to fight with Jude anymore.

"If you don't want us to do it, we won't. But we can make it work somehow. It is your store, so it's your call. And I'm sure we could get a bunch of people to help." He steps up and ruffles Charlotte's curls, and her bright eyes turn to him. She puts up a hand for a high-five, and Jude taps her hand with his. Why am I arguing with him like this?

Exhaustion overtakes me as I watch my baby daughter interact with Jude, and my chest tightens. I can feel my shoulders shaking before the tears even start flowing. The enormity of doing this all on my own for so long now is overwhelming, and the fact that Jude sees me struggling scratches at my soul. I don't ever want to appear weak or incapable of handling anything, but I can't keep up this façade any longer.

"I'm sorry..." I whisper, turning away from Jude and pulling Charlotte closer to my chest. I wipe at my tears with the heel of my free hand and try to take deep breaths, but my lungs keep hitching with sobs. The next thing I know, Jude is wrapping his arms around me, or us, from behind, and it only makes it worse. I bury my face into Charlotte's hair, inhaling her sweet baby scent, trying desperately not to think about Jude's arms around me on top of everything else. I want so badly to just lean back and melt into him. But no, I can't do that. *Friends don't do that.*

"What's going on, Ren?" The stubble on his perfect chin catches a little in my hair as he leans into me, and the compassion in his voice breaks me a little more. "I have a feeling this reaction isn't just about a store signing by my dumb rock band."

I glance down at his strong arms around us, his hands intertwining, and study his tattoos through my tears. Jude's arms are nearly full of color, except for the inside of his left forearm, which is still blank. I never thought anything of it before, but it's odd he's not filled in that spot. It's a distracting thought, anyway. A majestic, black-shaded dragon on his forearm stares up at me as it guards a hoard of gold coins.

"Are you ever going to fill that spot in?" I ask, between sniffles.

"What?" he chuckles, and his rumbling chest against my back feels so comforting. I think he's even wearing a cologne today, and the spicy fragrance is enthralling. "You're crying because I'm missing a tattoo? If I'd known you cared so much, I would have taken care of it by now."

"Yes, Jude. Your lack of a completely tattooed arm is irresponsible and very disturbing." I'm deflecting, and I know it. And Jude knows it too.

"So, back to what's happening with you here. What's got you so upset?"

I can't take his nearness anymore, and I move away, facing him.

"Are we starting with the word 'upset' again? I thought I banned that word."

His lips curve up into a smirk, but it's a smile on him.

"Well, maybe we should stop getting upset."

I bite the inside of my cheek, stopping myself from saying, *'well, stop doing upsetting things.'*

Jude can read my mind. Of course, he can.

"I will do what I can to not piss you off." I quirk a brow at him, and he qualifies, "Any more than I have."

I still don't say anything. Not making me mad is one thing, but he still needs to deal with this whole in-store signing mess. I keep my gaze steady on him while swaying Charlotte back and forth. Apart from my mini-meltdown, we still haven't addressed the matter at hand.

He leans back and crosses his arms, his body slumping. He raps the back of his head into the shelf behind him a few times with his eyes closed. I can't tell what he's thinking, which is rare. Something has been propelling him to be overly helpful with us, and I don't know what it could be. I am mostly grateful for everything, but my independence is starting to bristle.

"I'm sorry, Ren. I thought I was doing a good thing. But I am sorry I didn't talk to you about it first. I still think it's a good idea, so I hope you let me figure out how to make it work for you."

I can sense the tears about to well up again, and I force them back with a series of rapid blinks, which I'm sure doesn't look weird in the slightest, but luckily his eyes are still closed.

"You still haven't told me why you're doing all this, Jude. Not that I'm not grateful, because I am. But before I agree to anything, I need to know why I'm doing it."

He finally opens his eyes and turns his attention to Charlotte, who is now sleeping with her head on my shoulder. His gaze is so intense I have to shift my weight from foot to foot to avoid jumping out of my skin.

"Her."

twenty-three

REAL LOVE SONG

JUDE

"I'm doing this for Charlie." I hate I need to spell this out or explain myself. My reasons for helping shouldn't matter; just the fact it's happening should. But Ren isn't normal. She's always got to see who's performing the magic behind the curtain for everything. Everyone has an ulterior motive or will end up screwing her over one way or another. I get it. I know she's got trust issues, and rightfully so, but she shouldn't have them with me. "Because dickhead Brad isn't doing his job, and I know you won't take direct help from me. This is something within my power I can do for you guys to try to pick up some of that slack. Let me do this for you. If not for you, for Charlie."

I can't believe I'm begging someone to let me do something nice for them. When did this become my life? Leave it to Ren to be the subject of my pleading. She can be too stubborn for her own good. I can only hope she considers Charlie in this. I'm doing this for her. She's got to see reason in this.

Charlie's making little snoring noises on her shoulder, and now I think the growing size of my heart could give the Grinch a run for his money. This kid is going to be the death of me. Well, she *and* her mother. Seeing Ren vulnerable like this isn't something that happens very often, if at all, and it's doing something to me. While, yes, her rough edges are damned attractive, this smooth side is pulling out the protector in me I didn't know existed.

"I don't want to argue with you anymore, Jude." Her exhaustion is shadowing her eyes, and I think she may just have given in. "Fine. If we can figure it all out, I would appreciate it, but I have a condition."

I can't help but groan. Of course, there's a condition. I wouldn't expect any less from her.

"What's the condition?" I can't imagine what it could be.

"I won't accept charity." She straightens her spine and flicks her hair over her shoulder, back to the old Ren. "You guys have to take an appearance fee. You can donate that to whatever charity you like if you don't want it, but I need to pay you something. I'll be making enough from this to do that. I think."

I let out a sigh. I can live with that.

"Fair enough. I agree to your condition." Holding out a hand to shake, she takes it, and her warm fingers touching mine send a shockwave through me. I think it does for her too. Feeling her soft skin against mine, just through our palms, seems intimate and personal. A closeness that is foreign between us but not unappealing. Quite the opposite. It makes me want to find out what the rest of her skin feels like under my fingers and if her shadows are as soft as her highlights. These hands that I've known for over a decade and probably touched a million times before are suddenly brand new to me. They're now able to send vibrations to my soul that I've never felt before. Not what I should be thinking about of my friend. But is she thinking about me that way too? She hasn't let go of me either. We both stand and look at our joined hands for an awkwardly long time until she slowly drags hers away and drops it to her side.

I guess I was wrong before, and today is the true 'Let's Be Fucking Awkward Day.' I must have mixed up my calendar. *Jesus.*

Ren rushes past me to get back to the central area of the store, muttering, "I need to get out there." And I'm left to deal with a bunch of emotions I've never had before and don't know what to do with. I'm starting to drown in all things Ren and Charlie, and I'm not so sure it's a bad thing.

This whole time I thought I was basically the

Tin Man of rock 'n roll; no heart to be found. I'm the fucking notorious International Ladies' Man of Indigo King, and here I am, reduced to the back room of a record store, rethinking all of the life choices that led me...to what? Where am I in all of this now? Am I ready to admit to Ren I have feelings for her? Fuck no, I most certainly am not. Until I get a hint she might possibly be feeling the same, I need to keep that to myself. *Fuck. I hate this.*

Thankfully, my phone vibrates in my pocket, pulling me out of my own head and back into the present. It's our manager, Vanessa.

"Hey Van, what's up?"

"I'm fine. Thanks for asking." Her tone is so laden with sarcasm I'm surprised she doesn't die on the spot from its venom.

"Yikes." I'm used to Vanessa and her all-business attitude, which can sometimes be annoying, but this is another level. I can't think of anything I've done to put her in such a state. But who knows? "What did I do?"

"I'm sorry. It's not you." I can feel how deep her sigh is through the phone. "I've just had something dropped on my lap by the label I'm scrambling to figure out."

"Oddly enough, I've got something I'm working on that can use your expertise," I say before I even think, and I am now scared Vanessa will have a meltdown if I spring it on her. "But you go first. What does the label want?"

"It's not that they want anything. But there's an upcoming event you all will need to attend." Now she's hesitant all of a sudden.

"What event?" That doesn't sound too bad.

"The premier of the documentary."

"Okay, cool." We will see what Matt's fiancée, Samantha, filmed of us all summer on tour with Incendiary Ink. I've been looking forward to seeing it.

"On New Year's Eve."

"Wow. Okay. That's a weird date for a premier, right?"

"Well, it's kind of just a huge party with a red carpet. But this is a big deal, Jude. Everybody who's anybody will be there."

"Red carpet? Christ. I don't need to wear a tux or anything, right?" *God, no.* That will not be happening. I don't care if the label demands it. Jude Lockwood does not do tuxes. Or suits. Or ties.

She doesn't answer for an extremely long time. "...It's black-tie..."

"Fuck no, Van. Absolutely not. I forgot, I planned on having a super bad case of salmonella on New Year's Eve, so I won't be able to make this shindig."

"Jude."

"Actually, no, my bad. I scheduled a root canal on every single tooth in my mouth that day. I'm really looking forward to it and don't want to reschedule."

"Jude."

"Really, Van. I even asked for no Novocain, just so I can enjoy it more than...*wearing a fucking tuxedo*. " I can't believe this shit. I just won't go. It's that simple. "That was not in the contract we signed for doing the documentary. I know because I read that one before I signed, believe it or not."

Again, she's silent, so I wait her out. I don't want to keep talking because I know I'm about to say things I'll regret later, and this is not her fault. We know when the label says jump, we ask, *'How high?'*

"Are you done?" Her voice is clipped, and I think I may have finally gone too far.

"Yes. I believe I am."

"I'll be sending the details to the three of you via email in the next day or so. You need to let me know who your plus-one will be soon, too, so we can vet them and prep for the press."

"Woah, what? My plus-one?"

"Yes, Jude. That means your date."

"I know what the fuck it means, Van. But since when am I required to have a date for an event?" This is ridiculous. Who the fuck would I take to something like this? "And what do you mean they need to be vetted? By who? For what? That seems a bit extreme." Even if I wanted to ask one of my dating site prospects, that would be extreme trial by fire into the world of Indigo King. I couldn't do that to someone.

"Obviously, it's not a requirement, *per se*. But I'm told it's highly recommended. Their words, not mine. And the vetting is simply social media review for press optics."

"Would you be my plus one, Van?" It made sense in my head before I asked, but now I kind of want to take it back. Vanessa and I get along, but that could be weird.

"No, Jude. I have a date."

Thank God.

"Of course. I just thought I'd ask. You know. In case you needed someone to go with." Jesus, I'm rambling now. And I just asked her to be my date. "I didn't mean that as like a date...by the way. I just meant it as, like, friends. You know." *Shut the fuck up, Jude.*

Vanessa at least starts laughing at my discomfort, which I guess is a good thing after the intense mood of this call.

"Well, figure it out. What was the thing you had for me?" She's trying to change the subject. Admittedly, she's an expert at it.

"We need to arrange an in-store signing and acoustic show in the next couple of weeks at Vital Records LA."

"Oh, we do? Interesting. I don't remember scheduling that."

"Yeah, well. My friend owns the store, and the rest of the guys agreed to do it. We just need to work out the details. And we're not taking money for it. We're going to donate whatever our appearance fee is to charity. Which is where your expertise comes in." I'm hoping the last part helps sway her.

"Smooth, Jude." I think it's working. It's hard to tell. "You say your friend owns the store? Is this that girl that's your 'just a friend,' friend?" She sounds entertained.

I, however, am not amused, not after what just happened back here with Ren and me. I don't need to be reminded how one-sided my feelings for her are.

"Van."

"Alright, alright. I'm messing with you. I'd be happy to help out. Send me your 'friend's' contact information, and we'll arrange it."

"Thanks, Vanessa. It means a lot."

"Maybe she can be your plus-one?" She sounds hopeful. She'd probably love nothing more than for me to settle down, so she doesn't have to chaperone me on the road. The thought of asking Ren to be my date twists my stomach into knots. I've got a month or so to figure something out. Something other than asking Ren.

"Yeah, no." I need to get off this call. *Now*. "Thanks again. I've got to go, my dentist is calling. Probably about that root canal I mentioned. I'll talk to you later, okay? Love you, buh-bye." I hang up. I physically couldn't take any more of the conversation. Between tuxes and plus-ones, and store appearances, it was too much. It'll get sorted out. Somehow. By someone else, right?

twenty-four
HERE IT GOES AGAIN
REN

J ude leaves the store shortly after Pops shows up to take Charlotte and thank goodness. I couldn't take much more of him and his perfect chin, and wit, and charm, and cologne, and general Jude-ness. Another hour and I would have dragged him into the back room and not been responsible for my actions. All these crazy feelings and then breaking down like I did earlier in front of him. I have got to get my shit together when it comes to him. I'm becoming unglued. But then his holding us like he did when I was crying was above and beyond.

I decide to refocus on the dating site and try to connect somehow with one of the guys on there. That has got to be my only option to get Jude off of my mind. Bachelor #2 has been pushing for a meeting, so I think I'll do that and see where it goes. At this point, I've got to do something. I can't work. I can't sleep. I can't do anything without thinking about Jude, and it's got to stop.

When I get home in the evening, and Charlotte is settled, I find I've got messages from all three suitors. *Suitors*. And I'm thinking about Jude again. *Damn it*. Maybe I should be a Victorian governess. I always save Cool Dude for last since I enjoy our conversations more. I like to think of those as rewards for suffering through the other two. I try to tell myself I'm trying to be diplomatic and give them all equal time, but it's not any of that. I just like him better. I start with #2's message since he's the most eager of the bunch. Interestingly enough, I never gave him a nickname. I wonder if that means anything.

> #2: Hey Lady. Just checking in with you to find out how your holiday was. Did you spend it with your family? This is your child's first Thanksgiving and Christmas, correct? Are they able to appreciate any of it yet? If not, I'm sure the holidays will be a blast once they do. Something to look forward to, at least.

Have you given any thought to my request to get together? While these messages are great, I don't think they'll tell us if we have chemistry as humans. I already know I like your mind. I want to know if the rest is compatible as well. If not, I can be patient, but I'd be remiss if I didn't put myself out there. Let me know. My schedule is pretty open until the end of the year.

Yup. He's persistent. But I can't entirely fault him for it. Trying to connect with someone only through written words is a bit odd. We have had great conversations, and he is thoughtful, often remembering things I've said previously. What am I waiting for?

ME: Hey yourself. Yes, the holiday was spent with family, and we had a nice time. Nobody died of food poisoning, which is always a bonus. Hopefully, yours was good as well.

I think I am open to meeting up with you in a very public place. When is good for you?

There. I did it. I took the step. I jumped off the ledge. I can't believe I'm going to meet someone I met on the internet. I'm excited, scared, and disappointed, all simultaneously. I have to keep telling myself I'm not settling for these guys since I can't have Jude. Maybe once we meet in person, a switch will go off, and magic will happen. It's worth a shot, at least. Anything to get my mind off of Jude.

The following week is absolute madness as we prepare for the store signing with the band. The day before, I meet everyone from the band management and label, band members, and even the band's fiancées. Matt's fiancée, Samantha, will be filming the acoustic set as bonus material for marketing the band's documentary.

While they are perfectly lovely, I got a strange feeling from all of them. As though they were almost *too* excited and happy to meet me. I don't know what to make of it. Sarah finally drops the penny.

"We've all been dying to meet you."

"Really? Why is that?" I can't imagine anything about myself that would make meeting me so exciting. Unless Jude made me out to be something I'm not... "What did Jude say about me?"

Sarah and Samantha share a look and shrug.

"Absolutely nothing," Sarah says, glancing around to check if any of the guys are within earshot. "That's just it. We've only learned about you in the last couple of months. And how long have you guys known each other? Like a decade?"

"Yeah. Almost eleven years." I don't know why I'm shocked by Jude's silence about me. Not like I expected Jude to talk about me nonstop, but to not even acknowledge my presence the entire time he's been in the band? To be honest, I'm kind of hurt, but I can't let these two see.

"Well, Matt knew you existed, at least, I think. Since he and Jude live together." Samantha is smiling at me, and her bright eyes behind her glasses are so friendly that I can't stop myself from smiling back at her. Sarah is equally charming.

I get the sense they're trying to see more into my relationship with Jude than is there, so I shrug, "We're just friends. It's not that big of a deal. Though it is nice to meet you all now." I grin, hoping I've deflected the scrutiny of my feelings for Jude away. Even as I hear the words, they don't sound convincing to me either. They give each other another look, this one unreadable, but I don't have time to pursue the thought any further. My nerves are already on edge with the signing tomorrow and then the mystery date I arranged with #2 afterward since Charlotte will be with Pops for the evening; I don't need more fuel on that fire. I excuse myself and meet the delivery driver that walks in, who I assume, and hope has the records for tomorrow.

Technically, the store is closed today as we set

up for the event tomorrow, but once in a while, a customer shows up. Once they discover that all of Indigo King is in the store, they're star-struck, and the next thing I know, it's almost a party in here with all of the fans that have congregated and are either chatting with the band or each other. While all this is happening, the band's sound crew is trying to weave through everyone to set up the sound system. It's pure chaos.

I lean back on the counter, watching the groups of people talking and joking and taking pictures with the band, and I feel a sense of rightness flowing through me. This will be a fantastic event for the store, and I hope to do future events like it. I didn't think there was enough space for something like this. Vanessa came in like a Tasmanian Devil and basically snapped her fingers and wriggled her nose, and poof, there's magically a small stage for the band's set. And in front of it is a long table for them to sign albums and other things before the show.

"It's gotten a little out of hand, huh?" Jude's voice startles me from behind. I look over my shoulder, and he's leaning on the counter, watching the craziness with his typical amused expression.

"Not yet." I turn back to the crowd. "The chandeliers are still intact, so it's not really a party yet."

"We'll clear this out soon, don't worry."

"I'm not worried. Thanks for doing this. And

sorry again for being so uptight about everything at the start."

"Of course."

He goes quiet, and I turn to see what's wrong.

Shifting his gaze back to me, he asks, "Are you doing anything after the show tomorrow? I thought maybe we could grab some dinner or something. You said Art's got Charlotte overnight for the first time, right? May as well make the most of it."

Something in his eyes makes me want to believe he's asking for more from me when he speaks, but I know I'm wrong. I am so glad I made that date for tomorrow. I can once and for all stop all of this stupid wishing and hoping for something that will never happen.

"Actually, I have a date tomorrow night." I almost sound excited about it, which I guess is okay. I should be excited.

Jude's eyes widen, and his jaw clenches briefly at my statement. He quickly snaps his gaze away from me, and then his face is stoic and expressionless, void of all emotion. I wasn't expecting that reaction, whatever that was.

"Oh, yeah? That's cool. Yeah, I do too. I was just asking if you had anything going on because I didn't want you just sitting home alone on your first free night. If you wanted to hang out, I'd have canceled my date or whatever."

He's got a date too? Since when? Was he ever

going to tell me? To be fair, I wasn't going to tell him about my date either unless he asked. My stomach churns thinking about him out on a date with some internet troll. *This is why you started this in the first place. This is what you wanted. Deal with it.*

"Oh, cool."

Wow. I am a wordsmith if there ever was one. Future libraries will be built in my honor. But what the hell can I say? 'No, Jude. Let's ditch our dates and have the romantic evening we both know we want?' Please. I need to stop this right now.

Jude straightens and runs both hands through his hair, and I can't tell if he's mad, frustrated, or what. However, the energy pouring off him is dark and scary. He taps his hand down the top of the glass counter as he walks around it, the ring on his hand making a slight clinking noise as it hits.

"Jude?"

He flashes a quick smile at me but doesn't say anything and then heads to the exit, ignoring everyone else in the room as he leaves and slams the door on his way out.

Everyone in the room goes silent and turns to look at me as if I have any clue what just happened. I shrug my shoulders and shake my head. *What the hell was that all about?*

twenty-five

TAKE ME OUT
JUDE

I slam the door to the apartment shut, and the sound echoes around the empty space, amplifying the loneliness settling into my bones. My mind won't stop racing with thoughts of Ren going on a date with some strange dude from the internet with bad intentions. I don't like it. I'm tempted to tell her to call her date off. *What the fuck?* I have no right to say to her anything of the sort. And even if I did, what decade is my mind living in?

Ren's words, *'Actually, I have a date tomorrow,'* keep repeatedly playing in my brain and stomping on my heart with each play. I knew this was a possibility. Shit, it's the exact purpose for the entire exercise of the dating site. What did I think would happen? She'd never meet anyone from the site? That she'd keep her life on hold while I figured out what the fuck I'm doing with mine? That's not fair.

I need to face the fact Ren is just my friend. Nothing more. She's made it clear that's all she wants from me, so I need to respect that. I don't know when or why these new feelings for her popped up anyway. It's probably just a passing phase because we're going through significant life changes. She with Charlotte, and me with the band's success. Maybe I'm looking for comfort in the familiar I'm missing at the moment, and Ren is that source. She's a known commodity. A stable presence outside of my world of chaos. As I'm pacing, I get a text from her. Of course, I do.

> REN: Hey. Are you okay?

> ME: Yup.

> REN: Would you tell me if you weren't?

> ME: Yup.

Screw this. I grab a beer from the fridge and pull up the dating website on my laptop. If Ren can do this, so can I. The only difference will be she's excited about her date. I am not. Now, the question is, which one will I ask out first? All three have their own merits, but I think I'm going to go with Honey Bunny. Of the three remaining, she's the most outgoing. She'll be fun, at least. If she's available, of course.

> ME: Hey. Any chance you'd want to meet up tomorrow night for a drink or something?

Only a few minutes pass before I have a response. She must have been waiting by the phone. *That's a red flag if ever one was waved.*

> HONEY BUNNY: I would love to meet up with you somewhere! Just name the place and time.

Okay. So, she's eager. I can work with eager. I give her the name and location of an Irish Pub that's really not Irish, nor a pub on Fairfax Ave. It's near the bottom of my list of places I'd want to go on a date, and the fact she didn't blink an eye is one more strike against her. I'm totally going into this just looking for a distraction, which sucks for both of us, but there's not much I can do about it. I only hope this date does distract me. I can't keep going like this. The only problem now is, *Honey Bunny is a redhead too.* Could it be Ren? Did she lie about having a date earlier for some reason? To make me thing the site is actually working? I don't think Ren would be that eager for a date, but what the fuck do I know? I need a reality check.

The next day when I show up at the store, there's a line stretching down the street. That's crazy. I didn't count on this or parking problems because of it when I left. I was planning on being right on time for the event. Not early, and not late. I didn't want to give myself the chance to say something idiotic to Ren that would screw things up between us or make her hate me. It takes me forever to find a parking spot and make my way to the back entrance of the store. Vanessa is there to let me in, a disappointed scowl on full blast. I ignore her as best I can and join the others in the central area of the store.

My eyes find Ren right away as if supernaturally drawn to her. She looks outstanding today. Smiling so sincerely at everyone she speaks to, I'm sure they feel the warmth of her soul surrounding them while they're near her. Ren has one of those smiles that makes you want to smile along with her, even if you're in the shittiest mood. It's her eyes. They're usually so expressive, and when she's happy, everybody knows it and wants to be happy with her. *And I need to fucking stop. Damn it.*

After we take a bunch of group photos, we take our seats at the table, and security starts letting people in. We sign autographs and chat with fans for close to two hours. My hand is almost cramping too badly for me to play my guitar afterward. To be fair, I've been so tense all day. I had a death grip on the Sharpie I was using the whole time I was signing, which didn't help. I've been doing my best to avoid Ren without being obvious or rude about it, and so far, I've been able to successfully evade her. It's been too busy for her to pay too much attention to what we're doing.

I'm glad it's busy and a success. And I hope she does make enough from this to make up for her lackluster Black Friday sales. It makes me feel good I could do this for her. And I'm grateful to everyone else involved in making this happen for her. Sure, it's good for us as a band, but I think we'd have been just fine if this event didn't happen.

We take a quick break and let those with tickets for the upcoming set make their way in. Matt and Ryan and I step outside the back door for some fresh air and go over the setlist. I double-check my phone to see how we're doing on time. Considering the long walk I have to get back to my car, I might be cutting it close to meet up with my date.

"What's up with you?" Matt asks. "Got a hot date?" He and Ryan smirk at each other.

"Yeah, actually. I do."

Ryan slaps me on the shoulder, grinning.

"Dude, that's awesome. It's about time you and Ren got together. Matt and I had bets on how long it would take. I knew it would be before Christmas."

He turns to Matt with his hand out, palm up. "You owe me twenty bucks, man."

"What the fuck are you talking about?" I slap Ryan's hand away, and he takes a step back in surprise. Matt stiffens next to me, and I force myself to take a deep breath and bite the inside of my cheek to stop myself from saying something I'll regret. I throw my hands up. "Sorry. I'm sorry."

"Dude, what is up with you?" Matt has relaxed a little, but his body language tells me he's ready to deck me if I go off the rails. I don't want to give him a reason to do that.

I drag my hands through my hair and down my face, scratching at the stubble I didn't even consider for my date. Why am I bothering if I'm not going to make an effort in my appearance?

"Yeah, who is this hot date, if not Ren?" Ryan has forgiven my semi-violent outburst, thank God. I don't know what came over me. I lashed out when they seemed to joke about Ren.

I need to shift my gaze to the asphalt.

"I don't know yet. I'll find out tonight. We met on the internet." They both attempt to stifle their laughs but are hugely unsuccessful, almost doubling over. "Fuck off." I turn and open the back door to the store, ready to storm back inside and away from these assholes.

"Wait. Wait." Ryan is the first to recover. Ever

the diplomat. "Sorry, but what? Internet? What's that all about? You've never needed technological help to hook up."

I let the door shut and shove my hands in my pockets, warmth growing on my cheeks. *God damn it.* I don't talk about feelings or emotions like this with these guys.

"Ren made me sign up for this site, LastPerson-OnEarth.com, to try to find my person."

"Your...person?" Matt is incredulous. "Jude Lockwood, International Ladies' Man, is looking for 'The One?' Are you on shrooms or something? Feeling okay? Should we worry?"

"So, with a site name like that, is it full of orcs and trolls?" Ryan ignores Matt's snark and seems genuinely interested, which is strange on its own.

I stare at my shoes, push a suddenly very interesting rock around with the toe of my boot, and shrug.

"It's for weird book nerds like me. Ren found it, and we both signed up. And I don't know what it's full of. There are no profile pictures."

"Whoa. Seriously? You're going in blind?" Matt's tone pivots from amusement to worry. "What are you going to do... if they're... *unattractive*?"

Ryan and I stop moving and frown at him, not saying a word. Expressing our disappointment in him without a sound.

"What? We're talking about Jude here," he attempts to qualify. "Do neither of you remember the 'International Ladies' Man' moniker we just spoke of a minute ago? A self-appointed title, I might add."

"Fine. I deserve that." And I do. They have a right to doubt me, I guess. I have made a bit of a name for myself as a playboy, so I don't expect everyone to get it. Hell, I don't even get it. "I'm only doing this because Ren made me. I doubt I'm going to find my soulmate on the internet. I'm still me."

Matt and Ryan go pale and see something very frightening behind me. It's either Ren or one of the four horsemen of the apocalypse, and I'm betting on the former.

"Ren's right behind me right now, isn't she?" I can feel her glare through the fabric of the back of my shirt. *Shit*. I didn't hear the door open.

They both nod and present weak smiles to Ren as they pass me to head inside, leaving me to face her alone. I turn slowly on my heel, bracing for the worst, but she's smiling at me. It's an odd smile. I can't tell which kind it is. She has several in her arsenal to choose from. Why is she smiling at me? I think it's her customer service placating smile, and my stomach drops, knowing she doesn't mean the joy she's showing on the outside.

"We're ready for the set to start." All business. And still that smile. Something in her eyes hints at pain I don't understand, but I don't have time to ask since Vanessa comes out and drags me back into the store for the set. Keeping up this act that I don't have feelings for Ren is exhausting. I'll be glad when this day is over.

twenty-six

NOT IN THAT WAY

REN

I get it. I know Jude hates the dating site and everything surrounding it. I also know that he's only trying it because I asked him to and agreed to do it with him. What I didn't realize was *how much* he hates it. I figured his grumbling about it was Jude just being Jude. Plus, he made a date with one of his choices; he wouldn't do that if he wasn't interested. He's not one to waste time with uninteresting people. Wait. This is the only date that I know of. What if he's been going on dates with a bunch of them this whole time? He wasn't going to tell me about the date he has tonight; no reason he'd tell me about any others.

And what if he has been going on dates all along? It's none of my business. It's why I made him do this, so I should be happy. Why can't I be happy about it? I think my heart is defective, always wanting things I can't or shouldn't have. I'll learn my lesson from all this heartache one of these days. What that lesson could possibly be, I have no idea. Maybe just to keep my heart to myself from now on. That way, I won't be hurt.

While the band plays their set, I have time to settle the receipts for the day and resolve the band's fee with Vanessa. I finish in time to hear their last few songs, and Sarah waves me over to sit by her. The acoustic versions of their songs have been excellent, and it's been fantastic to see Jude playing a regular guitar instead of his bass. It's been a long time since I've seen him play like this. *Too long*. He used to bring his guitar to the store and work on songs in the sitting area while I worked, occasionally giving opinions if he asked. I miss that.

He seems to be enjoying playing now; he's keeping his eyes closed during each song, really feeling the music. He's enthralling to watch, and I can't look away. I can study all of him and get away with it since he's not looking up, and I take him in. His auburn hair is so dark that it's almost black in the chandelier's light. My fingers twitch with wanting to run through it and brush it out of the way to see all of his face. The song ends, and his eyes open and lock on mine for a split second, catching me staring at him. I look away quickly, caught in my silent admiration.

For the last song, Sarah joins them in singing

their big hit, '*Almost*,' and it's so beautiful that I can feel tears threatening. This time when I dare to glance in Jude's direction, his eyes are open and watching me as he plays. And this time, I can't look away. We both stare at each other, and it's the strangest thing. His face is expressionless, utterly void of any emotion. I think I'm as stoic as I wage an internal war to keep my tears from falling, but who knows what my face is doing. I just know I can't tear my gaze from him. We're having some sort of conversation, but I can't understand what he's saying. It's a language I don't know. His complete lack of emotion now hardens something inside me, something that was vulnerable, something that had hope. It's gone now, and the realization of it bursts the dam.

I hurry to the back room to pull myself together before they finish, and I'll need to close the event. I can't look like I've been crying when I thank everyone for participating in today's activities. I need to be professional even though I want to crumble into a ball in the corner. I don't know what just happened with Jude and me, but I need to keep it together for a bit longer despite how devastating it feels.

Wiping my eyes, I take a few deep breaths and slap on my customer service smile. I time it perfectly and return just as they finish their song. I take the mic briefly to thank everyone, and then off-mic, make sure to personally thank Matt, Ryan, and Sarah for coming. Jude must have taken off as soon as they finished because he's completely disappeared. *Good.* I don't think I could have faced him after that song. Once I finish my rounds with everyone and everything appears to be under control, I leave the rest for Sawyer to handle and head home to get ready for my date.

When I get to the bar where I'm meeting #2, I double-check my makeup and hair in the rearview mirror. After the dark emotions of the afternoon and Jude's aversion to even talking to me now, I may as well make the most of this. Maybe #2 is The One. It would be dumb of me not to at least try. So, here goes nothing.

I'm a few minutes early, but the bar is getting crowded when I walk in. #2 told me to look for a leather jacket and a hat, which shouldn't be too hard to find. I nervously pull on the hem of my royal blue dress that is now tighter than it was before I had Charlotte, making me self-conscious. I haven't worn anything so revealing in months and walking in heels is not at all like riding a bike. I feel like an uncoordinated baby giraffe in these things.

As I study the people at the bar, I spot a tall

man in a leather jacket and hat with his head lowered, scrolling on his phone and oblivious to the noise around him. I approach him tentatively and tap him on the shoulder, taking a step back. This has to be #2; no one else in here has a hat or leather jacket. I hold my breath when he turns around, and my jaw drops when I see his face. It's Jude. *What the hell?* He looks as surprised to see me as I am him.

I had a feeling this would happen. I had a feeling one of the guys I was chatting with was Jude. I can't stop the grin that spreads on my face as all the worry and doubts that I had throughout the day today melt away instantly. The site got it right. Jude is my person. I've known that for a while, though.

"I knew it," I sigh happily and wrap my arms around his waist tightly, leaning my head into his chest and inhaling his cologne. "I knew it was you."

It dawns on me he's not hugging me back. *He's not hugging me back. Why is he not hugging me back?* I open my eyes and see he's holding his hands up to purposely not touch me at all. I immediately let go of him and take a step back, my smile faltering. My confusion is deepening by the second. What is he doing? Why isn't he as happy about this as I am? *Shit. He's not happy about this.*

I dare to look at his face, and he's not confused at all. He looks guilty and can't meet my eyes. What the hell does he look guilty for? My head is spinning, and I don't know what is happening. *Oh my God. Oh my God. What have I done?*

"Jude?" He doesn't answer me but looks behind me. My stomach clenches, and dread consumes me. The bad feeling running through me morphs into something more potent as a nervous female voice behind me speaks.

"Wow. What are the odds of two redheads in this place?" Her sharp laugh stabs me in the back.

I turn and step further away from Jude, my mortification complete.

I force a laugh, "Oh God, no. We're old friends. That's all." I give her a swift once over, and she's pretty, with a seemingly perfect body and perfect makeup and hair. Totally Jude's type. Leave it to him to find the most gorgeous troll on the internet.

She holds a hand out to Jude.

"I'm Corbyn, but my friends call me Bunny." He takes her hand with an amused glint in his eyes. *Great.* Not only am I embarrassed, but the heart that was just on my sleeve has jumped to its own death in humiliation.

"Well, you kids have fun," I say, turning and walking away before Jude can introduce himself to Bunny. Amazingly I don't trip over myself as I make my way to the ladies' room to hide for the rest of the foreseeable future.

I can't stop shaking as I stare at my reflection in the bathroom mirror. I just revealed how I felt to

Jude and was flat-out rejected. There can no longer be any question if he feels anything more for me than friendship. This settles it once and for all. I should be happy that I don't have to think about that anymore. Maybe now I can focus on my actual date, who is allegedly out in the bar somewhere. *Shit. My real date.* I don't even want to go through with this anymore. I don't think I can handle any more rejection tonight, and with how awful I look in this dress, I'm sure #2 won't be impressed, either. *I just want to go home.*

After several deep breaths, I work up the courage to head back out into the bar and try to find another guy in a leather jacket and hat that isn't Jude Lockwood. Doing this without seeing Jude and his date, Bunny, is impossible. He appears to be enjoying his conversation with her as they lean their heads together to talk at the bar. My heart that just committed suicide a minute ago goes into death throes and stabs itself with a dull knife repeatedly for good measure. I'm not going to survive this night if I have to watch them fawn over each other the whole time.

I take a seat at a table and wait. And wait. After the first ten minutes, I start to get worried. I don't look in Jude's direction, though. I couldn't handle watching them have a good time while I sit here by myself, obviously being stood up. After the second ten minutes without a sighting of another guy in a hat and jacket, I give up. This night can't go any worse than it already has.

I want to run to the exit, but these damn shoes prevent me from progressing at any speed whatsoever. So, of course, I basically crawl past Jude and Bunny, and I have to force myself not to look in their direction. My focus is on the exit and getting to it without bursting into tears and falling flat on my face. It takes all my concentration to do both at the same time. I make it to my car without incident or tears, but that's where that ends. Once I sit behind the wheel, the floodgates open, and the tears come. *What a disaster.*

twenty-seven

I FOUND
JUDE

I can't do this. I've spent the last twenty minutes sorting out what happened with Ren earlier. She thought I was her date and was happy about it? Could that be true? Or was she joking? She laughed it off so convincingly when Corbyn showed up. I think it was just a joke. For a split second I thought my date was Ren as well, until I saw Corbyn approach with a confused look on her face. I knew right away I was wrong. Luckily, I didn't fall for Ren's joke and expose my true feelings. That would have been so awkward. And embarrassing. Not feelings I enjoy. I purposely haven't looked around the bar because I didn't want to see her having fun with her date.

But I just saw her leave by herself, and she looked like she was near tears. I don't see anyone interested in what she's doing, so did her date not show? Was she stood up? Who the fuck would do that? Even though her prank pretending to be my match hurt more than amused, she would never deserve to be stood up. Nobody would. It's fucking rude.

"...so that's how the buffalo got the name Chewie."

My attention snaps back to Corbyn. *What the fuck is she talking about? Buffalo?*

"I'm sorry, what?"

"You haven't been paying attention, have you?" While her words call out my distraction, her voice is sympathetic.

I can't lie. "No. I'm sorry. My mind is elsewhere at the moment."

"It's the other redhead, isn't it?"

"Is it that obvious?" And now I feel like shit for ignoring my date. I can't win tonight.

"Yeah. As soon as I saw you two together, I could tell that I couldn't compete with whatever was going on there."

"Well, now I feel like an ass. I apologize."

She laughs. "Don't worry about it. These are always a crapshoot. Plus, I now get to say I had a date with the bass player from Indigo King."

She is being exceptionally cool about this. I don't know if most women would be this nonchalant about their date being a dickhead like me.

"And I can say I had a date with a bunny." *It was funnier in my head.*

When I pull up to Ren's house, her car isn't here, and her porch light is on, but none of the house lights. She's not home. I know she left the bar alone. Where else would she go? This doesn't sit right with me, so I get out of my car and sit on the porch to wait for her to come home. Not only am I worried about how she's doing after apparently being stood up, but I'm a selfish bastard and need to find out for sure if she was joking earlier. I know deep down she probably was, but I can still feel her arms wrapping tightly around my waist, and the sweet smell of her perfume lingers around me.

There's an evil side of me happy her date didn't show up tonight. It's his loss, whoever he is. While I kind of want to hunt him down and lay him out for hurting Ren, I also want to shake his hand for allowing me to think I might still have a chance with her. It's the slimmest of possibilities, but until I know for sure otherwise, I'm keeping what little hope I do have alive for the time being.

After about fifteen minutes with no Ren, my anxiety starts to skyrocket. She should be home by now. She shouldn't be driving if she's upset. LA is full of horrible drivers with zero regard for anyone else on the road. My mind starts racing with grim scenarios of what could have happened to her. I can't take it anymore and send her a text.

> ME: Hey. Where are you?

Five minutes with no reply, I realize what an idiot I am. If she's driving, she's not going to text back. She could talk on the phone, though. I call, and it goes straight to voicemail, so I hang up. I guess her phone is shut off. That doesn't make sense. She wouldn't turn her phone off if Charlie wasn't with her in case of an emergency. I know Ren, and there's no way she'd go radio silent in this situation. Now I want to jump out of my fucking skin I'm so worried. Did she make it to her car at the bar? I didn't see her car, but I wasn't looking for it either. That starts another slippery slope for my thoughts to slide down.

Before I work myself into a full-blown tizzy, Ren's car pulls into her driveway. She stares at me, confused for a minute, before stepping out. Her eyes are red as though she's been crying, but she's still beautiful to me. *And that dress. My God, that dress. Bless whoever made that fucking dress.*

"What are you doing here?" She's standing next to her car, not moving to enter the house or get near me, for that matter. "What happened to your date with Rabbit or whatever?"

"Bunny. While she was perfectly lovely, we decided it wasn't meant to be and cordially went our separate ways." I move toward her, but she steps sideways and opens the back car door. I'm surprised to find Charlie in the back in her car seat, sleeping soundly. Well, she was until the overhead light blasted on. She squirms and whines a little at the annoyance. "I thought Art was going to keep her overnight?"

"I missed her too much, and I just want her here with me tonight," she whispers, carefully extracting the car seat and allowing me to carry Charlie into the house behind her. "You didn't answer why you're here. What's up?"

"Just checking on you. I saw you leave the bar..." I don't mention her date not showing up or her looking upset when she left. I don't want to rub salt in her wounds.

She takes Charlie gently out of her car seat and hugs her closely for a moment with her eyes closed, breathing her in. Her whole body seems to relax after that, and something in my chest implodes at the sight of them together. She senses me watching and gets self-conscious.

"I'll be right back."

As she takes Charlie to put her to bed, I make

myself at home and grab a beer and a seat on the couch, trying to act as natural as possible, though I'm feeling like a fraud for some reason. I had all this time while waiting for her to come home to prepare what I wanted to say and how to say it, but fuck me if I can remember any of it. The sight of Ren in that dress has fried my short-term memory. I don't think I settled on an approach anyway.

When Ren comes into the living room, the dress is sadly gone and is replaced with sweats and an old t-shirt. Her hair is pulled up into a loose ponytail, and I think she might actually be prettier now than she was ten minutes ago in that dress. All the years we've known each other, and somehow, I'm only seeing all this beauty in her recently. It doesn't make sense. What the hell have I been doing all this time?

"Jude. You checked on me. As you can see, I'm fine." She sounds annoyed. "You can go home or whatever."

Or whatever? What does that mean?

"Yeah, but I don't know if I believe it. Convince me."

She rolls her eyes and sighs heavily before going to the kitchen and coming out with her own beer. Sitting in the chair diagonal from me, she crosses her legs under her and examines me. I can't tell what she's thinking, and she's not giving anything away. The only light in the room is coming from the Christmas tree in the corner, and its softness creates a somberness to the mood. Again, without it being shoved in my face 24/7, I'd never realized there was a holiday coming up.

After a minute of scrutiny, she finally says, "Fine. I'm not okay. But I will be. Thanks for the concern, but you don't need to worry about me."

"Well, I do." It feels like she's trying to brush me off, but I'm not going that easily. Not when she's so down like this. I need to cheer her up somehow. "That was a good prank you played on me earlier."

Her brows draw together in confusion.

"What prank?"

I can't tell if she's seriously forgotten or if she's putting me on again. Why is she so hard to read lately?

"When you pretended to be my internet date. That was funny." I force out a laugh and a smile, hoping it lightens her up a little. "And what are the chances we'd pick the same bar tonight?"

She hesitates, picking at the label on her beer bottle.

"Oh, that. Yeah, that was funny." She's forcing her smile too, but I can't tell if it's because she's still upset about being stood up or something else. It falters as she goes on. "I thought you'd get a kick out of that. And yeah, super small world."

And there it is. My worst fear comes true. *It was a fucking joke.* And now I feel like a fucking joke. I should have known better.

It falls awkwardly quiet between us. We don't do awkward silences. It's not a thing we ever do. We do comfortable silences. We always have. The mood in the room has changed, and I'm getting the sense she isn't just brushing me off; she wants me gone. I swiftly rack my brain to think if I said anything insensitive or out of line, which would be totally like me, but I can't think of anything.

"Do you want me to go?" Maybe she wants to be alone, and it has nothing to do with me. I overthink everything. "I can leave you alone if you want." What I want to do is pull her into a big hug and tell her my feelings for her have grown into something much more than friendship. I want to kiss her tears away. I want to protect her from ever hurting for another second. But I know now that isn't what she would want. It's probably the last thing in the world she would want.

She looks up at me cautiously.

"Do you mind? I really just want to forget tonight ever happened and crash early."

As soon as she says she wants me out, I'm propelled into action. I jump up from the couch as if catapulted.

"Of course. No problem." I take my mostly full beer to the kitchen sink and pour it down the drain. She's been clear. She was joking earlier, as I suspected she was, and now doesn't want me hanging around. *Yup. Crystal clear. I'm a God-damned idiot.*

I mentally beat myself up the entire drive home for ever even thinking Ren might feel the same way about me. *How fucking dumb.*

twenty-eight

FIGURE IT OUT

REN

I t's Christmas Eve, and I haven't heard from Jude since the night I completely embarrassed myself in front of him and got stood up. That was almost two weeks ago. He didn't come for his usual Friday hang out with Charlotte, which is fine; he's not obligated to do it. But, strangely, he hasn't even texted. He's not responded to any of my texts, so I'm a little worried about him. I knew the disappearing act would kick in again at some point; it's just how Jude is. I was hoping he changed since it looked like he was getting a little attached to Charlotte, but it turns out I was right when I predicted he'd leave too. That makes me sad.

I closed the store early today for the holiday and am waiting for Brad to show up to visit with Charlotte. He reached out last week and said he wanted to spend some holiday time with her. I agreed, so long as I'm present to supervise. I need to know that he can handle her before letting him take her anywhere, but this is at least a start to their relationship. And, of course, he's late. *Surprise. Surprise.*

Fifteen minutes after his scheduled arrival time, there's a knock at the door, but when I answer it, Jude is there. Not Brad. I look outside to check if Jude scared Brad off or something, but I don't notice anyone.

"What are you doing here?" I'm astonished to see him since he basically dropped off the face of the Earth as far as I knew. He needs a shave, and he looks like he hasn't slept in a week.

"I brought this for Charlie." He pulls out a box from behind his back about the same size as Charlotte, wrapped in pretty Christmas paper with a big bow on top. "It's her first Christmas, so I wanted to get her something special."

I stare at the gift, stunned. We don't hear from him for two weeks, and he shows up with a Christmas present?

I reach to take it from him, but he pulls it back.

"Can I give it to her? I want to watch her face light up when she opens it."

"Oh. Okay." I'm suddenly aware that Jude will still be here when Brad shows up. This is not going to be fun. "Brad should be here soon, just an FYI."

His jaw tightens, and he raises an inquisitive brow at me.

"Oh?"

"To see his daughter." I can't believe I'm defending Brad in any way, but there it is. "We planned it last week, but he's running late, I guess." I step aside so he can come into the house.

Charlotte shrieks with joy when she sees Jude, and he screams back at her, and my heart cracks. The way these two interact is so extraordinary. She starts chattering at him in her long-winded gibberish, and Jude pretends to listen intently, nodding his head when she pauses. It's the damned cutest thing.

"That doesn't make sense to me, Charlie. But, then again, you are very small." He places her gift in front of her, but she doesn't know what to do with it. This is her first personal gift. I grab my phone from the kitchen and start recording. I'm such a dork. Jude eyes me curiously. "Why are you recording this?"

"This is her first time opening a present, so she might need some assistance." I wave at him to help her.

He starts tearing at the paper, and Charlotte quickly picks up what to do, ripping at it herself. A plain brown box is left when all of the paper has been torn off. Charlotte is not impressed with this and starts to whimper. I think she wants more paper to rip.

Jude pulls out his keys, cuts through the box's tape, and puts it back in front of her. She pats at the top, seeing an opening, but isn't sure how to get inside \.

"Alright, fine, ya lazy bum. I'll do the work for you," Jude says with an exaggerated sigh. He pulls the flaps back, and inside is a stuffed donkey almost as big as Charlotte. When she peeks over the edge and sees it, she shrieks again and lets out a huge belly laugh. Jude and I both cringe at the pitch and the volume but then laugh along with her. She obviously likes her present. He pulls it out of the box and hands it to her, and she eagerly takes it. He turns to me, still recording. "Her other donkey has seen better days. I figured it was time for an upgrade. Plus, it's damned cute, right?"

The emotions on his face are so complex I can't make out what he's feeling. It's almost relieved and part nervous. Maybe some pride thrown in and a bunch of other things I can't interpret. He's also avoiding meeting my eyes, and I wonder what that's all about.

I don't have time to wonder too much about it because there's a knock at the door. *Shit.* I am so not looking forward to this. I let Brad in and give him a warning glare not to start anything. I'd glare at Jude, but he's not looking at me.

Jude at least had a warning that Brad was coming. Brad didn't, and he tries to play it cool as if it's no big deal that Jude is here. And not only is he here, but he's on the floor with his daughter playing with a giant stuffed donkey that he gave her. It takes him a minute to acclimate to the tableau in front of him. He gives Jude a tip of the chin but doesn't say anything as he sits on the couch. Jude reciprocates the gesture, and I slowly let out the breath I was holding. There seems to be a strained truce at work between them. I have no idea how this will go, but at least it's not a contentious beginning.

Two hours later, I've shown Brad how to change, bathe, and feed Charlotte, and she's about to go down for the night. Jude is remarkably kind the whole time, offering tips that I didn't even know he knew, and Brad is amazingly receptive. There is no macho ego bullshit thrown around, and it feels like an actual team working together. It's odd but also a relief. I was apprehensive when Jude showed up out of nowhere that World War III was about to erupt in my living room. Luckily, all violence is avoided, and I think a good foundation for a future relationship between Brad and Charlotte might be in the works, which is even better. Of course, actual results are yet to be seen, but it's a start.

Once Charlotte is asleep, I kick both Jude and Brad out so I can have some peace and quiet. My nerves are shot from dealing with my ex and my unrequited in the same room for so long. There's nothing like having the guy who didn't think you worthy enough to be loyal to you, and another who just doesn't believe you are worthy at all, around you for hours to boost your self-esteem. I'm starting to ache all over, but before I take a long bath and soak away the day, I log into the dating site and see that I have a message from #3. Still, nothing from #2 since he stood me up, which is fine by me. He can eat dirt for all I care.

#3 is a strange one. He seems a bit egotistical, but it's hard to tell exactly. The way he phrases things makes me think he's full of himself.

> #3: I hope you and your family have
> a wonderful Christmas and New
> Year.

That's it. That's the entire message. It feels like a generic copy-and-paste note that probably went to all the women he's talking to. *Way to make a girl feel special.* I don't bother writing him back. There's a message from Cool Dude from a few days ago. I haven't had the heart to log into the site often since it's not been going so well. A pang of guilt hits me, thinking he's been waiting for a reply.

COOL DUDE: Before the craziness of the holidays takes over, I wanted to wish you and your family a Merry Christmas. Maybe sometime in the coming year, we'll get the courage to chat in person if we can make our schedules work. Or, we can keep this You've Got Mail thing going forever. You know, we have options.

ME: Thank you so much. And Merry Christmas to you and your family as well. I'll need to work up that courage to meet since my experience so far in that regard hasn't been the best. But it's always good to have goals! Happy New Year too!

I'm not sure I will ever get the nerve to try to meet one of these guys. While getting stood up wasn't the worst part of that particular night for me, it still stung. I don't want to go through that again. No matter how nice these guys are in chat, as #2 displayed, who they are in real life might be different. I'm not in the mood for head games. Besides, I'm still trying to get over Jude. It wouldn't be fair to anyone if I went into a relationship the mess that I currently am. *Ha. Currently? More like always.*

O n Christmas morning, I wake to an emergency text from Ren.

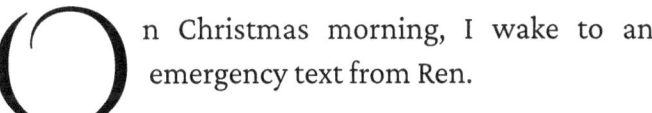

REN: Hey. If you're available, I could use help with Charlotte today. I've got a flu bug or something, and since you were here yesterday, you were probably exposed to it. I don't want Pops to get sick. Can you help? If not, okay too.

ME: I've always told you children are walking Petrie dishes. I'm on my way.

Of course, I'm going to help out. Because Ren never asks for help, the fact that she is means she must really be sick. I wouldn't want Art to get sick either, and it sucks he will have to miss Christmas with his family.

Shit. Family. I send obligatory texts to my parents and siblings and receive equally obligatory responses. What a happy fucking family we are. I don't think much more about it, throw myself together, and leave for Ren's house.

While I'm driving, I consider my situation. After basically getting my heart stomped on two weeks ago, I've been laying low and keeping away from Ren as much as possible. However, this is a physical and mental challenge at times since she and Charlie seem to consume my every waking thought. It's becoming a real problem and a little unhealthy. Things have been so strange between us since I came back, and I don't know how to fix it and put us back to where we were, or if that's even possible. Is our friendship ruined forever now?

That would be so like me, trash the one good thing, the one precious thing in my life, like the asshole I am. What did I expect would happen? My friendship with Ren is the longest relationship I have ever had outside of my family, and it only works because we don't put expectations on each other. Ever. I need to get my mindset back to that and clear it of any thoughts beyond friendship.

We're just friends. I'm Ren's friend, and she's mine. The end. Now let it fucking go.

When Ren opens the door to let me in, she

doesn't look like the same person I saw yesterday. She's super pale and has dark circles under her eyes.

"Wow. You look like shit."

She glares at me as I walk past her into the house.

"Thanks so much. Merry Christmas to you too."

"Hellooooo!" I say to Charlie in my best Mrs. Doubtfire voice. She screams back at me in response. We are kindred spirits and totally speaking each other's language now. I turn back to Ren, wrapped in a blanket, watching us from the hallway. "Yeah yeah, Christmas, shitmas. Go take your germs elsewhere, you grippe-ridden horror, and leave us be."

"Thanks, Jude." Her voice is hoarse and low, and when I glance at her, she looks as though she might cry.

"No problem, Ren. I got this." I step up to her and put a hand on her forehead; she is burning up. "What do you need? Do you have fluids? Need me to make some tea or soup or something?"

Her watery eyes finally meet mine, and a few tears do fall. I reach out and wipe them away and pull her to me. I've wanted to do this for weeks, but not under these circumstances.

"I'm sorry. It's her first Christmas..."

"I know. But she won't remember it, believe me." I smooth her hair, trying to think of how I can make her feel better. "Do you remember your first five Christmas's?"

"No." She sniffles into my chest, and I don't want to let her go. I want to hold her like this until she feels better, however long that takes.

"Well then, don't sweat it." I reluctantly release her and turn her toward the bedroom. She needs sleep. "Go rest. We'll be fine. I'm the Baby Whisperer, remember?"

"Jude. Wake up, sleepyhead."

I open my eyes and find Ren looking down at me, her brows furrowed and concern in her eyes.

"What is it? What's the matter?" I grab onto Charlie, sleeping on my chest, a little tighter. "Are you okay?"

"I'm much better, but what happened to you?" She points to the magic marker that now covers my arms and clothes.

"Mistakes were made." I thought Charlie would be better at coloring at this age than she actually is. Now I know she's still too young for that art project. "So, you're feeling better?"

"Yes, one hundred percent better." She examines my face, concerned. "How are you feeling? You look like shit."

As she says this, I take stock of how I'm feeling, and sure enough, I can feel the telltale signs of illness coming on; my entire body aches, and I'm chilled. I must be coming down with whatever Ren had.

"Take her." I almost throw Charlie at her. It's way too late to stop it, but I still don't want to be responsible for her getting ill. "I don't want to get her sick."

"We're past that point, I think. It's already in the house."

"Well then, I blame Brad the Dad. He looked a little sketchy yesterday." I frown. "I mean, he's always sketchy, but more so yesterday. Plus, he's a convenient target for my rage."

I sit up, and the room starts spinning, so I fall back onto the couch and groan.

"Oh, no." I grab at my head, that's now apparently been shoved into a vice. "Everything hurts, and I'm dying." *Fuck. This came on so damned fast.* "How can I be the picture of health five hours ago and now knocking on death's door?"

"I think you'll live."

"I want a second opinion."

"Fine. Taylor Swift is the most underrated song-writer of our generation."

"Not what I meant."

Charlie wakes up and starts gurgling around the fingers in her mouth.

"There's your second opinion, see? Even Charlotte thinks you'll survive."

"That's not what she just said. She said to tell you she hates peas, and if you don't stop forcing her to eat them, she's filing for emancipation forthwith. Or herewith. I don't know. She's kind of mumbled the ending."

"I think you're becoming delirious." A cool hand touches my forehead, and then my cheek, and then it's gone.

"Don't go. That felt good." I reach out to grab the hand and pull it back but touch nothing but air. I think she might be right; I'm delirious. I can't stop talking because if I stop talking, I'll have to focus on how shitty I feel, which is really shitty. "I need to talk to you about something anyway. I have a question." *Damn. I need to shut up.*

"Oh? What question?" She sounds distracted, but I'm not opening my eyes. The room is too fucking bright.

"I need a huge favor." *Am I really going to do this? Now?*

"Name it."

"Damn. Okay, so you agree to whatever it is before hearing what it is?" This might be easier than I thought it would be. *Nice.*

"Jude. Of course. You came to my rescue today, on Christmas of all days, when I needed you and got yourself sick in the process. What do you need?"

My dirty and sick mind runs through all the inappropriate things I could say I need but won't.

"I need a date for New Year's."

Silence. If I had a pin, I'd drop it just so I could hear it.

"Ren?" I lift my head slightly but still don't open my eyes. I know she's still here somewhere. I heard her gasp a little. *Shit. She's freaking out.* "Not a date. But a plus-one. For the label. The documentary premiere. It's black tie. I need a plus-one. You'd be a great plus-one. I'll pay for everything, even your dress, and stuff. If you agree, that is. Which you did. So, you can't go back on it now. Pretty sure out of all our agreements, that is indeed a contract."

"Um... I don't know, Jude." She sounds hesitant. "I'm not exactly in Hollywood premiere shape."

"What the fuck does that mean?" I can't believe she just said that. "You're fucking gorgeous. Shut up with that."

I hear a loud sigh.

"Jude..."

Peeking, I see her sitting on the chair with Charlie bouncing on her knee. Ren's forehead is creased with doubt, and it kills me she questions herself. How can she not know how fucking beautiful she is?

I close my eyes again, not having any of it. "Nope. We'll speak of it no more. It's been settled." The emotions running through me are so crazy; I don't know what is real and what is a fever dream. I'm ecstatic she's going to go with me. I feel a little guilty that I somehow conned her into it, but I can't figure out how. And I'm nervous she'll hate me for all of it since she's been more than clear she wants nothing but friendship from me. And, God damn, my head hurts.

"Let me get her situated, and I'll be back for you." A blanket is draped over me, and I turn on my side, pulling my knees up into a fetal position.

The next thing I know, there's something cool on my arm. Ren is rubbing my arm gently with a wet cotton ball when I open my eyes.

"What is that?" The feel of her soft hands on me is so soothing I'm falling into a trance with the sensation.

"Baby oil. It takes the marker off."

"What's in baby oil anyway? Sweat from slimy babies?"

I don't even hear if she answers my idiotic question. I fight with my body to stay awake to enjoy this, but I lose the battle, and I'm out almost instantly.

thirty

YOU DON'T KNOW ME

REN

I can't believe I agreed to this. I must have been out of my God-damned mind when I said I would go to the documentary premiere with Jude. As I stare into my floor-length mirror, I almost don't recognize myself. The kelly green velvet gown is backless, cut pretty deep in the front, and has a slit up one side almost to my hip. To say I'm self-conscious would be the understatement of the year. I still haven't shed all of the baby weight I gained while pregnant with Charlotte, and it bothers me every day, even though it shouldn't. And, I've never worn something so extravagant before, but it looks like it was made just for me.

Sarah and Samantha took me shopping for the dress, saying something about it being an Indigo King rite of passage or something. I'm not sure what that was all about, but they were a lot of fun to hang out with for a day. And I spent the entire day today getting buffed and polished and presentable enough for a Hollywood premiere. Even my crazy hair has been tamed and is up in an elaborate twist that I couldn't duplicate with a year of YouTube tutorials. I just hope these heels don't give me baby giraffe flashbacks.

Charlotte is with Pops for the night. Maybe this time will be when she finally gets a sleepover. All previous attempts were thwarted by some catastrophe or another. When Pops came to pick her up earlier before I went to the salon, he almost scolded me not to see him until next year. That's just tomorrow, but I get the point.

I will try my best to have fun tonight as Jude's friend, plus-one, or whatever he calls it. Whatever it is that doesn't involve the feelings I actually have. That's the one. I can do that for one night. He's going to be busy with the press and... *crap*. The press will ask who I am and what I am to Jude. All night long, I'm going to hear, *'She's just a friend. She's just a friend.'* I can feel the bruises on my heart start to bloom already. This is going to suck. Why did I agree to this?

The doorbell rings as I touch up my lipstick. I give myself a last once over and decide it will have to do. I have no tools to improve what the pros did anyway. I grab my wrap and clutch purse, and when I open the door and find Jude in a tux, my jaw drops.

He looks incredible. Amazing. Beyond words. It takes a while for me to notice that his jaw has dropped too. And he's staring.

"Holy fuck, Ren." His voice has grit in it now and is more of a growl. "Holy fuck." His eyes repeatedly take me in from head to toe and back, and I can sense their weight and maybe even a little bit of desire, but that's probably wishful thinking. "You clean up okay."

My self-consciousness starts to show, and I pull the wrap around my shoulders tighter. That's enough of that.

"You're not so bad yourself there." I wave at him, indicating his tux. I never in my wildest dreams ever thought I would see Jude Lockwood in a tuxedo, but it is definitely something the world needed. He is so damned handsome I can barely pull my eyes away from him. I've never been a girl that was attracted to the whole 'billionaire' suit vibe thing that some women like. It always felt too pretentious. But if Jude was their poster boy, I could be converted.

"Yeah, well. Not like us guys had a lot of choice on what to wear."

"You don't need a lot of choices when it looks that good."

He blushes a little, and after a few awkward moments, he waves to the limousine waiting at the curb.

"Shall we?"

He puts a hand on my lower back and escorts me to the limo. As soon as his fingers graze my bare skin, my knees give a little. Luckily, I don't stumble or fall on my face, but Jude notices and grabs me tightly around the waist for support. I have to stop myself from gasping aloud at his touch. If only he knew he was the one making me weak-kneed. I'm not going to survive this night. I don't know if I can do this. I can usually put on a good act to hide my true feelings to strangers, but not to Jude. He'll see right through any attempt at hiding that I try. I'll just need to avoid looking directly at him. All night.

We're awkward again on the ride to the theater. Mostly because I keep my gaze out the window to avoid showing him my emotions. As we arrive and our limo pulls up to the pre-carpet holding areas, Jude takes my hand in his and lets out a deep sigh.

"You ready for this?"

"No." *I am so not ready for this.*

"Good. Let's go." The door opens, and he slides out, leaning back in with an outstretched hand to help me exit.

Getting out of a limo in an evening gown with a slit up to your hip isn't something I've ever thought to practice in my life. And right now, in this very moment at a freaking Hollywood premiere, I guess I should have practiced. I'm trying to be as graceful and elegant as I can, and I don't know if I pull it off, but after a few failed attempts, I step out without exposing myself to the world. My hands start to shake, and Jude squeezes my fingers reassuringly.

He leans in, and his breath tickles my ear as he whispers, "I got you. I got you." What feels like hundreds of flashbulbs blind me, and I can't help but physically flinch at first. I'm sure those will be amazing pictures of me squeezing my eyes shut, surprised and frightened. *Awesome*. I wasn't expecting the press at the arrival area. That's not how these things go, but I guess all bets are off when it comes to Indigo King and their documentary, *Stage Left*.

While it feels like it in many ways, this is not my first event like this. When I was with vTV, I hosted several red carpet junkets for the channel. It has been such a long time; I almost forgot what it felt like. And this is the first time I'm on this side of the velvet ropes, ramping up my anxiety even more. I slap on my brand spanking new red-carpet smile and walk with Jude toward the initial holding area, where we'll meet up with the rest of the band and management and all the label representatives. With Jude being the Prince of Punctuality, we are the first ones here, and he grabs us some champagne. I guess that's one of the perks of being early. First dibs on the alcohol.

As I sip my drink, I do my best to stay out of everyone's way. The bustle of activity of the different people wranglers and agents, and other various label personnel is kinetic as more people arrive. I meet one of the label executives, Ian, who insists on a selfie, which is unexpected but cool. Apparently, he was a fan of my show, *Tour de Force*. It still surprises me for some reason when people know about that show. It's like it happened a whole other lifetime ago.

I'm a bit in my element as the crowd grows. While it's been a while, I'm able to slide into my extrovert side fairly quickly, and having Jude next to me the whole time is both comforting and distracting. Just his presence near me is enough to undo me. His hand is either on my back, around my waist, or caressing my shoulder as we chat with people, and it's not something I could ever ignore. It's electric whenever his skin slides against mine. Even the briefest of touches send shivers through me. I start to lean into him when his arm is around me, and I have to consciously pull myself away from him.

By the time we move out of the holding area to the actual carpet, I'm wound so tight I could snap. The people wranglers move us in and out of various combinations for photos against the media wall, and then Jude grabs my hand again, and we make our way down the press line.

Several reporters yell at Jude right away, "Who's your gorgeous date?"

"Has illusive bachelor Jude Lockwood finally been caught?"

He releases my hand and wraps an arm around me. I continue my grin but want to run for the theater behind me. This is the part I was dreading. This is where I get punched in the feels.

"This gorgeous woman is Rena Scott, former host of *Tour de Force* on vTV and current proprietor of Vital Records LA. For over a decade, she's been my best friend and was kind enough to escort my dumbass here so I didn't look like a total loser."

"Well, I can only do so much." I turn my shiny smile up to him, playing my part in the charade. The reporters laugh along with us, and we are moved down the line to the next group, where we do the whole thing again, with only slight variations on the theme.

By the time we enter the theater, my face hurts from the fake smile, and my feet are killing me from these stupid heels. Whatever idiot invented high heels should've been forced to wear them 24/7 as punishment.

Jude is still holding my hand, and he pulls me to the side of the large foyer, grabbing us more champagne. He holds his glass up to me and smiles, his eyes crinkling at the corners.

"Thanks for making me look good out there."

"You're welcome. It's a tough job." I clink his glass and take a sip.

"Seriously. You always were a natural at this

stuff." He leans against the wall, facing me with an intense stare. "Do you ever miss the TV life?"

"God, no." I can't help but scoff at the question. "There is no way I miss that constant scrutiny." I scrunch up my face, remembering the horrible internet trolls. "My hair was too red, my boobs too big, my boobs too small, my eyes looked funny one day, my voice was annoying, I was too fat, I was too skinny, I was too pale, my personality was the worst thing about me." I sigh. "And it got worse from there. I do not miss that at all."

"Well, I think you're perfect." He doesn't look away from me and unwaveringly holds my gaze. But damn it, I can't read him. I've never seen this expression on him before. I don't know what it means. It's too powerful to say whether it's positive or negative.

"Jude..." I can't help but blush from his words and the force of his gaze on me.

"C'mon, you guys, it's time to head inside for the show," Vanessa calls and waves us over.

Jude pushes himself off the wall, and I finish off my glass of champagne before he retakes my hand, and we head inside for the movie. Whatever that was all about will have to wait until after the show.

thirty-one

YOU CAN'T FIX THIS

JUDE

This is fucking perfect. I knew Ren would be the ideal date for this, or plus-one, whatever. Her experience at these types of events has been helpful as we are led around by our noses from one spot to another. She moves along smoothly as though it's all part of a bigger plan she's familiar with, but I'm lost and just following her lead. We're so in sync with each other, though; it's like we know what we're doing.

Never mind the fact she is absolutely ethereal in that evening gown. When she opened her door, I could swear I died and went to heaven. And having an excuse all night to be able to touch her bare skin whenever I want should be downright illegal. I kept looking at her and not paying attention to what was happening around me and got caught a few times while in the press line. Hopefully, I covered it up well enough not to be too obvious. I don't think Ren noticed, at least.

And she's still holding my hand as we're watching the movie. I don't want to let it go for fear she won't retake it. It's completely natural and isn't awkward at all anymore. It's like we're supposed to hold hands all the fucking time. I'm totally okay with that, too. And Ren seems to be as well, and I can't tell if it's real or her TV persona she's putting on for the cameras. There aren't any cameras in here, though, and she's still got my hand, so maybe I've been wrong, and there's hope for us after all.

I hear my voice, *"My goal this tour is to finish an interview without Matt dry heaving next to the bus. Can we do that, buddy?"*

The crowd gets a kick out of that. At least they're getting my odd sense of humor.

It's weird to see yourself on a big screen like this. It doesn't feel real; it's so much larger than life. Like it's someone else up there, not me. I've seen myself on TV plenty of times with all of our videos and press, but never like this. I sneak sideways glances at Ren to see if she's laughing at my jokes, and she is. She seems to be enjoying it.

Samantha, who filmed the documentary, did an excellent job. It hits on all the main emotional points, covering some pretty heavy shit with Matt, and ends with an optimistic outlook on the future for Indigo King. We couldn't ask for more than that.

When the lights come up afterward, everyone gets to their feet and gives her a standing ovation. It's well deserved.

Everyone is generous with their compliments on the film and our band's success as we all make our way out of the theatre. Once back in the holding area, we reunite with the limos that will take us to an estate belonging to one of the Blackmores of Blackmore Records in the hills of LA for the after-party.

Ren and I have another glass of champagne and toast the film's success on the way to the estate. We're still holding hands, and I swear I'm not going to stop so long as she lets me.

"Thanks again for doing this." I squeeze her hand, and she smiles at me.

"Of course, it's my pleasure. I'm having fun." She looks down at herself briefly, at her incredible dress. "Thank you for the gown. I could buy a decent used car for what this thing cost."

I take her in again. Her pale skin is luminous in the low light of the interior and looks so smooth I just want to run my fingers along all of it. Her eyes are bright, and her cheeks are slightly fired up from the champagne. Again, I want to reach out and touch her face to absorb the heat there; stroke her cheekbone to feel the angles. I want to run my lips along her exposed collarbone and give her goosebumps; breathe on her neck until she shivers.

"Earth to Jude. I think we're here."

Her voice cuts through my daydream and brings me back to reality. The sad reality where I don't get to do any of those things. *Fuck.* I do not like reality right now.

"Right. Cool. Let's party." *Yeah, and afterward, we'll go back to the fucking frat house and bust out a kegger and a beer bong. Jesus, man.*

This time we are not the first ones here, which means we are at a disadvantage in positioning. I like to get to things like this early to find a spot of power, somewhere you can observe from a decent vantage point and scope out the available women in the room and make your decisions and moves accordingly. Wait. What the fuck am I thinking? I don't need to do that tonight. I'm with Ren. I am so not used to being with someone at these things. I have been on my own for way too long.

"Judy! Judy! Judy!" I cringe at the name being called out from behind us but smile because I know it's my touring guitar tech and friend, Robert. He's the only one that could get away with calling me that.

"Roberta!" I turn to slap his palm and give him a half-bro hug. "I didn't know you'd be here for this."

"Are you kidding? I wouldn't miss this party for the world. There's supposed to be some choice cuts here tonight." He gives Ren a once-over that makes me twitch. "I see you've already found your prey. Quick work." He nods as if he approves.

"Robert. This is my best friend of almost eleven years, Ren." My tone is now as formal as I can make it. Impressing on him she is not some 'choice cut.' I'll not have him talking about her that way. "Ren, this is my asshole guitar tech and the lowest common denominator in any equation, Robert."

Ren giggles as his face turns red in embarrassment.

"Nice to meet you, Robert." She holds a hand out to him to shake, and I'm jealous he gets to touch her a second longer than I do.

"Sorry about that," he says. "Old habits die hard."

"Yeah, Yeah. Get out of here, Mr. Inspirational Quotes. You're cramping our style with your presence."

He wanders off searching for his next conquest, and Ren and I mingle for the next few hours. She fits in with everyone we talk to, listening to our crazy tour escapades or telling our own stories of our time before I landed in Indigo King. It's so easy with her, and I never worry that she'll say the wrong thing or offend anyone like I usually do. She's the good cop to my bad cop. We are bread and butter. Tacos and Tuesdays. Peanut butter and jelly. Alcohol and bad decisions. Sharks and tornados. We're all that stuff that goes together really well, and I love it.

And we still hold hands here and there, and I still get to touch her, so I do. I touch her as much as I dare without making her uncomfortable and crossing any lines. I'm trying to soak in as much of her as I can in this one night because I know tomorrow we're back to where we were, trying to date other random internet people.

Everyone starts to make their way out to the back terraces to prepare for the fireworks at midnight. I make sure we have more champagne to toast the New Year when it comes and pull Ren along behind me to the outside.

"This view is stunning." Ren is leaning against the glass railing and looking over the LA skyline, the lights of the city dancing in her eyes. "Can you imagine living in a place like this?"

I barely heard what she said, I was watching her lips move. Everyone around us starts counting down, but I can't take my eyes off her mouth. This whole evening has built up to this, and I'm not going to be able to stop myself. I need to taste her once and for all. I need to know what her lips feel like against mine and how her breath mixes with my own. I need *her*.

"Three, two, one. Happy New Year!" Everyone around us is cheering and celebrating the fireworks I think are going off somewhere.

I was right. I can't stop myself. I wrap a hand around the back of Ren's neck and gently pull her to me, my mouth caressing hers. Every cell in my body comes alive as we connect, and I slide my hand slowly down her back, reveling in the softness of her skin and pressing her against me even more. All of my senses are heightened; the smell of her perfume, the warmth of her body, it all overwhelms me. This is even better than I could ever have imagined it to be. Her in my arms, her body against me, her mouth on mine.

As our tongues collide and I taste the sweet champagne mingling in our mouths, it dawns on me Ren is probably tipsy. I'm taking advantage of her right now. *What the fuck am I doing?* I can't do this. I cannot do this to her. She's been clear. She doesn't want this. She's going to fucking hate me.

I forcibly tear myself away from her and take a step back. The sudden loss of her warm body against me gives me chills.

"Rena. I'm so sorry." I can't read her face. She looks shocked. *Oh shit.* What the fucking hell have I done? "Oh my God. Ren. I'm so sorry. I didn't mean to do that."

"Jude?" Her shock is morphing into hurt, and I can't watch this. I can't witness the death of our friendship out here on some strange millionaire's patio while fucking fireworks are going off and people around us are cheering. It's too gruesome. Eleven years flushed down the drain by my fucking impulsive libido.

"I can't. I'm sorry." I can't stop shaking my head in disbelief at what I just did. My best fucking friend. What the fuck made me think I could do that to her?

She silently searches my face for a minute, and I don't know what she's looking for. If it's guilt, I'm sure it's plainly there because that is all I am feeling. I am mortified. This is the stupidest thing I have ever done.

Her expression shifts again, and disappointment takes over her features this time, and I feel that in my soul. I never wanted to see that look in her eyes directed at me. *Ever.* She appears to shrink right in front of me, and I can barely look at her.

"Happy New Year. Goodbye, Jude."

It's so final, so certain, I almost don't recognize her voice as she speaks. The heartbreak in her words is crushing me and breaking my own heart. She goes inside the house, and I know chasing her would be futile. There would be no point. I just sabotaged the one good personal thing I have in my life. *I'll never be able to fix this.*

thirty-two

HURTS
REN

I expected awkwardness. Hell, I expected downright uncomfortable. What I did not expect was instant regret about a fantastic kiss. Jude's remorse, not mine. Well, that's not true. I guess I do now regret it since he does. As soon as he apologized for kissing me, I knew it was over. I could sense my world ending. The fireworks and cheers around us only added to the macabre feeling of the moment. I don't know how I made it home without falling apart on the limo ride. I didn't drop a single tear until I shut the door of my house behind me, and it echoed loudly. It was the loneliest sound ever.

It's been four days since the kiss of death, and I haven't heard a word from him. I'm starting to think I'll never hear from him again, and just the thought makes me so sad I can barely function. He regretted the kiss, fine. But now, it feels like he regretted our entire friendship. Rejection from the kiss is one thing, but now complete rejection is something else and cuts even deeper.

I can't stop crying. It's as though he died, and I'm mourning him, but I'm grieving the death of our relationship. Our friendship lasted longer than any I've had outside of family, and its loss is soul-crushing. This hurts more than when Brad and I broke up, and I didn't think that was humanly possible.

Maybe because I had hope. We were having such a great evening, and I thought we were blurring the lines of our friendship in such a natural and sweet way it would lead to something like the kiss. Little did I know it was the last thing Jude would ever want. He looked so mortified afterward I thought I would catch on fire from embarrassment in front of him and the entire crowd.

And now I can't escape the pictures of us on the internet. Everyone and their brother are interested in Jude's love life and who qualifies to be a part of it. The internet jury is still out on whether I do or not. When I saw the picture of us getting out of the limo and Jude whispering in my ear, I about had a stroke. I had thought that was going to be a horrible picture, but it, in fact, is the best picture of the two of us ever taken. And since I like to torture myself, I saved that one to my phone. All the rest have my TV smile and Jude's rock star persona and aren't as honest.

Trying to keep my sadness from Charlotte has been difficult, and she feeds off my mood all the time, so she's been out of sorts right along with me. It truly saddens me she'll now miss out on spending time with Jude since the two of them together were something so extraordinary. My heart hurts for Jude because he'll now miss all of Charlotte's future milestones. He was so excited to be there for her firsts; I swear I melted more at his reactions to them than to Charlotte.

I did receive several messages on LastPersonOn-Earth.com from Cool Dude and #3 this week, but I haven't looked at them. Something in me doesn't want to deal with anyone else right now, but I know I've got to move on from this. If that moving on is through this stupid website, then fine. I decide to keep to tradition and keep Cool Dude for last.

> #3: So I think we really should meet. Otherwise, we could totally be wasting our time, right? Why are we doing this if we don't know if we'll get along in person? Right? It's a new year. Time for a fresh outlook and approach. Wanna join me?

> #3: I haven't heard back from you
> on getting together, so maybe it's
> too soon? I can be a little more
> patient if needed, but I still think it's
> a good idea to meet sooner rather
> than later. Let me know what you
> think.

So, #3 really wants to meet. Okay. I'll think about that. It could be what I need to snap out of this depression. That is, if the guy doesn't stand me up. Something to consider, for sure.

> COOL DUDE: Holidays are over,
> thank God. I hope yours went well,
> of course. Personally, I'm happy to
> have them behind me.

Looking forward to picking up our conversation where we left off. If I remember correctly, we were discussing Abercrombie's First Law trilogy and the morality of barbarians?

> COOL DUDE: And ghosted. Damn.
> Didn't see that coming, but such is
> my luck.

> COOL DUDE: Please disregard my
> last message. I was having a
> dreadful week. Hopefully, you've
> read Harry Potter. Obliviate.

That makes me laugh. Poor Cool Dude, trying to

erase my memory. I wish that worked; I'd like to forget this whole week right along with him. It sounds like he's having a rough new year too. I write him back first.

ME: Forget what? 😊

ME: Sorry for the delay. I was having an equally poor beginning of the year. Barbarian morality can definitely be back in play.

I wonder what his bad week was about. Should I ask? Something niggles in the back of my mind that maybe this is Jude again. Could that really happen? No. I'm wishful thinking yet again. I really need to stop doing that. It's starting to get old, and even my own thoughts are wearing me down.

I move back to #3. What to say to him? Should I tell him I tried to meet someone else, and he stood mc up, so now I'm a little gun-shy? Actually, no. I need to go out and get over this. I can't mope around forever. I never gave #3 a nickname because he's the most vanilla of all three. Not a lot of personality, but that might just be the internet filtering it out. I guess meeting in person will test that theory to see if he's the same way in real life. Here goes nothing.

ME: Sorry. It's been a rough start to the year. I agree meeting sooner rather than later is a great idea. Weekends are better for me. When is good for you?

That should be enough to appease them both while I take a minute to breathe a small breath and pull myself back together. After all, I can only move so fast from one rejection to another. But I'm glad I'm taking this step and moving forward.

I pick the same bar as last time because I know Jude hates the place, and the likelihood of running into him is slim to none. It's not exactly my favorite place either after what happened last time, but it's familiar, and it's close to home should anything go wrong. I ditch the dress this time and go for a more casual style with jeans and a nice top. If I'm going to be stood up again, I don't want to waste my time dressing up for the honor.

I arrive early to pick a seat at a table with a view of the entrance. Surprisingly, there are quite a few empty tables tonight, which rarely happens here. It's usually standing room only. I don't think there are any bands scheduled for tonight, which might be the issue. I order a drink and settle in to wait for #3 to arrive.

The only description I got this time was tall with a blue shirt. A few minutes past the hour, a tall man in a blue shirt enters and looks around. He half waves when he spots me and walks in my direction with a small smile.

"Are you the last person on Earth?" he asks when he gets to the table. This has to be #3. He's smiling, and something about his smile makes my skin crawl a little bit. I think I might be right about this guy being full of himself. It's just a vibe I get from him.

"I've been called worse," I say, holding out a hand to him. "I'm Ren."

"Jimmy." He takes my hand and attempts to kiss the back of it. I slide mine away as smoothly as I can without offending him. He doesn't seem phased by it at all.

He sits and orders a drink, checking out the waitress as she walks away, and things are as awkward as possible. There is obviously zero chemistry between us. He's not ugly, but he's not Jude gorgeous, either. Blond hair, blue eyes, a stereotypical California dude. Nothing particularly interesting or extraordinary about him at all. Even his voice sounds bored. This will be a long evening if I have to keep up a conversation with him.

As Jimmy's drink gets delivered, I can't help but notice Jude enter the bar with his friend Robert I met on New Year's Eve. *Are you fucking kidding me? Here? Tonight? Now?* I quickly look away and pretend I didn't notice him and smile unnaturally wide at Jimmy across from me. I'm having fun. This is the best night of my life. *Wow, how fast Ren has moved on. Jesus Christ.*

Robert leads Jude to the table directly behind Jimmy because, of course, he'd sit there. There are only a million other open tables in this bar. I don't think Robert saw me, but as they're about to sit down, I can't help but glance up, and Jude's gaze meets mine. He instantly goes pale, shoots a surprised look at Jimmy, and then back to me. There's some kind of question in his eyes, but I immediately return my attention to Jimmy, who apparently said something amusing about himself. I force a laugh and a smile, calling back the TV persona I use in situations like this. Ones where I want to crawl under the table and hide for a year.

"So, why do you look so familiar?" He's rubbing his chin and squinting his eyes at me as he examines me closer. "Are you an actress or something? Didn't you do that one annoying toothpaste commercial that played all the time?"

I cock my head at him quizzically for a second. What the heck? Is that a polite way to ask someone that?

I clear my throat to stop from screaming. This

guy's only been here ten minutes, and it already feels ten minutes too long.

"No, I'm not that annoying actress."

"Okay, okay. I still know you from some-where...." He's not going to give this up. Fine.

"Did you ever watch vTV?" He nods. "I used to host *Tour de Force*. That's where you would know me from. Or perhaps my current business, Vital Records LA."

"That's it!" He claps his hands together like he is the one with the revelation. *What an idiot.* "You look so different from when you were on that show, though."

"Well, it was a long time ago." I try to keep my forced smile plastered on my face, but it's getting harder and harder to keep it in place. And now, knowing Jude is just on the other side of the booth I'm staring at is unnerving me more.

I haven't heard anything from Jude and Robert's booth, so either they're not talking or being very quiet about it. Not that I'd want to hear anything he had to say anyway.

After a long silence and an even more extended examination from Jimmy, he says, "So I thought six or seven months would be enough time for a woman to lose the baby weight. Is that not right? Or were you like this before? I don't remember you looking like...this." He waves a judgmental hand, indicating what I can only assume are my extra pounds since having Charlotte. A gasp escapes my mouth, and my hand flies to my throat in shock. I can't believe what I just heard from this man.

I don't get a chance to respond because the next thing I know, Jude is out of his booth and has Jimmy by the collar with both fists, pushing him against the wall at the end of his bench seat.

"What the fuck?" Jimmy squeaks, looking between Jude and me as if we're tag-teaming this situation. Robert has stood up, too, and is ready to back up whatever Jude has planned.

"'What the fuck' is right. How dare you speak to her that way." Jude is growling behind clenched teeth, a muscle in his jaw flexing repeatedly.

I can't do this. The insult was enough. I can't handle Jude being Jude on top of everything else. I get up without a word since I'm biting my tongue, and its pain makes my eyes water. I glare at Jimmy and Jude, still speechless, shake my head, and rush out of the bar. I don't make it to my car before the tears start this time. My heart is so trampled, and I feel so defeated.

Like every other date night in recent memory, this whole night has been a complete and utter disaster. I need to give this up.

thirty-three

J*esus Christ*. I can't do anything right. Robert drags me out of the bar in time to watch Ren's car drive away.

"Dude, what the fuck was that all about? Are you crazy?" He yanks on my arm and drags me to the car. "Did you learn nothing this summer? What if people recognized you?"

He's right. Of course, he's right. I can't be caught brawling with some guy in a bar. Not now I'm in a famous band. I couldn't help myself, though. I couldn't *not* do something. I saw red as soon as I heard what he said to Ren.

"That asshole disrespected my friend. I had to do something."

"What do you think your friend does when you're not around? Sit there calling out your name to dead air and lets herself continue to get insulted? C'mon, man. Wise up." He shakes his head as he surveys the parking lot, probably looking for anyone with a camera. "I'm sure Ren can take care of herself. She doesn't need a knight in shining armor to ride in and save the day. Or get caught up in a tabloid scandal on top of it. You know if you get named, she does too."

"Fuck me." I rake my hands down my face. He's right. I know he's right. Ren would be dragged into any story involving me tonight. "What was I supposed to do, though? I couldn't just do nothing."

"Actually, you could." He cocks his head at me. "What is going on with you, dude? You've been weird since you got home from Europe. And you were weird about Ren at Blackmore's on New Year's."

"What?" I need to change the subject and get out of this conversation. I do not want to talk about this, especially with Robert. He doesn't know Ren and wouldn't understand any of it. "Fuck you. I haven't been weird. Let's go and find another bar."

He raises an eyebrow at me but gets in the car. However, he's apparently not done with the conversation. *Fucking hell.*

"Seriously, dude. What is up with you? Is it Ren? Is something happening there?"

I start the car and pull onto the road, heading in a random direction.

"Man, I don't want to get into this now..."

"So, something is going on there," he chuckles. "Okay, that's a start. I can work with that."

"Leave it be, Roberta. I'm not in the mood," I warn. He doesn't really want to get into this with me. I've been avoiding this whole topic in my own head for days just so I don't have to think about it. I'm not very successful, but I try my damnedest.

"Well, you know, talking about it might be the better option versus physically accosting strangers in bars." He shrugs. "I'm just sayin'."

He may have a point, but fuck if I want to admit it. I keep driving for a while, not saying anything, trying to gather my thoughts. If I talk about this with him, I need to be sure about what I feel.

"So, let's start with when you got back from Europe." He took my silence as agreement to talk. Absolutely fabulous. "What happened when you got back that was different?"

This I know the answer to.

"Charlie. Charlie was different."

"Who or what is Charlie?"

My heart clenches thinking about her, slobbering all over my t-shirt while she naps, screeching when she first sees me, and our improvised game of backward Tag. I grab the steering wheel tighter, my knuckles turning white, and take and release a deep breath.

"Charlie is Ren's soon-to-be eight-month-old

daughter, Charlotte." He smirks at me sideways, but I catch it. "Shut it. She's a cool kid."

He lifts his hands up.

"Hey man, I didn't say a thing."

"No, but you were thinking something I'm pretty sure I'd kill you for."

"Okay, okay. So, Charlie is great. What does that have to do with you assaulting strangers in fake Irish pubs?"

"Nothing. Well, everything." God-damn it, this is not helping at all. "Fuck, I don't know, man. None of it matters, anyway. I fucked everything up on New Year's Eve."

"Oh? How did you do that? You guys were having a fun time together, from what I saw, which, I admit, wasn't much. I was otherwise occupied... But what I did see of you two looked copacetic." He pauses for a second. "Now that I think on it, you were overprotective of her then."

I cringe inwardly, thinking of how badly I fucked things up that night. After I kissed her, the shock and pain in Ren's eyes still haunt me.

"I kissed her." There. I fucking said it.

"And?"

"What the fuck are you talking about? *And?* That kiss ruined our entire decade of friendship, dude. That's a big fucking deal." I knew he wouldn't understand, which is why I didn't want to talk about this with him in the first place.

"Whoa, okay. What'd she do, slap you or punch you or something?" He directs me to turn right at the next light, apparently with a final destination in mind. Good. I need a drink.

"What? No. Nothing like that." Again, he's missing the point.

"So, she told you off? Did the whole 'I never want to see you again, you lecherous bastard' bit?"

"Again, no." He's starting to dance on my last nerve with his questions. It's making me feel worse about the entire thing. Something I didn't think was possible, so there are surprises for us all around.

"What the fuck, man? Did she kiss you back? That's the only option left here in this crazy multiple-choice game you're making me play."

He makes it sound like the last thing she would do under the circumstances when that's the furthest from the truth.

"She was tipsy on champagne, man. I took advantage of the situation. It was fucked up of me to kiss her like that. I apologized right away, but it was too fucking late."

"Wait, wait, wait. Let me get this straight. You kissed her, and I'm assuming she kissed you back because she didn't pull away or kick your ass or anything, and you then proceeded to apologize for kissing her?"

I consider his statement. It sounds about as good of a summary of the situation as any.

"Yeah, that's what happened."

He sighs and shakes his head, but I don't understand his reaction. This isn't difficult. I was an ass. It's black and white in my mind. I crossed a line that never should have been crossed.

"Dude. Do you not see what you did wrong?"

"Yes! I told you exactly what I did wrong, fuckhead. What don't you understand about any of this? Please tell me I'm not hanging out with the village idiot." How is this so complicated?

"No, fuckhead. *You're* the one being an idiot. She kissed you back, meaning... wait for it... she *wanted* you to kiss her." Again, he chuckles to himself, shaking his head at me like he can't believe I can be so stupid. "And then apologizing for kissing her, after she kissed you back... Dude, that's harsh. Even village idiots know that much. Way to make her feel like total shit. I can't believe you're so dumb."

Is that what I did? It is. I replay the entire scene again and picture Ren's surprise and hurt at my apology, not the kiss itself. *Holy fuck. Is that right?* Or am I twisting what happened into what I want to believe yet again?

I have to slam on the brakes to stop from running a red light while not paying attention. *Jesus Christ.* I need to pull my shit together. I glance over at Rob, still in disbelief he could be right about this.

He shrugs at me with a smartass smirk on his face.

"I'm sorry you're stupid?"

thirty-four
EITHER YOU WANT IT
REN

I can't believe Jude. Actually, I can. I can't believe Jimmy. Again, no, I totally can. I quit. I'm going to stay celibate for the rest of my life and collect thimbles or spoons, and cats or dogs. My heart can't take much more of this. What chances do I have if the 'last person on Earth' is a total asshole to me?

And, what was Jude thinking? Attacking Jimmy like that. He was utterly unbalanced and irrational, and out of line. How does he think he has any right to defend me? If that's what he was even doing. It's not jealousy because he's been more than clear he doesn't want a relationship with me. So, what, then? Some type of defense of my honor? Again, he has no right to do that. He, of all people, should know I can handle myself if I need to. He doesn't need to defend me. I don't want him to, either. After that display, I don't want anything more to do with him.

Regardless of my feelings for him, things like this only make me hurt worse. Because I want him to have the right to defend me. I want him to be in a position to be jealous. I want *him*. And the only way I'm going to get over him and the loss of our friendship, which is even more devastating, is to forget about him and keep him in the past. I can't do that if he's popping up during my dates and fighting over me.

When I pull into my grandfather's condominium parking lot, I need to steel myself for the questions he will inevitably ask. And with Pops, I can't shrug him off or avoid answering. He's always been able to get me to talk to him, even when I don't want to. It's annoying sometimes. I check my watch. I've only been gone barely two hours, which is not long enough for a date. He's going to know something happened. The guy was a jerk. No big deal. I don't need to bring up Jude at all.

He opens his door with Charlotte bouncing on his hip, and her smile when she sees me makes everything that happened tonight completely meaningless. Those guys don't know what the hell they're missing.

"Gimme, gimme," I say, holding out grabby hands for Pops to hand her over. Once I have her, I squeeze, breathing in her calming baby scent, and glance up at Pops. "Guys are jerks, you know."

He chuckles and steps aside for me to enter.

"This is not news, Rena. What happened?"

"Oh, you know. Typical jerky guy stuff." I put Charlotte down and start gathering her things to go home.

"Rena, it's been an age since I dated. I have no idea what constitutes 'jerky guy stuff' these days. Enlighten me, please." He squats down and starts entertaining Charlotte while I pack her bag.

I roll my eyes at him and sigh.

"Pops. Things aren't that different from when you dated."

"Then, humor an old man's curiosity." He smirks. "That would be me. I know I don't look it, but I'm the old man in this scenario."

"Fine." I knew he would drag this out of me. My skin itches to go home, have a massive glass of wine and start forgetting this night happened, not relive it again. "He made a rude comment about my baby weight and how long it's taking for me to lose it." It smarts to remember it. I can still picture his smug face when he said it. This brings up visions of Jude springing up and practically jumping on the asshole.

Pops' eyes go wide in disbelief.

"He did what? Are you serious?" He shakes his head in disbelief and stands up, putting his hands on his hips. "Men of my generation would at least have manners. Well, mostly. So, what did you do? I hope you told him to go kick rocks."

That makes me laugh. Telling someone to *'go kick rocks'* might not have the impact he thinks it would, but I appreciate the sentiment. Leave it to Pops to make me smile somehow through this. My laugh turns into a sigh. I was afraid this would happen. I'd have to mention him.

"Well, Jude happened to be in the booth behind him." An eyebrow raises, but I ignore it and go on. "He heard what the jerky guy said to me and proceeded to jump up and attack him right in the booth." There. It's out. I can move on now. Pops will have some pearl of wisdom to pass on, and that will be that.

But Pops doesn't say anything right away. He merely rubs his chin and nods as if something I said confirmed something for him.

"Good." He's still nodding and smiling a little bit. While he thinks this is good, Pops doesn't know what happened between us on New Year's Eve. I never worked up enough nerve to talk about it. When I picked up Charlotte on New Year's Day, I didn't mention it and still haven't.

"No. It's not good, Pops. And I certainly don't want or need Jude fighting my battles for me. I can take care of myself."

"What do you mean? Real men stand up for

people they really care about. It's the honorable thing to do."

"Well, that's where you're wrong. Jude definitely doesn't care about me like that." I thought perhaps talking to Pops about this would make me feel better, but the opposite is happening. Tears are threatening again as I relive the evening and remember locking eyes with Jude. I still don't understand the questioning look he gave me, but it doesn't matter.

"What makes you so sure?" Charlotte is getting antsy, and he picks her up and starts swaying with her on his hip. He's so amazing with her.

I'm going to have to tell him, damn it. I guess it was inevitable.

"He kissed me on New Year's Eve, Pops, and was sorry for it right away. I left the party and haven't heard from him since. Well, until I saw him earlier at the bar." I swallow back the tears. "If someone is sorry they kissed you, it's fairly obvious they don't care about you."

He gets super quiet, and I have to glance up to see what he's doing or feeling. He's still dancing with Charlotte, but his forehead is creased as though he's confused. What on Earth could he possibly be confused about?

"What is it, Pops? You look like I've puzzled you." I let out a long sigh, put Charlotte's bag over my shoulder, and reach out for her again. I'm anxious to get home. After this evening and now this conversation, I feel like a sponge that's been wrung out so tightly that it doesn't remember what fluids are.

"I think you're wrong about Jude, is all." After planting a kiss on her forehead, he hands Charlotte over carefully and then does the same with mine. He's so damned sweet. "I think maybe Jude cares too much, and it scares the bejeezus out of him. Just something to think about."

"Yeah, okay." I open the door to leave and wave one of Charlotte's hands at him. "Say goodbye to the crazy-talking old man."

He's still laughing as he closes the door behind us. *Very funny, Pops.*

thirty-five

HOW I MISS YOU

JUDE

I spend the next few days trying to get my head straight. I've even taken to writing songs on my six-string, which I haven't done since Indigo King's first album. We each play stuff we've been working on at our next band meeting at our apartment, and after Matt and Ryan hear my songs, they both glance at each other and then give me strange looks.

"What? They're not that bad." And they're not bad at all. They're some of the better songs I've ever written.

"We didn't' say they were, man." Ryan's hands are up.

"Then what the fuck was that look?" I know I'm not paranoid. There was a definite look.

"Who are all these songs about?" Ryan's voice

switches to compassion. What the fuck is that about?

"What does it matter who they're about? Are they good enough or not?" Subjects have always been non-relevant in our songs, except for the few Ryan wrote for his fiancée Sarah.

"It matters because whatever happened to inspire these songs sounds pretty fucking devastating." The concern on his and Matt's faces takes me back. I've never been considered this way by them before, and I don't like it. "Is everything okay with you?"

"I'm fine. And I repeat, are the songs good enough or not?" The steely edge to my words finally cuts through to them.

"Well, yeah, they're great, but I don't know if we want to use all of them." Matt's brow furrows as he speaks, he's still studying me, and it's unnerving. "We're not writing an album to play at funerals. Maybe pick just one thoroughly morose song to completely depress our fans?"

"They're not that sad."

"Have you read these lyrics?" Ryan chuckles, holding up the notebook with my chicken scratch on it. They might be right. The songs are a little on the dark side. "I'll ask you again, is everything okay with you? Did something happen with Ren?"

My head snaps up.

"Why would you ask that?"

He shrugs.

"Whatever the fuck happened on New Year's, which, yes, we noticed something was wrong after midnight, and now these songs... One plus one kinda equals Jude's got girl problems."

I bury my face in my hands. *Fuck me running.* I can't seem to avoid this, no matter how hard I try. I still don't know what I'm going to do about any of it because I'm still sorting through what happened and how I feel about everything. I don't want to fuck things up even more than I already have.

"Fine. Yes. Something happened on New Year's Eve, and now I have a bit of an issue with Ren, but I'm sorting through it."

"What kind of issue?" Matt grabs a beer from the fridge and hands me one, giving Ryan a soda.

"I kissed her at midnight and then apologized for it, which I now have come to understand was the absolute wrong thing to do, so don't fucking jump on my case about that, thanks. And now Ren isn't talking to me, and I sort of attacked her date the other night in a bar."

Ryan whistles and Matt shakes his head. Their reactions are not helpful in the least.

"Dude..." Ryan looks like he's having a hard time holding back a laugh. "That's a lot."

"Fuck you. Do we want to go over the perfect events making up the love story in Vegas between you and Sarah just over a year ago?"

"Jude." Matt steps toward me, but I'm not done. Fuck this. And fuck them for laughing or thinking this is somehow funny.

I turn to Matt. "Or how about how you broke Samantha's wrist this past summer? That was the most romantic start of a relationship I've ever fucking seen."

"Jude." Matt's tone is warning, but I don't give a shit.

I stand up and meet him where he stands.

"No. Don't *'Jude'* me. I have been nothing but a fantastic fucking friend to both of you, and you're going to sit here and laugh at my situation? And my songs? Fuck that. And fuck the two of you." I slam my beer down on the table. "Just go ahead and write the fucking songs and tell me when and where to play them. I'm done."

I move to step around Matt to leave, but he steps in my way. I don't want this to turn physical. He'll kick my ass without breaking a sweat, and I really like my face the way it is.

Ryan stands, too, and uses his arms to divide us and move us back from each other.

"Yeah, no. we're not going to have internal fighting in this band. Sorry about your luck, guys." He turns to me, puts his hands on my shoulders, and looks me in the eyes. "Jude, I totally deserve your anger. I am sorry I laughed. It's not an excuse, but the thought of you in a real relationship, having real relationship problems, is a little hard for my tiny brain to wrap itself around. I'm going to need a bit of an adjustment period since this is such a new and novel concept."

I stare at him long and hard and then let out a sigh. He's got a point. I am not, nor have I ever been, a relationship guy. And it's admittedly new for me too. *I'm* still getting used to the idea. And I shouldn't have lashed out with my cruel words.

"I'm sorry too. That was out of line by me." I glance at them both and can see the forgiveness right away. "But like you said, this is new to me, and I'm freaking the fuck out, guys. I don't know what to do. And you're not being very fucking helpful."

"Well, let's have a seat and try to help you figure it out." Matt pats my shoulder with a commiserating smile. I love this chosen family of brothers. Not many people I could blow up like that with and get this kind of response.

An hour or so later, armed with advice from my two engaged friends, I decide to reach out to Ren to see if she'd even be willing to talk with me so I can explain myself to her.

> ME: Hey. Any chance we could get together to talk?

After another hour passes with no reply, I'm pretty sure that it's entirely over between us. I've lost her for good.

thirty-six

BELOVED FREAK

REN

I can't. When I got Jude's text, I couldn't respond. I don't have anything to say to him and can't imagine he has anything to say I want to hear. And on top of that, my heartbreak is still way too fresh to start picking at the scabs. I am not made of stone; each time I try to ignore my feelings and just be his friend, it tears my soul. If I keep it up, there's not going to be anything left of me.

I know Jude will say he wants us to be friends again like we were, but I can't do that. I can't go back to platonic anything after what happened between us. He kissed me, and I kissed him right back, and it was the best kiss I've ever had. It was the best kiss in the history of kisses nationally, if not worldwide. And he was instantly sorry he kissed me. I can't recover from that. I don't think I ever will.

So, no. I'm not responding to Jude. And thankfully, he's not pressing the issue either. He's not one to chase, thank goodness, so I can move on without being bombarded with messages or calls from him. He respects people's decisions, whatever they are, which is something else I love about him.

I'm currently waiting with Charlotte outside of the Mother Goose Daycare, waiting for Brad to meet us so we can check if this place will be a good fit for her. We're early, so we take a seat on a bench in front of the building. I can hear the nursery rhymes and games being played inside and can't help but smile. My little girl might make her first friends here. I wonder if someday she'll make friends with her own Jude and stay friends for over a decade. Regardless of how things ended with Jude and me, I truly hope she does. Everyone should have a friend like Jude. Just don't be dumb like me and fall in love with him because that's fatal, for the friendship and your own heart.

Brad shows up on time, and Charlotte is happy to see him, making my heart pang a little. Maybe she'll have a somewhat normal childhood after all. Who freaking knows. Brad seems to have cleaned himself up quite a bit and is being consistent with his visits with Charlotte. Even his coming today isn't the surprise it would have been a few weeks ago. He's even paying for daycare, if we agree that we like it. Luckily, it goes well with the daycare, and we sign her up to start in a few weeks. That gives me time to get used to the idea of being without her during the day. Yes, I'll be able to work more productively at my store, but I'll miss her terribly. I've gotten used to having her with me all the time. I need a break, sure, but I also don't want one. It's a curse.

We go for coffee to discuss future arrangements with Charlotte, and every time he calls her 'Charlie,' I flinch a little, hearing it in Jude's voice in my head.

"Please don't call her that." I'm trying to be nice about it without explaining why I don't want him using that name. "Her name is Charlotte."

"Doesn't Jude call her that? I think it's cute." He's oblivious to my physical reaction to Jude's name. He really isn't the sharpest tool in the shed.

"Not anymore; he doesn't," I say it matter-of-factly while leaning over to play with Charlotte to keep from having to look at him.

"Oh? How come?" And he sounds concerned, which might be a first for him. I'll need to mark this date on my calendar.

"Reasons that are none of your business," I say, slightly sharper than intended. I'm not sure I care, though. "Just please don't call her that. Okay?"

"Yay. Biting my head off. Just like old times." He huffs like a little boy not getting his way. I am so grateful I no longer have to sleep or cohabitate with this man. What I ever saw in him in the first place continues to elude me. "Awesome, Ren."

I glare at Brad but ignore his comments. We've

been getting along lately, and I don't want to start anything, especially not in the middle of a coffee shop or in front of Charlotte.

"So, you're not going to tell me what happened with Jude?" He seems surprised I'd hold anything back from him. That's interesting of him. "How come?"

"Because it's none of your business." My TV smile comes out yet again. It's been getting quite the workout. "Nothing about me outside of Charlotte is your business anymore if you've forgotten."

He looks a little stunned, and I cheer a little on the inside at being able to stand up to him. Not that I couldn't before, but my confidence in being a mom has climbed a few rungs since we were together, and it feels good to finally be steady on my own two feet.

ME: So, serious question time. Have you ever missed someone you care deeply about? They're alive, but no longer in your life? If so, how did you deal with it? Since we're probably never going to meet, I figured we could start asking the hard-hitting questions.

COOL DUDE: Never going to meet?? I'm wounded. Actually, I'm with you on that. Meeting in person probably isn't in our cards. Hopefully, you're on board with that, and I didn't just ruin another friendship. Think I might scrap this whole experiment soon.

To answer your question, yes, I have and do miss someone who I care deeply about, and they are no longer in my life (see ruined friendship above). As for advice on how to handle the situation, you are barking up the wrong Ent. I am as lost as you are on this particular aspect of this thing called life.

ME: I am so sorry to hear you are going through a similar situation. If we can't advise each other, maybe we can commiserate instead? At least until we both move on? I'll start first. What is it you miss most about them? For me, it was their sense of humor. They had the quickest wit and sharpest tongue, combined with the most off-the-wall references to make me constantly laugh around them.

COOL DUDE: Damn. You're going to make me type these things out, huh? Okay. Fair play. What do I miss the most? Shit. I'm sitting here having a hell of a time trying to think of just one thing; there are too many to pick just one. If I had a gun to my head, I'd say her warmth. She makes everyone around her comfortable and welcome. When you're in her presence, you feel special, like the only person in her world. I miss that feeling.

Okay. It's my turn. When did you know you cared so much about them? I will say when I saw the broken parts of her, and I wanted to pick them up and put them back together more than I wanted to breathe.

ME: Aww. That is so sweet of you. Whoever she is, she is definitely missing out. When did I know I was doomed to the pit of despair, you ask? That's an easy one. When I saw them interact with my child. As soon as I knew my baby loved them, I did too.

I guess it's my turn again. Do you think there's any hope for you to reconnect? For me, or us, I'd say no. A line was crossed with us that can't be uncrossed, and it hurts my heart it can't be undone.

COOL DUDE: Okay, lots to unpack. First, a question before my answer – you keep referencing "they/them/their" pronouns. Is your friend non-binary? No judgment if they are. I'm just a curious bastard.

As for the question of hope, I understand your answer and see how you might lose hope. Not knowing the situation, I mourn for your loss. As for me, I keep a sliver of hope alive because I apparently am a masochist. I thought I was a realist or pragmatic, but I can't help but hope a miracle will happen in this situation.

My turn again. Let's turn it on its head. What do/did you like least about them? For me, it was her stubbornness. I get independence and all that, but when you obviously need help, fucking take it when it's offered, you know?

ME: Last response for the night. I'm starting to fade here. As for the pronouns, no, they are, in fact, a "he/him." I only used "they/them" to keep another layer of anonymity here on this lovely internet. Sorry if there was any confusion.

As for the dislike, oddly enough, it was his white knight complex. I'm a big girl and can take care of myself (and do). I will ask for help when I can't handle something on my own. So there! (just kidding) Have a good night.

COOL DUDE: Fair enough. Good night. Keep your face shiny.

thirty-seven

I DON'T MISS YOU AT ALL

JUDE

Long hours in the studio aren't enough to distract me from missing Ren and Charlie. I've been pulling sixteen-hour days and could go the other eight per day if it wouldn't make me literally insane. The good thing about this is the new album has my fingerprints all over it. Way more than the last one. Ryan's fiancée Sarah, who helped produce our previous record, is producing again on this one. She's got a knack for finding our sound or our vibe for each album, and while this one is entirely different, it's still clearly an Indigo King record. I like that.

It's a whole fucking family affair. Not only is Ryan's fiancée working with us, but Matt's fiancée Samantha is filming us again, too. This time she's capturing us creating and recording the album. I'm not sure what it's for exactly, but I don't pay attention to any of the marketing shit anyway. I show up, keep my head down, and do my thing.

The only things keeping me distracted are my chat messages with Catfish on LastPersonOnEarth.com. We've gotten into some deep-diving conversations about relationships and life. I don't think I'm relationship material, but I'd still like to meet up with her at least once before I shut down my account. I won't be using the site anymore to meet chicks. At least not for a long time.

I have a feeling it's going to take a while for me to get over Ren and Charlie. I guess the good thing that came out of all this is I know now the Tin Man has a heart. I wasn't so sure before. I kept it locked up so deep I almost drowned trying to pull it up. And now I don't know what to do with it. Lock it up again? Or gamble with it? I don't think I'm in a place where I'm willing to risk it again. Not yet. Not ever, maybe. Who knows?

I do know I feel empty, hollowed out like there's a humungous hole in my soul where Ren and Charlie used to fit perfectly. If I could cry, I'd be balling tears all over the fucking place, but I do *feel* like I'm crying on the inside. It's the weirdest, most sad feeling in the world. And it's the closest I've been to real tears since I was a little kid. My mind and heart are consumed with their loss, absence, and the void left by them. My mind has also started to play cruel tricks that make me feel like I'm going fucking crazy. Sometimes when I think about Charlie, I can smell baby powder out of nowhere, and there's obviously no baby powder around. And other times, when I think about Ren, I can smell her perfume. It's fucking nuts. It's like my body is revolting against me and haunting itself, which is craziness.

ME: Do you ever think of someone and then smell their cologne or whatever? Or vice versa? Like out of the blue? That's so fucking weird.

CATFISH: I have done that, and yes, it is bizarre. A brain is a weird place. I looked it up and found that memories associated with smells were "not necessarily more accurate, but tended to be more emotionally evocative." I'm not sure what it means about the accuracy, but I totally get the emotional part.

ME: I like the word evocative. The brain is indeed weird and also very dumb. Kudos on the research.

CATFISH: Did you just call me dumb?

ME: NO! Of course not. I said the brain is dumb.

> CATFISH: So you're calling me brainless instead? Hardly an improvement.

> ME: Yes. I was saying you had no brain. I've been carrying on this entire conversation with an anencephalic twat. (sarcasm emphasized)

> CATFISH: Wow. That word is way too big for my brainless head to comprehend. (note - I'm referring to the word "twat")

> ME: I'll type slower next time so you can understand easier.

> CATFISH: Oh my gosh. That had me laughing so hard I had tears. Thank you for that. I needed it.

> ME: Well, admittedly, tears were the ultimate goal, so I win.

At least I made somebody laugh today, even if it's a stranger on the internet. I haven't felt humorous lately, so that was a nice exchange. Maybe I'll give Catfish my contact info when I quit the site. She seems like a decent pen pal, at least. Sometimes the anonymity of the internet allows for more honest conversations, I think. I like that about our messages.

After almost everyone leaves at the end of the second week in the studio, Sarah pulls me aside. I've been anticipating this and am frankly surprised she's not done this earlier. It's just how she is.

"Ryan told me what's going on with you and Ren, and I wanted to check on you and see how you're doing."

Of course, he did.

"Why, do I not look okay?" I run a tired hand through my hair and rub the days-old scruff on my chin. "I thought I looked pretty stellar this morning."

"Well, that was a million hours ago, and no, you look like shit." She leans forward in her chair, tilting her head. "Do you want to talk about it?"

"Not particularly, no." I'm trying to forget, not constantly talk about it.

"Well, like it or not, I'm going to give you some unsolicited advice. Call her. Or go to her. But one damn text asking to get together isn't going to cut it. Especially with the time that's passed since New Year's Eve." She reaches out and puts a hand on my knee. It's comforting, but only so much.

"And what am I supposed to say when I call or see her? Sorry I said I was sorry? I'm not really sorry? See my dilemma?"

Sarah takes a deep breath and lets it out in a huff.

"You can start by telling her how you feel about her, then work your way to fixing the kiss situation. If you tell her the truth, the rest will make sense to her. Trust me on this."

"And what if she doesn't want to listen to me or let me talk?" I can picture not getting an opportunity to start talking. Ren is stubborn. If she doesn't want to hear from me, she won't. Even if I'm standing in front of her.

"You know how there's the whole myth about what women want?" I nod. "It's really simple. We want the truth. So long as you guys tell us the truth, we'll deal with it no matter how shitty it is. Maybe not right away, or the way you expect, but there is nothing more important to us. And, let me tell you, a guy baring his honest soul to a woman is the hottest thing on Earth to that woman. Instant aphrodisiac."

I arch an eyebrow at her, and she blushes slightly.

"Let's not cross into TMI, okay?"

She laughs and gets up to leave.

"Fine. But think about what I said. I like Ren and I think you two are perfect for each other. I don't want to see it end because you're a chicken shit to tell her how you feel."

"Thanks, Sarah." She ruffles my hair and leaves the studio, leaving me by myself.

I need to make some choices and finally take some risks. I can't live like this anymore. Knowing she doesn't know how I feel about her is my biggest issue. If, after telling her, she wants nothing to do with me, then I can figure out how to live without her. Right now, though, I need to stoke that little flame of hope I keep burning for her and put on my big girl panties and fucking tell her how I feel.

I think I need some tattoo therapy.

A s the weeks after New Year's go by, I'm convinced that the whole Jude incident was just a dream. It never really happened. Outside of one text, I've not seen hide nor hair of him. Not that I expected him to reach out again, but I think deep down, I wanted him to at least try a little harder. But we don't always get what we want.

I'll be losing another friend soon, too, since Cool Dude is shutting down his account on LastPerson-OnEarth.com. We talked about exchanging socials or emails, but I don't know. We're discussing possibly meeting in person as a final official sendoff. I'm still considering that. I like the idea, but I don't want to ruin the Cool Dude's mystique, either. In my mind, he's kind of epic, but maybe he's a jerk in real life. That would be too disappointing with everything else going on.

It's been a debate between us all week, with each taking different arguments and playing Devil's advocate for both sides.

> ME: But what if you're an asshole? I'll have to hate you for the rest of your life. That's an enormous burden to impose on me, you know. And not very fair since I'm basically perfect.

COOL DUDE: While you are undoubtedly perfect by your own standards, you may not be ideal to me and mine. Also, I never claimed not to be an asshole because it was never directly asked of me. I can guarantee you that I am an asshole, and I wear my badge proudly (we get them at our five-year anniversary meeting).

> ME: You go to the meetings? Pfft. Loser.

COOL DUDE: You sound like a recruit-in-waiting. I can send you a brochure if you're interested.

> ME: Keep your propaganda. I know it's all a front for the Illuminati.

COOL DUDE: And what, you don't
want to join?

ME: Is there free daycare?

COOL DUDE: Unfortunately, no.
And the health insurance is terrible.

ME: Then I'll have to pass.

COOL DUDE. Okay. Obliviate.

It goes like that for days until we finally agree to meet briefly this weekend to say we did before quitting the website. This works out well for me since Brad is stepping up and taking Charlotte for her first overnight with him. I'm nervous as all get out about it, but I've been working on my separation anxiety since she started daycare. She's been fine; I've been the one freaking out when I leave her. Spending time with her dad will be good for them both. They need to bond more than they have.

I'm still pining for Jude. I can't help it. Every Friday, I approach the store with a wish that I'll find him leaning against the door, ready to tell me I'm late, and he'll be surprised and disappointed that Charlotte's not with me but at daycare. But every Friday, nobody is waiting by the door of my store, and my heart craters for the rest of the day.

I still daydream about our time at the premiere, the party afterward, and how easy it was between us, even though we weren't really a couple. It felt like we were for a few hours, and it was beautiful. And the kiss... the kiss is bittersweet. It was the most amazing thing and the worst thing ever at the same time.

My phone rings in the middle of my fantasizing about our kiss, and when I check the phone screen, it's Jude. *It's fucking Jude. Oh my God. It's Jude.*

Do I answer? Do I let it go to voicemail? If I answer, what do I say? How do I sound? Mad? Aloof? Busy? *Shit. Shit. Shit. Fuck it.*

"Hello?" I try not to sound too eager.

"Ren, I didn't think you were going to answer for a minute there."

"Yeah, I almost didn't."

"Fair enough. How are you? How is Charlie?"

"Charlie... I mean, Charlotte is good. She's at daycare today."

"Daycare? Oh wow. That's a massive change for you guys, huh? How does she like it? And how are you doing without her during the day?"

Of course, he knows I'd be climbing the walls without her. Damn him for being so thoughtful.

"She's doing great there. She's game for anything, though. I'm the one with separation anxiety. What do you want, Jude?" I can't keep the impatience out of my voice. The longer we talk, the more my defenses fall down, and I can't fall back to how we were. It's impossible. He's quiet for a second before answering.

"I wanted to see if you were available to get together this weekend to talk. There are some things I need to say to you, and I need to say them in person."

"Jude... I don't know..."

"Ren. After almost eleven years, please just give me a few more minutes."

Damn it. Him and his reasonable request. Am I being unfair? He's right. After so many years as friends, the least I can do is give him a little more time. It will be excruciating and the most painful thing I ever do, but I can prepare myself for it at least.

"Fine, Jude. I'll meet up with you."

"Thank you. I appreciate it."

We make arrangements to meet at the same place I'm meeting Cool Dude. If I meet Jude beforehand, I'll have a reason to keep my shit together for the second meeting. That makes sense, right? If anything, it gives me a goal to get through the Jude talk.

Both conversations are going to have my head spinning, I'm sure. I almost wish Cool Dude was a date and not a 'nice-to-know-you goodbye.' While we connected on many things, my heart isn't in it to try for anything more with him. My emotions are way too fragile to even think about starting another relationship. To try now wouldn't be fair to anyone involved, especially them.

So, Saturday is going to be a big day for good-byes for me. Awesome. Hopefully, after this weekend and all the pain involved, I can get on with my life, however that will look without Jude. The thought of it makes my heart heavy, and my hand goes to my chest to try to calm down, and I notice my hands are shaking. I don't know if I'm nervous, excited, relieved, or just plain old anxious, but I don't like it. It's probably all of the above. I have to admit, I'm a freaking hot mess.

The sooner I can get all of this behind me, the better.

thirty-nine

SORRY

JUDE

s soon as I see Ren when I walk into the fake Irish pub that has witnessed so many insane moments lately, my throat tightens, and my palms start sweating. This is probably the biggest night of my life, and I'm a nervous fucking wreck. I need to be so careful with my words, and I am not one to be cautious, ever. I usually say whatever pops into my damn head, and that will not work in my favor tonight. *This has to be perfect.*

She looks fantastic, with her red curls cascading down her back. My fingers itch to run through them. She's studying something on her phone, and I could stand here and watch her all evening. I never tire of staring at her. She puts the phone down and glances around, and finally spots me, still at the entrance, watching her. She gives a small wave and a half-smile that rapidly fades as she catches herself. That makes my heart skip. She's not happy to see me. That's clear. I need to get this right.

I take the seat across from her, shifting uncomfortably. It's hard to be comfortable when the person you're sitting with doesn't want you there. I take a deep breath, trying to build up my nerve. I gave myself a pep talk in the car before coming in, much to the amusement of a couple of teenagers in the parking lot, but that momentum took off as soon as I walked in and saw her.

"So, how have you been?" I ask, my voice a little shaky through my nervous half-laugh. That's a good opening question, right? *Fuck. I'm screwing this up already.*

"Fine."

She doesn't elaborate or ask how I'm doing. And she's still not meeting my eyes. How the fuck am I supposed to do this if she's not receptive at all? This is like trying to play water polo with my hands tied behind my back and wearing cement boots. *Jesus.*

"Good. Good. I'm fine too, thanks."

She lifts her gaze and glares at me, but at least I got her to make eye contact with me. That's all I wanted. I smile, and her lips twitch ever so slightly, and she quickly looks down at her hands on the table.

"Please say what you wanted to say, Jude. I'm meeting someone here shortly." Her voice is flat, lacking all emotion, and her words stab me right in the fucking heart.

She's meeting somebody else tonight? Holy shit.

I hesitate. Questioning my intentions and my options. I came here to clear the air. To tell her how I truly feel about her, regardless of how she reacts to it, I need to get it off my chest or go to my grave with regret for never telling her. I don't want to do that.

"About New Year's Eve." It's somewhere to start. She lifts an eyebrow but continues to rip small pieces of the napkin she's holding into tiny bits. "I need to explain what happened because I think there's been a gargantuan misunderstanding between us."

"A misunderstanding?" She's doubtful. I get it.

"Yes. I misunderstood everything, Ren. I fucked up. I fucked everything up."

"Go on."

Okay. This is good. She's at least going to listen.

"When I kissed you, I thought I was taking advantage of you being tipsy. I thought I crossed a line between us that should never be crossed, and you would regret it and hate me for it when you sobered up. When I said I was sorry, I didn't mean I was sorry for kissing you. I was trying to apologize for taking advantage of you and the situation."

I take off my hat and run a shaky hand through my hair. I think I'm doing okay. Fuck if I know, but I think I'm doing alright. *Jesus, this is nerve-racking.* A waitress comes by, and I order a beer.

"So, you weren't sorry for kissing me?" I can't read her face. She's wary and cautious, but she's covering it well. I don't blame her.

"Are you fucking kidding me? No way. That was the best kiss I ever had the privilege of being involved with." I instinctively reach out for her hands, and she doesn't pull away. *She doesn't fucking pull away, and her skin feels divine.* "Ren. I thought you only thought of me as a friend. A buddy. A pal. Never somebody you'd want to be romantically entangled with. So, when I kissed you, I was mortified I ruined even that, let alone any chance to be more."

"Romantically entangled?" She chuckles, still looking at our joined hands with a small smile playing on her lips. "What is this, Melrose Place?"

"You have to admit, this sounds like it would make a great episode."

She nods her head from side to side, considering. "I guess."

She still hasn't responded to what I've said. Not directly, anyway. I give her hands a squeeze, pulling her attention back to the matter at hand.

"Ren, if I thought for a second you felt about me the way I feel about you, I would never have apologized for kissing you. In fact, I would still be kissing you."

She squeezes my hand back, and that's got to be a good thing.

"What makes or made you think I don't?" There's a challenge in her question I don't understand. Was I supposed to see some sort of sign from her? If so, I totally missed it.

"Seriously?" Now I'm bewildered. "Ren, you made me sign up for a fucking dating website. There isn't a more obvious sign you don't want to date me than that."

She pulls her hands from mine and buries her face in them, groaning.

"Oh my God. What a freaking nightmare that was."

"Speak for yourself. I did okay on there."

"What, with what's-her-name? Rabbit?"

"Bunny. And I'll have you know she figured out how I felt about you as soon as she saw us together. That's why our date ended early that night."

She drops her hands from her face onto the table, incredulous. "Really? Wow. I'm now Team Bunny. She can have my pink fur hat."

"So, does this mean you forgive my complete and utter lunacy on New Year's?" We're joking, but I need to know this is fixed. I need to know what she's thinking.

Grabbing my hands again, she says, "Yes, Jude. I forgive you. And thank you for explaining what happened. When I thought you regretted kissing me for me, I was utterly devastated. I felt we were really connecting that evening, and when you apologized, I was so deeply hurt I couldn't stand it. I had to leave. I couldn't face you anymore after that. I was humiliated." She glances down at our hands, sadness filling her eyes as she recalls the evening. My stomach churns, knowing how badly I hurt her without realizing it.

"Jesus, Ren. I am so sorry I hurt you like that." Now I can't meet her eyes. I knew I'd hurt her, but I didn't know how much. And hearing the magnitude of it breaks something in me. Something I didn't think I had left to break. "I understand if you want nothing more to do with me after that, Ren. *I'm just glad you let me explain myself and tell you what I was thinking that night.* I am so sorry about the whole thing."

She leans across the table, cupping a hand on my cheek and her touch is like a soothing balm for my soul.

"Jude, I wasn't saying that to make you feel worse. I was just telling you what I went through."

I close my eyes and lean into her hand, feeling its warmth and reveling in her touch and her words. *This is happening. This is fucking happening. Is this fucking happening?*

"Does this mean you're feeling the same way about me...?" I can't believe I just came out and asked that, but I need to fucking know where we are in this. I'm not dealing with my imagination anymore. I want to hear these things from the source.

"If you mean falling head over heels, then yeah, I'm feeling the same way." Her smile is so sweet it hits me right in my soul.

My jaw drops, and I have to physically shut it again with my hand.

"Are you serious right now? Because if you're fucking with me, I might just have to run into Fairfax traffic."

"Jude, I'm serious." She's full-blown laughing now, and it's the most outstanding sound in the fucking universe.

"Good. I was a little worried, not gonna lie."

Ren gets serious suddenly, and I worry now that she's played a cruel joke. All of this was for a laugh at my expense. Probably for fucking up so badly on New Year's. I can't believe Ren would do that though. That's not like her at all.

"I am worried too, Jude." She starts to wring her hands, and my stomach clenches in fear. This could be turning all wrong. "I worry because you're not exactly known as the Relationship Guy, you know? I don't want to just be an experiment or something for you. I've never seen you serious for anyone before."

I nod. She's right. This is all new to me, but that doesn't mean it isn't real.

"I understand your fear, believe me. I'm the first to admit that I'm scared too. I'm going to need your patience through this to help me be what you need."

She sighs a little, her eyes getting watery. *Shit.* Did I say the wrong thing again?

"Jude. That is so damned sweet." She grabs my hands again. "I love that you don't even know when you're being so amazing. The great thing about a relationship is that each of us helps the other person be better, so no problem on the patience, if you'll do the same for me."

"Of course." This is going too well. I feel like lightning is going to strike or something, or some other massive calamity is going to fall upon us since we're both finally happy. I hope I'm wrong. I can only keep my fingers crossed for so long.

She glances at her phone. "Shit, I'm meeting someone in a few minutes, but it's only for a second to say hello and goodbye. Can I kick you out of the booth for a little while so they can come and go?"

"Come and go?" I lift a brow and can't help the smirk that accompanies it. She just tossed a softball right into the fucking strike zone. I can't help I knocked it out of the park.

"Jude. Please." She's laughing, though, and the flush between her freckles is so attractive I want to kiss every single one.

"Fine. I'll be at the bar if you need me." I slide

out of my seat but point a playful warning finger at her. "No funny business. I'm watching."

"Okay, okay. Get lost." She shoos me away with exaggerated arm swings.

This is going to be good.

Well, this has been an interesting turn of events. How could the explanation for all that hurt be so simple? And how could something so simple cause so much pain? And now it hurts to know that we could have fixed it all right there if we just would have said something about how we felt. We were both so afraid of ruining the friendship; we did just that by denying our stronger feelings for each other. It's crazy.

I study Jude at the bar, his back to me, and it's a rather stunning view if I do say so. He's wearing the cowboy hat that we picked out at the Santa Monica Pier, and God damn, does it look good on him. I'm excited that I'm actually allowed to think these thoughts about him now. Not that I needed permission before, but at least now I'm not riddled with guilt about our friendship because of it.

Checking my phone, Cool Dude should be here any minute now. I'm kind of nervous about meeting him but anxious to get it over with so I can go back to spending time with Jude. We have a few weeks to make up for being apart like we were. The bar is getting crowded since a band is scheduled tonight in the attached event room. I keep glancing at the entrance every time someone comes in so I can catch sight of him as soon as he arrives. I am kind of dying to know what he looks like.

Jude comes back to the table and hands me a drink refill, and he's got an odd expression on his face. I can't tell what he's thinking, but he's amused as usual.

"Are you sure I can't interest you in joining the Illuminati? I think you'd be a great fit."

I don't think I hear him correctly.

"What?"

"I have those brochures I told you about in my car; I can grab you one." He sits down, a huge grin spreading across his smug face.

"You? You're...?" I am completely stunned and speechless. I did not see this coming.

"The only guy in here wearing a hat...?" *And holy crap, he's right.*

"You're Cool Dude?"

He starts laughing, "CD13978 in the flesh. Is that what you called me? Cool Dude? I should be flattered, I guess."

"Oh my God, Jude. You're Cool Dude!" I'm still in shock. I remember thinking it might be him initially, but I didn't think it would ever really be him, never in my wildest dreams.

"I mean, it's not the most original nickname, but it's appropriate, so I accept."

"Well, what did you call me? If anything?"

"You're Catfish," he chuckles as if to an inside joke and shakes his head, and there's that adorable blush again. *Damn.*

"Why Catfish? That's an odd name." That is weird. I am dying to know where that crazy name came from. And how it applies to me at all.

"Because you were too perfect to be true. I mean, come on. *'May your face be shiny?'* That's pure Tolkien comedy gold right there. I thought for sure you were a nerd-programmed AI."

"When did you know it was me?" This is utter madness. I can't believe the damned site got it right. I might have to write a glowing review and testimonial.

"Not until you said you were meeting someone after our talk because I was doing the same. It all clicked into place for me then. But I didn't know how the talk would go, so I was hedging my bets on revealing myself depending on whether it went badly. Lucky for me, it went well."

"Well, lucky for me too. But I'm trying to

remember all that we chatted about. We had some great conversations. I might miss them."

"We could keep up the dating site charade...it could be kind of kinky." His smile turns wicked, and he gives me a devious wink. Something deep in my spine tingles.

The noise in the bar is rising, and it's getting to where we need to raise our voices to be heard over the din. People are also beginning to give Jude sideways glances, so I think he's about to be recognized.

I lean across the table and get close to his ear, my lips barely brushing his skin.

"Want to get out of here? I think you're about to be swarmed."

He turns his head to me and catches my lips with his. I wasn't expecting a kiss right here in the bar, but his mouth takes mine, a hand rising to brush my cheek, and I can't do anything but give in to it. The sensation of his lips brushing softly against mine and then pressing harder little by little throws me into a tailspin. He pulls away slowly, heavy-lidded eyes studying me. He looks almost half asleep.

"You okay there?" I smile, still feeling the warmth of his mouth on mine. *It's delicious.*

"Let's go." He grabs my hand, pulling me behind him quickly to the parking lot.

When we reach his car, I lean back against the passenger side door, and he places his hands on either side of me. The streetlamps cast a yellow hue on the night, deepening the contrast of the shadows around us. I snake my hands around his waist, finally feeling that incredible six-pack I noticed along the way, and it feels just as defined as I thought it would.

He lets out a small gasp, and his stomach muscles tense as my fingertips graze his skin. The sound is one of the sexiest things I've ever heard. He leans his head down to mine, kissing my forehead, then my nose, then my chin, and then back up to my mouth. He kisses me gently at first, then becomes more possessive and passionate. I pull on him to get closer, but he's still not leaning into me like I want him to. I want to feel his whole body against me. I arch a little to meet him halfway, and he pulls away.

"Nope. Cool your jets there, Ren." He smiles, and this time it's not wicked at all; it's sweet and vulnerable. He's definitely got my attention.

"What's wrong?" I thought for sure this would be exactly where this would head. I mean, this is Jude. "Did I do something?"

"No. No. Not at all. My God, no. I want to do this right. You are now my first girlfriend in a very, very long time. I need to relearn how to do all of this. And I'll need your help with that. As much as I'd love to get into your pants right now, and believe me, I *really* want to get into your pants, I don't want that to be what we're all about."

I just fell in love with Jude Lockwood. I fell in love with my best friend and internet pen pal, Jude Lockwood, in a cheesy pseudo-Irish Pub parking lot. This reinforces for me that he has changed. Maybe the two of us really can work in a romantic relationship. He seems to have his priorities in order for a change. I'm still completely nervous about it, but maybe I don't need to be.

I must take too long to respond because he suddenly looks distraught.

"That's okay, isn't it? To take things slowly between us?" The worried crease on his brow is so precious I just want to hug him, so I do. I pull him so close and so tight it's hard for him to breathe.

"Yes. It's perfectly okay."

"Cool, then please stop trying to strangle me." He pries himself out of my death grip around him while fake coughing. He reaches behind me to open the car door for me with a hopeful expression. "Let's go hit the Pier, and people watch. That would make a good first date, right?"

This man. I want to melt into a puddle in this parking lot. "Yes, that would be a fantastic first date."

I'm going on a freaking date with Jude Lockwood.

forty-one

WILD CHILD

JUDE

The drive to the pier is electric, and we hold hands the entire time as we play our old license plate game on the way. The new combination of our long friendship and this unfamiliar level of involvement is exhilarating. While most of it feels like a natural blending of the two, some of it is awkward, and I worry I'm going about this all wrong. I don't know what the fuck I'm doing, and with how devastating New Year's Eve was, I'm afraid anything I say could ruin it instantly. Ren seems happy with how things are going, so I need to chill the fuck out and stop overthinking.

To even consider this kind of relationship could be a possibility between us just a month ago was pure folly. But here I am, holding Ren's hand, on our way to our first date. It's surreal. I'd pinch myself, but I don't have a free hand. Add to everything the fact that she is Catfish, who I was more honest with than myself sometimes, and this couldn't be more perfect. The magnitude of how important this relationship is could overwhelm me if I let it. And not only with Ren, but with Charlie too. It's not just the two of us, we are now a trio, and the thought fills me up with emotions I don't know the names of yet, but they are the most amazing feelings I've ever experienced.

And I must seriously have it bad if I turned down being intimate with Ren. *Jesus Christ.* I may need to rethink that part. Now that this is a thing, I don't know if I'll be able to keep my hands off of her. It sounded all admirable and noble in my head when I said it, but I don't know if I'm going to be able to live up to it. She's too beautiful to not want my hands all over her. *Fucking hell.*

When we arrive at the pier, the atmosphere is different somehow. Things were different last time we were here, but those changes are now officially cemented. The midway is closed at this time of night, but the boardwalk is always open, so we walk. Actually, we *stroll*, leisurely taking our time as we meander around the park, making up Life Stories for the people we pass by. Ren is amazingly good at this.

We spot a couple, probably not much younger than us, pushing a stroller. The mother looks especially haggard.

"Their baby has a bad case of colic, and the only

way it will sleep is if they come out here and walk it every night."

I shake my head.

"That's too obvious. I think you're slipping."

"Oh, but I wasn't done. The baby in the stroller isn't theirs; it was switched at birth with their perfectly happy baby who falls asleep like clockwork without any help and then stays asleep all night. They suspect they've been cursed but truly have no idea what they're missing." I didn't think you could giggle wickedly, but Ren pulls it off.

"Damn, that's harsh. Those poor people. Should we tell them?"

"Oh, no. Never tell people what they're missing." She's dead serious, and I want to kiss her all over her freckled face. "That would be cruel and unusual."

The breeze picks up, and Ren shivers.

"Don't you own any jackets?" I joke, taking mine off and helping her into it. "This chivalry thing only goes so far. I'm beginning to think it's a conspiracy to steal my clothing piece by piece."

"What's this?" She grabs my left arm and turns it, palm up, running a finger along the new forearm tattoo I got a couple weeks ago. It's a wide outline drawing of Charlie's stuffed donkey.

"Oh, just something I got a little bit ago." Like an idiot, I hadn't considered Ren would see it. It might be too much, too soon.

"Jude, that's Charlie's donkey." Her fingers trace

the ink outline, and the sensation of electricity skims across my heart. "It's unmistakable with that wonky eye." She glances up at me, her bright eyes questioning. "You got Charlie's donkey tattooed on your arm?"

I swallow hard. I didn't want to show her this yet. I was right. It's too soon. And I can tell she's freaking out a little bit. *Shit.* I stumble with my explanation but keep it honest. I need to always be honest with Ren from now on.

"Well, yeah. After our failed coloring experiment, I thought I'd give her something to practice on." I shrug, knowing how lame that sounded. It is what it is, though. "But, it's also in my final free spot. I've been saving it for something special like this. It's prime real estate since it's what I see the most when I hold my guitar to play. So, every time I'm on stage, I'll think of her."

Her eyes fill with tears, and I don't know what the fuck I just did to make her cry. *Jesus Christ, I suck at this.* I am the worst boyfriend in the history of boyfriends.

"Jude, you didn't even know if we would work out our problems..." She seems confused. A tear slides down her cheek, and I quickly wipe it away, thankful for an excuse to touch her. This entire situation is confusing me.

"And? This wasn't about you and me. This was about Charlie and me. I wanted something to remind me of her." I shake my head. "I don't understand why you're crying, Ren. What did I do?"

She throws her arms around my neck and pulls me down into a kiss, which really fucking confuses me more, but I'll go along with this part happily. I don't know what I did to deserve this level of affection being thrown at me, but whatever it is, I'm going to keep doing it.

Pulling away from me, she frames my face with her hands, searching my eyes for God only knows what. I hope I have whatever it is she's looking for.

"For a super-intelligent guy, you are fucking dumb, dude." She shakes her head with a smile and a sigh. "How do you not understand that this tattoo is the sweetest thing in the whole God-damned world? Jesus, I want to jump your bones right now."

I lift a brow.

"So sweet that you're calling me Jesus now? I don't know. I think Cool Dude was more fitting..."

She attacks my mouth again with hers, and the joy filling me up, knowing I inadvertently made her want me, is so satisfying it's hard not to smile while I'm kissing her. I'm thinking maybe I should rethink the 'taking it slow' speech I gave earlier because that's starting to become a problem for me.

A phone starts ringing somewhere around us, and Ren pulls away to reach into her purse.

"Hold that thought. Shit. It's Brad."

She takes the call, turning away, and I replay the

entire evening that has led us to where we are now, on a date at the pier, kissing on the boardwalk. I shove my hands into my jeans pockets and turn to gaze at the ocean, forbidding in the moonless dark, and realize that I feel like a whole person. I don't think I realized how incomplete I was before.

"We need to go pick up Charlotte," Ren says behind me, her voice anxious. "She must be cutting another tooth or something. He can't get her to stop crying."

I smile, taking her under an arm and heading back to the car.

"This sounds like a job for the Baby Whisperer."

W hat a whirlwind the last couple of weeks have been. Ever since Jude and I admitted our true feelings, it's been like we're living in a fairy tale. I don't see much of him since the band is wrapping up the new album in the studio, but we have a constant text conversation all day long. It sometimes calls back to our anonymous internet chats, and the topics can get serious, but mostly its sarcastic banter back and forth. I find myself laughing out loud at something he's said at least three times a day. One thing is for sure: this relationship will never be boring.

> BIGDICK69: Hey. How was
> dropping off Charlie this morning?
> Is that tooth still bothering her?

Jude. Oh my God. I can't even.

> ME: Did you change your name on my phone again?

BIGDICK69: By your avoidance of my question, I will assume Charlie is fine. And, maybe.

I change it to something more fitting.

> ME: No worries. I've corrected it. How is the final mixing going? Almost done?

JUDE THE PRUDE: NOOOOOO. WHAT DID YOU CHANGE IT TO? And, tremendous and yes.

> ME: I need some secrets. You already know me too well. Well, almost…

JUDE THE PRUDE: Damnit woman. Tell me. BTW, Art is taking Charlie this weekend. I have a surprise for you. Maybe. Only if you tell me my new name.

Shit. Now I want to know what the surprise is; it sounds intriguing. I can't stop giggling as I take a screenshot of my phone and send it.

> JUDE THE PRUDE: Ha. We'll just see about that.

ME: Okay… what's the surprise
then? I gave you what you wanted.

JUDE THE PRUDE: I didn't say I'd
tell you the surprise, only that you'd
get it. And, gave me what I wanted?
Woman, you have no idea. 😒

Shoot. Him and his wordplay. I can never win
against him when it comes to that. He's too slippery
and precise at the same time. He should have been a
lawyer, constantly reciting the fine print. He probably reads Terms of Service agreements.

ME: Oh, I have ideas...

JUDE THE PRUDE: Ren… Don't do
this to me. I'm begging you.

ME: Begging might be involved. If
you're good. And you better be
good.

JUDE THE PRUDE:
Fuuuuuuuuuuuck.

ME: 😊 And you better get back to
your record.

JUDE THE PRUDE: I severely
dislike you right now.

ME: No, you don't.

JUDE THE PRUDE: I know. Quite the opposite.

It goes like this all day, every day, flirting like mad until the weekend arrives. I still have no clue where we are going or what we're doing, but I was told to pack an overnight bag. So, whatever this surprise is, it involves a sleepover. I like the sound of that.

When Jude arrives to pick me up, he's leaning on the door frame, and when I open the door, I am instantly swept up into a kiss and pressed against the wall in the foyer. I barely catch my breath before his mouth is on my neck, and his hands are in my hair.

"Hello to you too," I giggle. Though, I think I like his version of a greeting better. He releases me, and I regret saying anything. That felt so good.

"Sorry, I've missed you." He's leaning with his hands on either side of me, trying to catch his breath. "And your texts are fucking torturous."

I place a palm on his chest, his heartbeat racing underneath my fingers.

"Well, tell me the surprise, and I'll stop the torture." I lick my lips and run a finger down his chest to his waist, his muscles twitching as I go.

He squeezes his eyes shut and exhales. Biting his bottom lip, he pushes off the wall. Damn, that's hot. This torture goes both ways.

"Right. Let's go." He finds my overnight bag and takes it out to the car as I lock up the house.

As I head to the car, I skip a little and say, "We're going on an adventure!"

"That confirms it. You are totally a nerd AI." The grin spreading on his face is so full of...everything, I almost lose my footing. I am in danger of over-heating merely looking at him. I don't know how I'm going to get through this mysterious evening.

I squeal and gasp when we pull up to the Hotel Casa del Mar. I have always wanted to eat or stay here. It is so beautiful, and I'm sure the views of the ocean are amazing.

"Jude. I'm not dressed for this." I glance down at my ripped jeans, then over to his. "And neither are you. You didn't tell me to dress up or pack anything formal." I sound a little too tightly wound, and I definitely feel that way.

He laughs and rubs my thigh, pulling on a thread from one of the ripped areas of my jeans.

"Don't worry, commoner, we'll be eating en suite this evening." He wiggles his eyebrows suggestively, and the super-heavy French accent he uses makes me chuckle.

We check in, and when we get to our suite with

an absolutely stunning ocean view, my breath catches. It's so beautiful and better than I pictured in my head. We can see the Santa Monica Pier from our room, and there's even a telescope to get a better look.

Jude comes up behind me while I'm leaning over the telescope, sliding his hands around my waist under my shirt, his fingers skimming across my stomach. I jump from being ticklish with a squeak but turn to face him. He hooks his thumbs through my belt loops and pulls me against him, looking down at me with so much desire and heat in his eyes that I could strip for him right here and now.

"What do you think?" He slips his hands around me and up my back, then down my spine, sending teasing shivers through my entire body.

"I can't."

"You can't, what?" His brows draw together in confusion.

"I can't think. Brain. Broken."

"Uh oh, there's a glitch in the matrix, huh?" He runs his tongue along the shell of my ear, and I can't help the gasp that escapes my lips.

"Must be some wires crossed somewhere..." I lean into him, find his collarbone, and lick, then graze it with my teeth. If he's not going to play fair, neither am I.

He groans and pulls me harder against him. His solid muscles are taught and possessive as he holds me, his fingers exploring wherever they can reach. His hand is in my hair again, and we're devouring each other's mouths when there's a knock at the door.

"Fuck. That must be our dinner." We're both panting and disheveled, and neither of us moves to answer it. "I hereby renounce my admiration of punctuality and wish a pox on the house of anyone who is ever on time for anything ever again."

"Damn, you could just say you're horny and don't want to answer the door." I slap his chest lightly and move around him to let whoever it is in with our food.

"Point taken."

Room service enters with a cart loaded with food and proceed to plate our food for us. Then a bottle of champagne is opened and poured, and I give Jude a questioning glance. They leave the cart, which still has dessert on it, and after Jude tips them, they exit.

"What's the champagne for? Are we celebrating something?" I'm racking my brain, trying to think if this is a special day that I've forgotten or something. I don't think it is, but I've not been thinking very clearly lately.

Jude raises his glass to mine.

"We officially finished the record today, so I thought a little bubbly was in order to mark the occasion."

"Shouldn't you be celebrating with Ryan and Matt, though?"

He shrugs with a smirk.

"They're hanging out with their women, and I wanted to hang with mine."

"Oh, I'm your woman, huh?"

"Damn straight." He leans over and pecks my cheek. How he can go from a sex-crazed mouth devourer to a sweet and vulnerable cheek kisser is astounding, and I love that about him. I love how open he is about who he really is and doesn't give a damn what anybody thinks about it.

"Just don't call me your 'Old Lady.'"

He gets a look on his face like he's about to make a sarcastic comment about me being older than him, even biting his lip to hold it back. *Damn that's sexy.*

"What? I didn't say anything." He's trying to look all innocent but failing miserably.

"You didn't have to. We share a brain, remember?"

He chuckles. "Whatever you say, Old Lady."

I throw a grape tomato from my salad at him, but he ducks out of the way. *He's lucky he's cute.*

When we finish our meal, we sit and watch the sunset, the pier midway silhouetted against it, and it's a strange full-circle moment. We spent a lot of time as young friends out on that pier in the early days of knowing each other. We had nothing but dreams in front of us back then. And now here we are, overlooking that same pier from a hotel suite that probably costs more for one night than both of our rents back then combined. And we're looking at it as boyfriend and girlfriend, and me now as a mother.

"Can I afford your thoughts yet?" He reaches over and brushes my hair off my shoulder. His touch is always soothing, no matter how slight it may be.

"For you, they're free today." I smile. "I was just thinking about how far we've come from our early days hanging out at the pier. I never could have imagined we'd end up here."

"Me neither." His face grows contemplative.

"I know you're way out of my price range, but any discounts on your thoughts?"

"I'll take an I.O.U. This time. It's been a long, strange trip, but it's been worth it to end up here with you. I only wish we'd done this sooner, but if we had, you wouldn't have Charlie, and that's not an option, so it has been worth it to wait and get here only now." He takes in a long rush of air and laughs. "You know what I mean." His cheeks are heating, and I can't think of anyone more perfect than him at this moment.

I trace the tattoo on his forearm, and my eyes get misty, knowing just how much he loves my daughter. He would and has done anything for her that she needs, and I know he will always be there for her no matter what. The way he has handled Brad, first getting him to be involved in Charlotte's life in the first place and then being a sort of mentor to him in her care, has been the single best thing anyone has ever done for us. And it will have rippling effects throughout the rest of our lives that he can't even comprehend.

"What do you say we take dessert to the bedroom?" He stares at me seductively, then grabs a tray off of the cart and whisks it into the bedroom before I can even see what's on it. I don't hesitate and jump up to follow him, champagne in hand, anxious for the next part of the evening to commence.

When I enter the bedroom, I notice the tray on the bed has a large container of strawberries and a bowl of dipping chocolate. This could get interesting. And I have a fun surprise for him, too.

He's taken his shoes off, so I do the same, lining mine up next to his under the window. When I turn to face him, the sunset shines through the windows and onto his face, highlighting the dark red in his hair. He almost glows in the warm light and is so beautiful; I've never seen him like this before. My heart stutters, and my stomach flips in anticipation of what's ahead.

I push through my sudden shyness and step up to him, placing a palm on his cheek and studying his intense gray eyes examining mine. This is the point of no return. If we stopped now, we might still be able to salvage a friendship out of whatever remained between us, but anything more, and we're in it completely. I can see he understands the huge risk we're taking now, but it's worth it.

"Ren?" He's asking if I want to go any further, wanting to be sure.

"Shut up." I run my hand through his hair and grab the back of his neck, pulling him down and into an answering kiss that can leave no doubt about what I feel. I want this as much as he does, if not more.

Our hands become frenetic, grabbing and clawing at each other's clothes to get them off as soon as possible until we stand before each other in our underwear. This is the most exposed we've ever been to each other, and I'm self-conscious, positioning my arms to cover myself as much as possible. The sunset that was beautiful a moment ago is now too bright and exposes all of my faults and imperfections.

"Stop it. Don't you dare hide yourself from me." He quirks a small smile and steps up to me, pulling my arms away and around him. "Do you know what I've gone through to finally see this gloriousness? Quite a lot, I tell you. And fuck, it was worth it. Rena Scott, you are simply ravishing. I want to see all of you."

My mouth goes dry, and all of the air seems to have left the room. His words are perfect. Exactly what I needed to hear to calm my nerves. When he kisses me again, I melt into him, our bare skin touching for the first time, sending thunder waves through my veins and weakening my knees. Before they can buckle, Jude walks me backward to the bed, never breaking our kiss and deftly removing my bra on the way. I'm reminded of how much more experienced he is at this than I am, and I get nervous again as self-doubt creeps in. Am I going to measure up? I'm sure he's had some wild and fantastic sex, and I just...haven't. I've had mediocre sex. We are not on the same level.

He must sense my apprehension because he pulls back.

"Ren? What is it? What's wrong?" The concern in his eyes makes me want to curl up in a ball. It's almost as though his worry magnifies my doubts.

I try to shake my head to tell him it's nothing, but my tears betray me. Fucking tears.

"It's nothing. I'm fine." I try to say confidently, but it comes out as a whisper. I want to cover myself up all over again. This is crazy.

"Rena. Talk to me, please. If we need to stop, we can stop. Just say the word." He brushes my jawline with his thumbs, the callouses giving me goosebumps.

"I don't want to stop, Jude." I lean into his hand and close my eyes. "I just worry that I won't meet whatever standard you're used to when it --"

His mouth crashes into mine before I can finish, our teeth clashing and our tongues dancing as he pulls me against him. The kiss morphs into the most gentle and barest of touches, and the transition leaves me wanting more. But he leans away from me, making sure he has my attention.

"Don't, Ren. Don't ever do that." He shakes his head fervently. "Don't you ever compare yourself to anything or anyone. You are what I want. You are enough. You are everything to me."

I nod because I have no more words. He gently lowers me to the bed, settling over me, careful not to disturb the tray.

His hands sweep across my skin, leaving bliss in their wake, while his tongue expertly finds and worships every erogenous zone on my body and even creates some new ones, I think. As he takes a breast into his mouth, I wrap my legs around him, rocking into him, my back arching. He groans as he sucks on the nipple, making it taught, and I think it's the perfect time for my surprise.

"Duuuude..." I moan breathily, my eyes closed, and put as much ecstasy into the word as I can.

He freezes, not moving a muscle, and I hold my breath, wondering if he's forgotten the whole 'I say 'dude' during sex' conversation. Shit. He forgot. I look like a God-damned idiot. I bite the inside of my cheek, trying to control my own laughter because I think it's fucking hilarious.

His shoulders are starting to shake, and a laugh erupts in his chest so deep it's vibrating against my stomach. Then he lets the laughter loose, burying his face into my side. I join him, relieved that he remembered. I was starting to get worried.

"Oh my God, Ren," he chokes out between laughs, "that was perfection." He's laughing so hard now he's wiping at his eyes, and I'm right there with him. He moves to put his weight on one elbow and accidentally pushes on the tray. In his attempt to avoid toppling the contents onto the bed, he falls onto the tray; the side of his head gets dipped in chocolate, and the strawberries go flying.

This throws us into further rounds of laughter to the point of tears. I don't think I've ever laughed this hard, and my stomach is starting to hurt. The situation is too surreal and too funny.

"Are you okay?" I catch my breath and try to survey the carnage of the upset tray. It looks as though the mess is limited to just Jude. I wipe some chocolate off his cheekbone with a finger and taste it. It's not bad.

"I'll be fine. I just need to clean up." He starts to push off the bed but hesitates, eyeing me curiously. "Care to join me?"

I arch an eyebrow, considering. The idea is intriguing.

"I think I'd like that."

"Oh, I think you'll like it a lot." He pulls me off

the bed and leads me to the bathroom, where he turns on the showerhead and glances back at me, chocolate dripping from his hair onto his shoulders. I giggle. "Here goes nothing."

He leans down, steps out of his boxers, and looks expectantly at me. While I briefly inspect and appreciate his manhood, I'm captivated by his entire demeanor. The melted chocolate, the smile that I've known for so long but is now so different in the best possible way, this kind and snarky soul in front of me that makes my own weightless on my worst days. This man who makes me feel safe in a world that isn't. This is so much more than sex. I think it's true for him too.

I step out of my panties and take his hand as he leads me into the shower.

"Just so you know, I'm tested regularly and am clean. I've not had sex since my last test. Are you on the pill?"

I cock my head at him, curious.

"When was your last test? And yes, I'm on the pill."

"When I got back from Europe."

"Oh." Wow, that was a long time ago. Well, for him, I'm sure it's a long time. Three months maybe? That's a lifetime in Jude sex years.

As the steam billows around us and the water sprays on our skin, our eyes meet, and nothing else needs to be said. He leans back quickly to get the chocolate out of his hair, and I take advantage of the position, running my fingers down his chest, along his spectacularly defined abs, and along his hip bone, his muscles flexing as I go.

He grabs my wrists and holds them against the shower wall, the cool tiles against my back, as he retakes my mouth, possessing it, taking from me what he wants, what he needs, and I give it. He traces a line of kisses down my neck, grazing my skin with his teeth, sending shudders through me. As I arch into him, he takes a breast into his mouth, his tongue flicking and teasing my sensitive nipple relentlessly until I can't take much more.

He releases one of my wrists and uses that hand to find my center and firmly massage my clit. Rubbing and pressing in circles until I gasp for air and quiver with pulsating waves running through every nerve ending.

I take him in my hand, the smooth skin of his cock exquisite beneath my fingers. He's hard and straining against my touch for more.

He pulls my leg up from behind my knee, opening me up for him, and he slides in slowly, eyes closed, and jaw clenched. Once he sinks in entirely, he lets out a long unsteady breath and opens his eyes to gaze at me. Our eyes never waver as we explore each other's familiar yet strange bodies. Alternating between timid and bold, hesitant and demanding, tender and savage.

The intensity increases as we rock together, our wet skin sliding against each other until we build up to an orgasm that meets the others' and releases. Each of us cries out at the power and strength of the ecstasy and euphoria flowing through us. I can still feel the spasms throbbing around him long after he's spent, and we're frozen in the hot water's spray, trembling and trying to catch our breath.

"Dude," he says roughly with a grin, pressing his forehead to mine, and we both burst into laughter. He pulls me closer, wrapping his arms around me and kissing me deeply. When we separate, he gazes at me long and hard. "I love you, Ren. I think I always have. I've just been blind."

I stare at him, surprise overtaking me. I did not expect that.

"You don't need to say it back to me. I just needed to say it to you. Don't feel obligated..."

"I love you too, Jude." And I do. "I think I always have, too. But you've just been blind."

We both crack up laughing yet again until we calm down enough to kiss. And kiss. And kiss. And more. And more until the water starts to run cold.

We've finished rehearsals for our upcoming headlining tour, and we're pushing heavy with the press stuff Vanessa is making us do. I know it's part of the whole gig, and I didn't use to mind it, but now it's taking me away from Ren and Charlie, and we have such little time left before we leave. This will be my first time on tour with someone waiting for me at home, and I'm not looking forward to it. I'm not worried I'm going to stray or anything like that. I am afraid I'm going to miss them so much I'll up and quit the fucking band when I can't take it anymore. Ren has promised to video chat with Charlie every day, so maybe that will help keep me sane.

We are house shopping in preparation for the new album release and tour. Apparently, Matt and I can no longer live in our duplex because our address got out or some shit, so now there are people camped out in the front yard every day. I've been staying with Ren, but I'm being super careful. With pictures of us together on the internet from the documentary premiere on New Year's Eve, she's had some random weirdos come into her store, asking about me and our relationship. It made her uncomfortable, and I don't blame her. People are fucking scary and can be unhinged. It's something more for me to worry about while I'm on the road, so we are looking for a house with a gate. A solid gate. A gate that cannot be breached. I asked the realtor for a home with a moat, but I guess there aren't any in LA. I'm actually kind of surprised by that because there is some crazy shit here.

We're on the fifth or fiftieth house, I lost count after two, and they're all starting to look the same to me. I'm tempted to let Ren figure this out. She has better taste than I do, anyway.

"This one is a four-bedroom, five-bath, modern architectural home with a three-story atrium in the center, with an adjustable skylight." Theresa, our realtor, rattles off facts and figures about each house, but I think she's just making shit up because she never checks any notes. "This one has a walk-in rain shower and a soaking tub..." I arch an eyebrow at Ren, who bites her lip to keep from laughing. "There's a lap pool and a rooftop deck with a view of the ocean and the pier."

"Hey, I see a gate. Sold." I'm a simple man.

"And, there's a lower level with soundproofing, so it's perfect for a musician if you wanted to build a studio of some sort," Theresa continues. I don't think she heard me just buy the house.

"What's the list price?" Ren is always the pragmatist.

"This one is five point three million, but the seller is very motivated."

"Motivated by money..." I grumble. I'm getting hungry, and I don't like shopping of any kind, to begin with. So, purchasing a big-ticket item like a house on an empty stomach is not going to go well for any of us in this car.

Ren squeezes my fingers as Theresa punches in the code to open the gate to the property, and I squeeze hers back. Once the gate is open and we pull in, Ren's grip on my hand becomes vice-like. Her other hand goes to her throat as the house comes into view, and I think I just bought this house for the second time in one day.

"Jude," she whispers, not taking her eyes off the house. "It's perfect."

I lean over to see what she's seeing, and sure enough, it is perfect. Walls of glass and steel with a ton of natural light pouring in. It's surrounded by banana trees, palms, and other lush green foliage. If there's even a hint of a yard in the back, I'll buy this house a third time.

Ren and I get out of the car and take it in, arms around each other. I can feel her excitement though she's not saying anything. We don't have to step foot inside; this is going to be our first house together. Maybe even our last. She puts her head on my chest, and I hug her tightly to me. This doesn't seem like a big step for us, just the next one. And it's not like we're going to be living together in earnest until I'm home from tour. I just want to know she and Charlie are safe while I'm gone, and Ren agrees.

"I know it's a formality at this point, but we should probably look around the inside for squatters or something," I deadpan. She crushes my waist and jumps up to kiss my cheek before practically skipping to the front door where Theresa is waiting.

I just bought a fucking house.

Three weeks later, we're standing in the same spot in front of the house, holding on to each other for dear life while trying to keep our shit together as we say goodbye. I already said my goodbyes to Charlie, who's in the house with Art, who stopped by to see me off. I have never felt this dread of being apart from someone before, and it's devastating. I feel like I'm going to die. My brain knows this is only temporary, and I'll see them every day in video chats, but it doesn't seem like that will be good enough to keep me sane.

Our foreheads are pressed together, and Ren's tears are flowing so freely I can't stop them all. Seeing her so sad is breaking something inside of me. Letting go of her and turning to get in the car that's been waiting too long will be the hardest thing I've ever done in my life. We just started this. It doesn't seem fair we have to separate right away.

"I will talk to you every day, I swear." I'm trying to be the strong one, but I am not feeling very strong right now. "Take this time to get you and Charlie settled in the house. Have a séance or something to get rid of the ghosts." Ren is convinced the house is haunted because she didn't know the cabinets and drawers were self-closing. I haven't had the heart to tell her it's not.

She nods and sniffles.

"I ordered some sage."

"Good girl." I rub her back, trying desperately to work up the courage to go.

"And I know about the self-closing cupboards and drawers, nimrod."

I throw my head back and howl with laughter. We really do share a brain.

"On that note, I'm going to go." I lift her chin up, taking her and every single freckle on her face in, trying to memorize all of it. "I love you, Ren."

"I know."

She did not just pull a Han Solo on me. Holy shit. She starts giggling.

"Laugh it up, fuzzball," I quip, running my hands through her hair and pulling her into a kiss. I am going to miss this. Her smell, taste, touch, and things that can't translate in a video chat that make her my Ren. I breathe her in one last time, this woman that has completely changed my life, and I turn to go.

epilogue - two months later

MY GIRL TONIGHT

REN

Today is Charlotte's first birthday, and we're getting ready to video chat with Jude. He's on the road between Kansas City and somewhere else and said the reception might be horrible for the call. And sure enough, it keeps getting rejected. This makes me sad. I know Charlotte won't remember this, but it hurts my heart. Jude will miss seeing her on her birthday. He was so excited about it.

"When is the cake?" Pops has asked this question every hour on the hour all day. I love the man, but this is getting out of hand. I sigh.

"After we eat lunch, we'll have cake, Pops. Same answer as last time."

"Fine. Fine. Still can't get hold of Jude?' He eyes my phone as I pass it from hand to hand nervously.

"No. But he said he might be unreachable." I

shrug it off, trying to convince myself and Pops it's not a big deal. "We'll try again later. That's all."

"Maybe he's with another woman and doesn't want you to know, so he's avoiding your calls."

I roll my eyes. My grandfather has been saying stuff like this since Jude left on tour, and it is weirdly helpful in preventing any irrational jealousy that may arise. Something about the way he says it makes it sound so absurd it would never be believable. I love he can do that for me.

"Maybe." I agree with a nod and wipe at Charlotte's chin. "She's a lucky woman, whoever she is."

"How lucky, exactly?" a voice says from behind us. Jude's voice. *Jude's voice.*

I turn, and there he is, in the flesh. I yelp and hand Charlotte to Pops and run to him, launching myself into his arms. He catches me and spins me around, and the feel of his muscular body against mine after months apart is sublime. Charlotte screeches her typical greeting on seeing him too. It must be a Scott women thing.

Jude drops me and grabs Charlotte from Pops, spinning her around the same way he did me, and the screeches turn into belly laughs.

"There's the birthday girl! Look at how big you've gotten in two months. Holy shit."

"Jude." I chastise. He needs to stop swearing around her. She's going to pick it up and start cursing if he's not careful.

"Ude," Charlotte murmurs, running her sticky hands down his face.

Both of our jaws drop open, and we stare at each other.

"She said, 'Jude,'" He is beaming brighter than a lighthouse. "She said, 'Jude.'"

"No. She clearly said, 'dude.'" I put a hand on my hip. I'm messing with him, but it's too fun not to.

"I heard 'rude,'" Pops chimes in with a shrewd smile on his face. "Probably in response to the swearing thing."

I pick up my phone and start recording.

"Say it again, Charlotte," I coax, wanting it recorded not only for posterity but also to clarify what she actually says.

She looks up at Jude; her bright eyes are so full of joy at seeing him in person again after such a long time. My heart swells just watching her. I hold my breath, waiting for her to say something.

"Ude," she repeats and laughs, smacking his cheeks.

"Yup. She totally said, 'Jude.' You got that, right?" I can see his chest puff up with pride from here, and I just fell in love with him all over again. I don't think I've ever felt so much love for a person in my life outside of Charlotte.

He walks over to me, bouncing her on a hip, and gives me a quick kiss.

"Don't worry; she'll say your name soon."

"What? Oh no. She said, 'Mama' last night." I grin at him. I was going to tell him, but Charlotte beat me to it.

"Mama," Charlotte says as if on cue while pulling at a strand of my hair.

"See?"

Instead of being jealous or deflated, 'Jude' wasn't her first word; he gets misty-eyed and nuzzles his face in her neck, making her giggle.

"She's talking."

"She is. And she's copying what we say, so no more swearing."

"Yes, Mama."

"Mama."

After dinner, we take a walk down to the pier while Art watches Charlotte, giving us some time alone. It's nice to walk the boardwalk hand in hand again and people-watch like we love to do.

"Those two are obviously KGB." He points to a couple leaning against a nearby building under a streetlamp, facing away from each other, looking suspicious as all get out.

"Obviously. Go on." I can't stop the smile from spreading on my face. I love this.

"They're preparing to meet with their CIA counterparts, but they really suck at being spies and are too dumb to stand ten feet away in the shadows."

The laugh that comes out of my mouth is accompanied by a very ungraceful snort, and I have to cover my face. I have missed him and his sense of humor so much. I throw my arms around his neck and bury my face in his chest, taking a deep breath to pull all of him into my senses. I want to remember this day. I want this moment to be a core memory of being incandescently happy.

"I'm glad you still find me amusing," he whispers, kissing the side of my head.

"Amusing? Jude, you're freaking hilarious. You always have been. It's one of the things I love most about you." I glance at him, the streetlamps casting sharp shadows. "One of many, many things."

"Oh, really?" He steers me toward the pier again, moving us along. "Tell me about the other things..."

I list about seventy-five things as we walk to the midway and approach the arcade, and he agrees with every one. Of course, he does.

"Yeah yeah, I'm awesome. Let's shake things up and take the Ferris wheel for a spin tonight." He smiles, but he's got an odd glint in his eyes. I don't know what it's about; maybe he's just tired from all the traveling he's done today.

We grab tickets and head to the ride. It's not very crowded, being a weeknight, so we don't have to wait too long. Before we get on, he takes off his jacket and helps me into it.

"Since you're always stealing my jackets, may as well get that part of the evening out of the way now."

I laugh and pull it tighter around me. He's right. I do always forget my jacket when we come here and end up wearing his. After we're locked in and start moving, he puts an arm around me and kisses the top of my head.

"Whatever you do, don't go rifling through my pockets." The corners of his mouth twitch a little; he's obviously trying to hide a smile.

Of course, the first thing I do is start checking the pockets. I can feel something in the inner one, something kind of small and box-like. I reach in, and it is a box. A jewelry box. More specifically, a red leather Cartier ring box.

I gasp and grip the box tighter, afraid to drop it. My eyes dart up to his, dancing with amusement at my reaction. I'm scared to move, and I don't know what to do. He's just sitting there watching me freak out. What is this box? Why am I holding a box? And why does it totally look like a ring box?

"Jude. Do something, please." I glare at him. "I'm freaking out, and I don't want to drop this. Whatever this is."

He finally relents and takes the box from me,

chuckling to himself. I try to sigh in relief, but I don't think any air comes out.

"Do you know how long we've known each other?" It's an odd question.

"It was eleven years on May the 4th."

"That is correct. That was four thousand and thirty-five days ago. Or, if we're using your bad mother's month chart thing, one hundred thirty-two months and seventeen days."

"That's a lot of numbers."

"It is. But it goes to show how long we have been building up to this moment." He opens the box, displaying an absolutely stunning pear-shaped solitaire ring set in platinum. My hand flies to my throat as I'm in awe of its beauty. It takes my breath away. It's simply gorgeous. "This ring here is a culmination of over a decade of friendship, and love, and loyalty, and trust, and all the crazy and beautiful things that make up a lasting relationship. Things you and I have perfected over the years. We always joke we share a brain, but I think we share more than that. We share a heart and maybe even a soul. You made me consider I had a 'person' somewhere just for me. Little did I know you were that person. You're my person. And I want to share the rest of my life with you and Charlie. I want to spoil the fuck out of that kid while you keep her in check with all the morals and stuff. I am not perfect. In fact, I'm extremely flawed, but when I'm around you, I'm the best version of myself I can be. You make me want to be better. For you."

He takes the ring out of the box carefully and clears his throat. I hold my breath, amazed that this is even happening.

"Rena Scott, would you do me the extreme honor of sharing the rest of your life, and Charlie's too, with me? Well, until she's eighteen, then she's on her own."

I have to laugh through the tears of joy streaming down my cheeks.

"Did you come up with all of that on your own? Or did you read it somewhere and memorize it or something?"

"Answer the damn question, Ren. Marry me? Yes or no. It's multiple choice."

He's looking nervous as if he's not sure I'll say yes. How can he be so daft? I would marry him this second if given the opportunity to, and if a Justice of the Peace didn't mind heights.

"Of course, I'll marry you."

He slides the ring on my finger, and it fits perfectly. I barely glance at it, though. I'm too busy kissing my fiancé on a Ferris wheel.

Cheers erupt from the ground, and we pull apart and look down to find Matt and Ryan with their fiancées, and even Pops is there with Charlotte. All of them are clapping and shouting congratulations up to us. I look to Jude, and he shrugs.

"They're family. They wanted to be here for this."

"And now, they're my family too."

"And Charlie's."

"And Charlie's."

He arches an eyebrow at me, questioning my use of the nickname I've fought against for months.

"What? It's growing on me."

"I knew you'd come around to the dark side eventually. Welcome, Soon-to-be-Mrs. Lockwood."

"Soon, huh? What's the rush, Mr. Lockwood?" I can't seem to stop smiling, and I don't care.

"I think eleven years is enough of a wait, don't you?" He pulls me closer and kisses the top of my head.

"It is. But all is well that ends better, and I'm pretty sure this will have been worth it."

-THE END-

barely playlist

S **potify:**https://open.spotify.com/playlist/
1sjChR17fho8ahmUBna2QW?si=
d81d271e184c482f

1. *The White Stripes, We're Going to Be Friends*
2. *Weezer, My Best Friend*
3. *The Hives, Hate To Say I Told You So*
4. *Nickel, Stupid Thing*
5. FINNEAS, *Die Alone*
6. *The Damned, Alone Again, Or*
7. *Local H, Bound For The Floor*
8. Aimee Mann, *Save Me*
9. The Murder City Devils, *Boom Swagger Boom*
10. Azure Ray, *Displaced*
11. Supergrass, *Alright*

12. Suzanne Vega, *Left of Center*
13. *Joey Ramone, Stop Thinking About It*
14. Civil Twilight, *Human*
15. *Nikka Costa, Everybody Got Their Something*
16. *Rosie Thomas, Have You Seen My Love?*
17. *Kris Allen, I Need to Know*
18. Katy Perry, *Roar*
19. Jonas Brothers, *Sucker*
20. *Dishwalla, It's Going To Take Some Time*
21. Kaiser Chiefs, *Ruby*
22. Florence + The Machine, *Breaking Down*
23. Nothing But Thieves, *Real Love Song*
24. *OK Go, Here It Goes Again*
25. Franz Ferdinand, *Take Me Out*
26. *Sam Smith, Not In That Way*
27. Amber Run, *I Found*
28. Royal Blood, *Figure It Out*
29. Ed Sheeran (feat. Ella Mai), *Put It All On Me*
30. *Jann Arden, You Don't Know Me*
31. Stevie Nicks, Dave Grohl, Taylor Hawkins, Rami Jaffee, *You Can't Fix This*
32. Emeli Sandé, *Hurts*
33. Dean Lewis, *7 Minutes*
34. *Royal Blood, Either You Want It*
35. Foo Fighters, *How I Miss You*
36. *Garbage, Beloved Freak*
37. *FINNEAS, I Don't Miss You At All*

38. Cattle & Cane, *7 Hours*
39. Nothing But Thieves, *Sorry*
40. The Walkmen, *Heaven*
41. The Black Keys, *Wild Child*
42. Nothing But Thieves, *Lover, Please Stay*
43. Plain White T's, *Hey There Delilah*

Epilogue: Jon McLaughlin, *My Girl Tonight*

also by amy booker

Near Miss Series

Almost

So Close

Barely

Near Miss Rock Star Collection

Drive Me Wild Series

Ms. Fortune

Ms. Chief

Ms. Lead

Ms. Take

The Mischief Motors Collection

Upcoming Rhapsody Series (2023)

Coda

Reprise

Overture

Waltz

Sustain

All books are stand-alone, but set in the same

universe, so you can pick them up wherever and whenever!

Sign up for my VIP mailing list here! You'll be the first to learn about new releases, sales, available preorders, and freebies. Note: Be sure to add admin@amybookerauthor.com to your contacts before signing up to ensure the emails go straight into your inbox.

Books are available in audiobook and paperback. Please go to my website for links or to buy direct!

contact amy

My website: http://www.amybookerauthor.com

Facebook: www.facebook.com/amybookerauthor
Instagram: www.instagram.com/
amy_booker_author/
TikTok: www.TikTok.com/@amybookerauthor
Email: amybookerauthor@gmail.com

Add my books to your Goodreads

Join my ARC/ALC teams

Join my Facebook Group